VALERIE

VALERIE

or

THE FACULTY OF DREAMS:

AMENDMENT TO

THE THEORY OF SEXUALITY

SARA STRIDSBERG

TRANSLATED FROM THE SWEDISH BY
DEBORAH BRAGAN-TURNER

FARRAR, STRAUS AND GIROUX
NEW YORK

Farrar, Straus and Giroux
120 Broadway, New York 10271

Printed in the United States of America
Originally published in 2006 by Albert Bonniers Förlag, Sweden,
as *Drömfakulteten—tillägg till sexualteorin*
English translation originally published in 2019 by MacLehose Press,
Great Britain, as *The Faculty of Dreams*
English translation published in the United States by
Farrar, Straus and Giroux
First American edition, 2019

Library of Congress Cataloging-in-Publication Data
Names: Stridsberg, Sara, 1972– author.
Title: Valerie : or the faculty of dreams : amendment to the theory of sexuality /
Sara Stridsberg ; translated from the Swedish by Deborah Bragan-Turner.
Other titles: Drömfakulteten, tillägg till sexualteorin. English
Description: New York : Farrar, Straus and Giroux, 2019.
Identifiers: LCCN 2018060814 | ISBN 9780374151911 (hardcover)
Subjects: LCSH: Solanas, Valerie—Fiction.
Classification: LCC PT9877.29.T75 D7613 2019 | DDC 839.73/8—dc23
LC record available at https://lccn.loc.gov/2018060814

Designed by Abby Kagan

Our books may be purchased in bulk for promotional, educational, or
business use. Please contact your local bookseller or the Macmillan
Corporate and Premium Sales Department at 1-800-221-7945, extension 5442,
or by e-mail at MacmillanSpecialMarkets@macmillan.com.

www.fsgbooks.com
www.twitter.com/fsgbooks • www.facebook.com/fsgbooks

1   3   5   7   9   10   8   6   4   2

Hope was never a thing with feathers.

—CLAUDIA RANKINE

Valerie is not a biography; it is a literary fantasy derived from the life and work of Valerie Solanas, American, now deceased. Few facts are known about Valerie Solanas and this novel is not faithful even to those. All characters in the novel should therefore be regarded as fictional, including Valerie Solanas herself.

This also applies to the map of America, there being no deserts in Georgia.

CONTENTS

BAMBILAND

THE OCEANS

THE FACTORY

LOVE VALERIE

VALERIE

A hotel room in the Tenderloin, San Francisco's red-light district. It is April 1988 and Valerie Solanas is lying on a filthy mattress and urine-soaked sheets, dying of pneumonia. Outside the window, pink neon lights flash and porn music plays day and night.

On April 30 her body is found by hotel staff. The police report states that she is found kneeling by the side of the bed. (Has she tried to get up? Has she been crying?) It states that the room is in perfect order, papers neatly piled on the desk, clothes folded on a wooden chair by the window. The police report also states that her body is covered with maggots and her death probably occurred around April 25.

Some weeks earlier, the report goes on to say, someone on the hotel staff had seen her sitting by the window, writing. I imagine piles of paper on the desk, her silver coat on a hanger by the window, and the smell of salt from the Pacific. I imagine Valerie in bed with a fever, attempting to smoke and make notes. I picture drafts and manuscripts all over the room . . . sun, perhaps . . . white clouds . . . the desert's solitude . . .

I imagine myself there with Valerie.

BAMBILAND

NARRATOR: What sort of material do we have?

VALERIE: Snow and black despair.

NARRATOR: Where?

VALERIE: The crap hotel. Last stop for dying whores and junkies. The last epic humiliation.

NARRATOR: Who's in despair?

VALERIE: I am. Valerie. I always wore rose-pink lipstick.

NARRATOR: Rose-pink?

VALERIE: Rosa Luxemburg. The Pink Panther. Her favorite roses were pink. Someone bikes away and burns down a rose garden.

NARRATOR: Anything else?

VALERIE: People lying dead in the desert and I don't know who's going to bury all those people.

NARRATOR: The president, maybe?

VALERIE: Death is seldom in the same place as the president. All activity has ceased in the White House.

NARRATOR: Where will you go now?

VALERIE: Nowhere. Just sleep, I suppose.

NARRATOR: What are you thinking about?

VALERIE: The girls from the underworld. Dorothy. Cosmogirl. Silk Boy.

NARRATOR: Anything else?

VALERIE: Prostitute stuff. Shark stuff. Me reeling at the prospect of all this eternity.

The day Dorothy is interviewed by *New York* magazine over a bad telephone line the sky above Ventor is the same pink as a sleeping tablet or old vomit. No one ever comes to fix the lines in Ventor anymore; desert birds have eaten the withered black wires, distorting conversations and laughing at Dorothy and the way she persists in her role as the victim of unfortunate circumstances. Her words flutter like wrapping paper in the wind.

NEW YORK MAGAZINE: Dorothy Moran?
DOROTHY: Yes.
NEW YORK MAGAZINE: We'd like to talk to you about Valerie.
DOROTHY: Yes.
NEW YORK MAGAZINE: It's three years today since she died.
DOROTHY: I know.
NEW YORK MAGAZINE: Tell us about Valerie.
DOROTHY: Valerie . . . ?
NEW YORK MAGAZINE: Your daughter. Valerie Solanas.
DOROTHY: Thank you, I know who Valerie is.
NEW YORK MAGAZINE: Tell us something . . .

DOROTHY: Valerie . . .

NEW YORK MAGAZINE: Why did she shoot Andy Warhol? Was she a prostitute all her life? Did she always hate men? Do you hate men? Are you a prostitute? Tell us how she died. Tell us about her childhood.

DOROTHY: I don't know . . . We lived here in Ventor. I don't know . . . the desert. I don't know . . . I burned all her things after she died . . . papers, notebooks . . .

(*Silence.*)

NEW YORK MAGAZINE: Anything else?

(*Silence.*)

DOROTHY: Valerie . . . used to write . . . fancied herself as a writer . . . I think she had t-t-talent . . . she had talent . . . She had a fantastic sense of humor . . . (*laughs*). Everybody loved her . . . (*laughs again*). I loved her . . . She died in 1988 . . . April 25 . . . She was happy, I think . . . That's all I have to say about Valerie . . . She was dedicated, reaching for the sky, the way I see it . . . I guess that's how it was . . .

NEW YORK MAGAZINE: Was she mentally ill? People say she was in and out of mental hospitals throughout the seventies.

DOROTHY: Valerie was *not* mentally ill. She even lived with a man for a few years. In Florida. On the beach. Alligator Reef. In the fifties.

NEW YORK MAGAZINE: There is evidence she was in Elmhurst Psychiatric Hospital. We know she was in Bellevue. We have reports she spent time in South Florida State Hospital.

DOROTHY: That's not right. Valerie was never mentally ill. Valerie was a genius. She was an angry little girl. My angry little girl. Never mentally ill. She had some strange experiences with strange men in strange cars. And once she pissed in a nasty boy's juice. She was a writer. You can write that down . . . I'm hanging up now . . .

NEW YORK MAGAZINE: It's alleged that she was subjected to sexual assault by her father. Did you know about that?

DOROTHY: I'm hanging up now . . . Put down that she was a writer . . . Put that she was a research psychologist . . . Put that love is eternal, not death . . .

(Call ended—)

The blood flows so slowly through your body. You claw at your breasts, weep and cry out, fumble with the bedding. The hotel sheets are dirty, gray with age, and foul-smelling, urine and vomit and vaginal blood and tears, a golden cloud of pain floating through your mind and gut. Blinding streaks of light in the room, explosions of agony in your skin and lungs, pitching, plunging, blazing. Heat in your arms, fever, abandonment, the stench of dying. Slivers and shards of light still flickering; your hands searching for Dorothy. *I hate myself but I do not want to die. I do not want to disappear. I want to go back. I long for someone's hands, my mother's hands, a girl's arms. Or a voice of any kind. Anything but this eclipse of the sun.*

Dorothy?

Dorothy?

The desperate screeching of desert animals. The sun burning over Georgia. The desert house with no pictures, books, money, or plans for the future. The swollen pink Ventor sky pressing against the window and everything again overlaid with a mantle of merriment, warm, moist. Dorothy has found some singed old dresses in a suitcase and you are probably on your way to the ocean again, to Alligator Reef and endless skies, just the two of you. She twirls in front of the mirror with cigarettes left burning all over the room. In plant pots, on the bedside table, in her compact.

VALERIE (*chuckles affectionately*): You little pyromaniac.

DOROTHY: All these dresses have black marks on the cuffs. Look at this snowy white one. It looks as though it's been through a nuclear war.

VALERIE: You always were kind of like a nuclear war.

DOROTHY: It's strange how you can forget one of your favorite dresses. I can't remember where it came from. I just remember how everything around me was made completely white and scrubbed clean when I was wearing it. The sky, my breath, my teeth . . . Do you remember when I forgot all the candles in the bar and the curtains caught fire?

VALERIE: I remember you setting fire to that old guy's beard when you were lighting his pipe.

DOROTHY: Do you remember when I set fire to my hair?

VALERIE: You were always doing it and I was always running for water to save you. I remember forever saving you.

DOROTHY: You did.

The glint of skyscrapers and tarmac in the darkness as the airplane continues its circling over Kennedy Airport; factories working, surfers gliding along beaches, fields of cotton, deserts, towns, New York traffic edging slowly forward. Splinters of light and memories glimmering faintly in your consciousness. The dark red-light district outside, neon lights, girls chasing the wind through the streets, skin and sparks of life, seductive smiles and puked-up dreams.

And if you did not have to die, you would be Valerie again in your silver coat and Valerie again with your handbag full of manuscripts and your building blocks of theory. And if you did not have to die now, your doctorate would shimmer on the horizon. And it would be that time again, the forties, fifties, sixties, Ventor, Maryland, New York, and that belief in yourself: *the writer, the scientist, me.* The great hunger and swirling vortex in your heart, the conviction. Slogans echoing between the buildings on Fifth Avenue and the president crouching behind his desk in Washington. There are only happy endings.

A girl can do anything she wants

You know I love you

The shouts die down and the heat evaporates, the smell of New York full-blown and burning. Fifth Avenue is sucked into a blackness, a narrow, foul-smelling underground tunnel, only the sour taste of deadly disease and never-ending porn music. And there is daylight in the Tenderloin with vomit-colored curtains at a smeared window, piles of notes and your bloodied underpants over the back of a chair, and on the bedside table a bottle of rum you will never manage to drink. The itching has taken over your body. It is worse than the pain in your chest and the difficulty breathing and the fact you have long ago lost all sensation in your hands and feet.

Mason Street is deserted, no shouts, no traffic, but a short distance away is the real city with real people and sun and trees and girls cycling with books on carrier racks, and farther away the cold ocean still pounding against the shore. The salty breath of the Pacific sweeping over sandy beaches, the sharks' expectation in the deep. Death by drowning, suffocation, lying on the beach, murdered, raped. April has always been the cruelest month. *I wish the daylight would vanish, that someone would hang a blanket in front of the sun and the neon signs, that someone would switch off the porn music and this incurable disease. I do not want to die. I do not want to die alone.*

There is a flash of Ventor and Dorothy in the room—a strip of burning paper flaring up and dying out in a room that's completely dark—the desert sand always blowing into your eyes and blurring your sight. The sand turning everything to a sweet, hot mist, a drug that numbs and soothes.

It is such a long time since your last visit to the desert and the yellow dive in the middle of nowhere. The porch facing countless hours of sun, a hidden winemaking machine in the corner and one long season of heat and parched grass. A bowl of golden light, a light that was yours until you ran away into the desert and wanted never to come home again.

Do you remember, Dorothy?

Do you remember how we would go to the river together?

The top down and a new guy at the wheel. Your scarf flapping in the wind. Your fair hair, newly washed. The song. You, singing and chattering in the front seat.

You and I beneath the crazy sky.

BRISTOL HOTEL, APRIL 7, 1988,
A FEW WEEKS BEFORE THE END

The manifesto has disappeared among the sheets streaked with dirt and brown fluid oozing from your vagina and rectum, a burning, vile-smelling outpouring of loneliness, a seeping humiliation. *If there are more ways to humiliate me, bring them on.* It is not like you to lie in a hotel room raving to yourself when you know you are alone, about to die; it is the fever, making you delirious. All you want is to stay in this room, not fall into the darkness and through the smell of forest and lemonade and stagnant river water and sunlight spilling onto the picnic blanket, the strong synthetic light of the forties.

Valerie, sugar

Time for food now, Valerie

Dorothy shouts from a blanket by the river where the sun's intensity has turned the grass into withered brown tufts. Behind her, columns of sunlight stand between the trees, and she waves away midges and dragonflies trying to nosedive into the picnic. America has just dropped the atom bomb on Nagasaki and still it is that time, a forgotten age of car rides with the top down and fried chicken sandwiches on the backseat and Louis in shorts with his shirt undone, stretched out on a blanket. An age when nights are deepest blue and crystal clear and little desert holes like Ventor have no electricity for months on end, and it is still all right to drink from the river and Louis drives back and forth to the textile mills to lay cables and you stopped calling him Daddy a lifetime ago.

You run under the silver-leaf maples, in your white dress again, the one that is really too thin and too childish and has lucky threads of gold and silver sewn into the petticoat and you only wear it because Dorothy likes it so much. Your feet sweating in your gym shoes and in your mouth the taste of metal and blood and something strange, choking. It is so quiet when you run, all sounds around you muted and only the blinding light cascading from the trees and the fateful dress swirling, far too tight across your chest and shoulders.

The forest invaded by dead animals and the soft smoky light motionless, lingering between the trees. And, when you think of it now, Dorothy's face is above the treetops and her dress smells of sex and sugar, her arms perspire as she reaches out to you, and she swears at the sun-bleached umbrella blowing over all the time, and her hands and arms are covered in liver spots. The sun burns so fiercely through the treetops and her eyes are black lakes you want to drown in and she strokes the fabric of your dress, stars and smiles and snow, and she swats the bluebottles away from your face.

Dorothy?

Dorothy?

Are you there, Dorothy?

DOROTHY (*over by the hotel room window*): I'll do whatever you want, my sunflower.

VALERIE: As long as you don't wear those vile pearls.

DOROTHY: My white pearls. They're my favorite pearls.

VALERIE: Not at the funeral, not at my funeral.

DOROTHY: Whatever you want. No artificial pearls, no plunging necklines, no fur, no makeup. Tell me what to put on and I will.

VALERIE: Dorothy?

DOROTHY: Yes, Valerie?

VALERIE: I'm so scared of dying. I'm so scared of dying on my own.

DOROTHY: It's only heaven, my darling . . . only heaven can love you for yourself alone and not your yellow hair.

VALERIE: I don't have yellow hair.

DOROTHY: I know, but never mind. It's just a metaphor.

VALERIE: I don't have yellow hair.

DOROTHY: It doesn't matter anymore, Valerie. It's not important what you call it. You're my little yellow-haired girl.

VALERIE: But I think I'm gray-haired now. And it's getting thin. It's falling out, horrible piles of it lying on the sheet when I wake up.

DOROTHY: Don't be afraid, baby.

VALERIE: I'm so light now, just a cloud. I have no hands. I miss my hands so badly.

Valerie

The sun burns through the umbrella. The brown, ferrous-smelling river water unmoving, stagnant. Dorothy and Louis still down by the riverside on their day out, drinking beer and lying outstretched on a blanket in the heat. Transistor radio, sweaty cheese, beery kisses, picnic.

You go down to the river's edge alone. Your feet in dark mud, in river slime, birch trees reaching for water, specks of rotting surface pollen. You will remember forever the magical light, the sludgy water creatures, distant birdcalls, rolls of ponderous clouds above. The shade of the trees, a shimmering green yearning and for what, you do not know, just a beast in your stomach wanting out and shafts of light descending through the green darkness. Just a song somewhere that sounds like a legend, but not here; a garden full of kindling, a waste-land, a leap of snow leopards hunting across the plain. You want only to hold that song, to possess that foreign language and the legend living and breathing in the river.

Your feet slide in the brown, vile-smelling muck and you do not know how you are going to catch up with all the longing and how you will cope with it if you do. You just know there is a song, like a legend, but not here, not now, only green darkness. The swaying crowns of the trees, dapples of light all around, making you tired and dizzy, and when you fall asleep by the river you dream you are flying high above snowcapped mountains and people applaud you far below.

And when you wake, Louis is under the treetops and the heat has gone and the sun is embedded in flashes of light shooting into your eyes as you open them and the backs of your thighs are stuck to the shiny surface of the backseat and covered in pondweed and mud and the unreal intensity of the light serves as darkness when you later recount it to Cosmogirl:

> *the darkness descended when I was nearly seven. We were on a picnic by the river. Dorothy was there. Louis was there. The light was so strong I didn't know which way to turn. When I woke, Louis was next to me. I didn't see Dorothy. The leaves cast shadows on his hands. I was lying on my back and Louis was there. My dress was pure white. I never had a white dress after that. He put his hands underneath my white dress. I let him. I let him. Then darkness. The light through the trees on his hands.*

Apparently it is raining outside, which concerns you not in the slightest, because inside the courthouse there is no weather at all, just stone and wood and dark suits and the sweet little traffic officer, William Schmalix, in his white gloves. All the questions are the wrong ones and outside in Madison Square Park you have kneeled and reached into the pants of untold strangers. You are wearing Cosmo's yellow top and underneath it nothing moves.

MANHATTAN CRIMINAL COURT: Judge David Getzoff summons Valerie Solanas in the case of *New York State vs. Valerie Solanas.*

VALERIE: Thank you so much. It's not often I shoot someone and have the honor of coming here.

MANHATTAN CRIMINAL COURT: Everything you say here can later be used against you.

VALERIE: I don't doubt it.

MANHATTAN CRIMINAL COURT: Personal circumstances of the accused. Valerie Solanas. Age: thirty-two. Address: none.

Marital status: single. Profession: unknown; the accused states she is a writer. No previous criminal record. Born in Ventor, Georgia, April 9, 1936.

VALERIE: Hey, hey, hey you. Mister. What do you know about love?

MANHATTAN CRIMINAL COURT: You are accused of homicide or attempted homicide. The charge is not yet established.

VALERIE: Aha.

MANHATTAN CRIMINAL COURT: Do you know what day it is?

VALERIE: I know I should have done a bit more target practice, mister.

MANHATTAN CRIMINAL COURT: Do you know where you are?

VALERIE: As far as I can see, I'm not anywhere I want to be.

MANHATTAN CRIMINAL COURT: Do you have a lawyer?

VALERIE: No, but I have no objection to appearing outside history.

MANHATTAN CRIMINAL COURT: Do you need a lawyer?

VALERIE: I need a kiss.

MANHATTAN CRIMINAL COURT: I'm asking if you need a lawyer.

VALERIE: I regret that I missed. If a lawyer can help me undo that, I'll gladly have a lawyer.

MANHATTAN CRIMINAL COURT: Do you remember why you shot Andy Warhol?

VALERIE: Unfortunately, I tend to remember slightly more than I need to. And in this case there was someone who had too much control over my life and I found it rather hard, to cut a long story short, to adjust to.

MANHATTAN CRIMINAL COURT: Why did you shoot Andy Warhol?

VALERIE: You should read my manifesto if you're interested in joining SCUM's supporters. It will tell you who I am.

MANHATTAN CRIMINAL COURT: You handed yourself in to a traffic officer yesterday on Fifth Avenue. Why did you do that?

VALERIE: Because I wanted some company. Because I was fed up. And he seems really nice, William Schmalix. And clever. I've never seen such a tiny policeman before and he still managed to arrest me.

MANHATTAN CRIMINAL COURT: This is the final time I will ask about a lawyer. You will need defense counsel. Can you afford a lawyer?

VALERIE: I want to defend myself. This, unlike so much else, will remain in my own competent hands.

VENTOR, GEORGIA, SUMMER 1945
MEN BACK IN THE FACTORIES AFTER THE WAR

The tarot cards are lying fanned out in strategic places around the house. Dorothy predicts that everything will be fine and there will be new children in the house and new desert flowers and the house will stop being a shithole and Louis will stop staring into the distance and the grapes and wild animals will survive out there where there is only sand and stones and merciless sun. As long as Louis is there, she is happy and busy and convinced she will succeed in growing sunflowers and sweet peas. As long as Louis is there, she drenches the house in soap and washes the sheets and nightshirts overnight and serves cornflakes with milk and syrup for breakfast and forever has new projects: a bath in the kitchen, a saucy hat, piles of dead butterflies in glass jars, solar panels on the roof, a new flavoring for the winemaking machine, and myriad underwater dreams of a future for Valerie somewhere else. A shift in the breeze inside you when she gazes at you with her dark eyes, convinced you are a changeling in need of special sustenance and special books and games, a stranger to her, unexpected but secretly wished for, like winning on the horses without having placed a bet.

DOROTHY: Nine years old and the prettiest in all America.

VALERIE: *You* are the pretty one, Dorothy.

DOROTHY: Louis thinks I'm beautiful. I intend to carry on being beautiful until I die. I have no intention of accepting the march of time, of my face looking like a war zone. Louis will stay with me as long as I'm radiant. Don't forget to be radiant, Valerie. Don't ever forget.

VALERIE: You're radiant.

DOROTHY: But I've had to work at it. Beauty doesn't come free, pretty eyes aren't free. What would you like for your birthday?

VALERIE: I'd like you.

DOROTHY (*spreads her arms wide*): Happy birthday.

VALERIE: And I'd like it if we didn't live with Louis.

DOROTHY (*crestfallen, lets her arms drop to her sides*): He's your father, Valerie.

VALERIE: He might be. But I don't like him.

DOROTHY: Without him, I'm nobody.

VALERIE: Okay.

DOROTHY: Without you, America is nothing.

And you return from the river in Louis's car, but Louis is not there, only Dorothy and you, and she continues to sing at the top of her voice, roughened by sweet wine and cigarettes, as the roads disappear behind you, poplars and telegraph posts and deep black shadows, and she sings like a gushing waterfall and holds your gaze in the rearview mirror. On the shoulder the remains of dead animals flash past—foxes, dogs, and snakes— and on the porch of the desert house Louis waits for you both to return and for Dorothy to go back to her work at the bar. And on the backseat huge bloodstained tears of wretchedness and no way to get around the simple facts of Louis and Dorothy and Valerie Solanas. Dorothy falls to pieces without Louis and Valerie falls to pieces without Dorothy. So Dorothy carries on singing and driving, knowing all about the world, but not wanting to know, and as she whistles and hums and casts fathomless glances in the rearview mirror, she wishes it were possible to keep everything and lose nothing.

Dorothy

Dorothy

Nightfall takes such a long time, and when you come home someone has taken your collection of snake skins; it must have been a desert dog. After Dorothy has melted away to the bar in her leopard-skin dress with her leopard-skin bag, Louis lies on the porch swing drinking beer and the night is black with insects, total darkness without stars or lamps. For the last time he takes his chicken soup out into the garden. For the last time he shouts to you to come out of the house. With a beer in your hand you walk slowly across the sand, still hot from the sun, and the heat has burned all your thoughts away and when it is dark outside you might as well be dead.

Afterward he smokes a cigarette and watches the smoke blend into the night. When the dark recedes and the hens wake, he packs his things and disappears into the distance. When Dorothy finally returns, she is tired after the night and smokes a cigarette on the porch and listens to the birds fly by in the first light.

Then she walks slowly through the rooms and she already knows, but does not want to know, and she shouts and weeps and goes through his empty drawers and none of his clothes are there and no money in the cake tin under the sink, only the forsaken wedding ring, lying in the sun. In Hiroshima shadows of fleeing people are seared onto buildings forever. You tell Cosmo about it later:

it was nothing special, it was just that Louis used to rape me on the porch swing after Dorothy had driven into town and the treetops wafted about in the night sky and the seat creaked in resistance because it needed oiling again and we were always waiting for new light bulbs for the garden and Louis should have done a bit more exercise because the flab on his arms wobbled when he strained on top of me and his chest against my face heavy and suffocating and he was a jumbled agony of tears and lust and the seat cover fabric was a mesh of wild pink roses that Dorothy had embroidered at night and I counted the roses and the stars in the sky and all flesh was sun-scorched grass and the dark took its time and my eyes pricked and burned and the desert dogs in their deepest sleep were chasing the wind and the stars in the sky had long been dead and I rented out my little pussy for no money and afterward he always wept and tried to untangle the knot of chewing gum in my hair and I don't know why it always got stuck in my hair while I was counting wild roses that were blood roses and death roses and the gum always fell out of my mouth and afterward my hair smelled of menthol and his shirt was marked with chewing gum and the stars were still dead in the night sky and remnants of cloud had caught in the trees floating above and Louis cut out the stickiest menthol snarls and chain-smoked long afterward and I smoked his cigarette butts and we listened to the geckos chirping around us and there was nothing left to cry about except America would keep on fucking me and all fathers want to fuck their daughters and most of them do and only a minority refrain and it's not clear why except the world is always one long yearning to go back

MANHATTAN CRIMINAL COURT, JUNE 3, 1968

The hearing continues after a short break. You refused to answer "adequately" and "properly" to the questions of the court
and it withdrew for a while. Silver clouds dart like shadows on
the ceiling. It is hard to decide if they are balloons or silver
cushions or if they are floating mirrors that have escaped from
the ladies' toilets. A daydream running alongside all the other
daydreams, a land of mirrors outside time, and around you only
black holes opening in the marble floor, and a hundred thousand silver wigs falling from the sky. An echoing courtroom
and endless rows of benches in different kinds of dark wood
and someone holding your arm all the time. Andy is obsessed
with death; he loves making screen prints of electric chairs and
suicides and crashed cars. Cosmo would have laughed at his
phony art and the hearing, and this proceeding feels as if his
silver wig were being rammed down your throat.

MANHATTAN CRIMINAL COURT: Will the accused, Valerie
    Solanas, please stand.

VALERIE: Remember, I'm the only sane woman here.

MANHATTAN CRIMINAL COURT: You have the right to a lawyer. There are people prepared to pay to defend you. Monsieur Maurice Girodias, proprietor of Olympia Press, has offered to pay for your defense.

VALERIE: I don't want his lawyers. I did the right thing. I regret nothing. I had plenty of reasons. It's not often I shoot someone. I didn't do it for nothing. They had me tied up and it wasn't very pleasant. They were going to do something that would have ruined me.

MANHATTAN CRIMINAL COURT: Redact all the defendant's statements.

VALERIE: Redact nothing. All that has to be recorded. I repeat. I will continue to repeat. I can repeat any number of times. I did the right thing. I regret nothing. I had plenty of reasons. It's not often I shoot someone. I didn't do it for nothing. They had me tied up, a very unpleasant experience. They were going to do something that would have ruined me. I want you to write that down in the record of proceedings.

MANHATTAN CRIMINAL COURT: No statements by the accused will be recorded. Hearing terminated; court adjourned. The accused is to be taken into psychiatric care for observation.

VALERIE: I refuse to be redacted and censored in this way.

MANHATTAN CRIMINAL COURT: The defendant will leave the courtroom.

VALERIE: I'm going nowhere until I'm included in the record.

MANHATTAN CRIMINAL COURT: Court is adjourned until further notice.

VALERIE: I demand that all my statements are documented in

the record. I am not leaving this court until I know my statements have been included.

Decision of the court: All statements by the accused are to be redacted from the transcript. Valerie Solanas is to be taken to Bellevue Hospital for observation.

VENTOR, SUMMER 1945

And the world is always one long yearning to go back. The river, Ventor, treetops, blood roses, those skies that never will return. Flimsy shreds of clouds reflected in the river, black branches in the murky water. The trees bowed toward the river, their roots engulfed by dark water, their crowns longing to be drowned, and Dorothy walking into the river wearing her clothes. She has pulled together her prettiest things, her brilliant white dress and designer handbag that looks like an aspirin tablet and is stolen from some bar in Ventor. Her hair in perfect curls under a scarf and the sun shining on her face. Dorothy steps into the river in her dress, the water streaming into her underclothes and eyes; she walks until she can no longer touch the bottom and she cannot swim so she just carries on into the deep, dreaming of winning everything and losing nothing (winning Louis and not losing you, losing Louis without losing herself).

You will always wish it was not your fault Louis left and you will always save her when she walks out into the water and the sun spots touch her pale hands so tenderly when you pull her onto the edge, onto the earth and grass and rubbish of a riverbank that has no beauty, only the stench of stagnant water and old underclothes and a strange, acrid chemical smell. And the black shadows of the towering trees shelter you from the sun, and while you wait for her to wake up again the cold comes. Slowly her pale freckled hands begin to move, opening and closing like night plants, and her dress is dark with mud and sand. When she comes round she vomits water and sand and wine and pie and tablets and blood. Her mottled pink chest heaves violently, her breath cold and blue, the dress ruined forever, makeup all over her face. She cries then because someone threw her handbag into the water while she was in the river. Taking your hand, wretched with shame, not even good at drowning.

DOROTHY: Sorry, Valerie, little one. I shouldn't have eaten that pie.

VALERIE: You shouldn't have gone in with your clothes on.

DOROTHY (*closes her eyes and fumbles for your face*): Free fall.

VALERIE: What do you mean?

DOROTHY: Free fall into the light. Dorothy's dead to me. Radiant. Radiant. I will always be. Happy. So happy. Happy and free.

VALERIE: You're talking nonsense, Dorothy. You're not dead yet, you're here, normal as ever, you haven't changed. You've got vomit on your hands. Wash yourself and stop your babbling. You didn't turn into a poet in the river.

DOROTHY: I turned into nothing in the river. How's my dress?

VALERIE: Fuck the dress. It's dirty, you'll have to wash it. And your makeup's a complete mess.

DOROTHY: I'm an idiot.
VALERIE: You're an idiot, Dorothy.

You walk home hand in hand. Dorothy has washed herself and her dress in the sweet, dark river water. The house in the desert is full of goodbye letters. Dorothy writes hundreds of farewell pages on pink paper before sealing them with a parting kiss. *Valerie, my love. It will be better for you when I am no longer here.* And then she burns them all behind the house and swears on her breasts that she will never do it again and she laughs at the smoke, as if there were no danger. Then she starts to set fire to the sleeves of her dresses again, to scarves, coats, tablecloths; she sets fire to curtains in the bar, to items in shops, and she goes home with a stranger and burns down his rose garden.

BRISTOL HOTEL, APRIL 9, 1988, YOUR BIRTHDAY

NARRATOR: Happy birthday, Valerie.

VALERIE: Are they funeral flowers?

NARRATOR: I don't really know. I brought them for you because I liked them. They smell so nice, a birthday smell. They can be funeral flowers if you want.

VALERIE: I don't like flowers.

NARRATOR: There are only one or two magnolias.

VALERIE: I don't want to have a religious funeral. I want to be buried as I am. I don't want them to burn my body when I'm dead. I don't want any man to touch me when I'm dead. I want to be buried in my silver coat. I want someone to go through my notes after my death.

NARRATOR: My faculty of dreams—

VALERIE: —and no sentimental young women or sham authors playing at writing a novel about me dying. You don't have my permission to go through my material.

(*Silence.*)

(*The narrator picks at the flowers.*)

NARRATOR: Can you hear the ocean?

VALERIE: I can hear the ocean and I don't want to hear it.

(*More silence.*)

VALERIE: I used to read from the manifesto at lunchtimes in Manhattan restaurants until I got thrown out.

NARRATOR: I can imagine. Did they like it?

VALERIE: You bet they did! They loved it. Who lives here apart from me?

NARRATOR: Junkies and down-and-outs. Prostitutes. AIDS sufferers. Mental-health cases with no hospital to go to. Ailing bag ladies.

VALERIE: Do you like them?

NARRATOR: I don't know. I've not met them.

VALERIE: Tell them we'll be out again soon. Tell them I'll arrange a day trip to the ocean for them. A day of blowy umbrellas and summer drinks for dying whores.

NARRATOR: My dream is for another ending to the story.

VALERIE: You're not a real storyteller.

NARRATOR: I know.

VALERIE: And this is not a real story.

NARRATOR: I know. And I don't care. I just want to sit here with you for a little while.

VALERIE: I don't have much to add.

NARRATOR: I don't want to live in a world where you die. There must be other endings, other stories.

VALERIE: Death is the end of all stories. There are no happy endings.

(*Silence.*)

NARRATOR: I just want to talk to you, Valerie.

VALERIE: And I don't want to die like this.

You and Dorothy in the kitchen. It is hot and sticky and there are black flies everywhere in this never-ending summer. It is the first summer since Louis left and you have to duck to avoid Dorothy's jungle of flypapers to reach your place at the table. She has emerged from her bed, emerged from the black river water, and bought a new plastic handbag. The old one has water stains and stands on the kitchen windowsill with a bunch of wild roses stuck in the opening. The flowers in her garden are dead, but she cooks again and laughs again, incandescent with despair.

DOROTHY: Eat up, my little pony, and you'll grow.
VALERIE: Is it flies or people you're intending to catch with those flypapers?
DOROTHY: Fellers.
VALERIE: I thought you'd gone off them.
DOROTHY: There's men and there's men.
VALERIE: Yeah.
DOROTHY: You have to beware of certain men.
VALERIE: Yeah.

DOROTHY: All men are not pigs.

VALERIE: Nah.

DOROTHY: Your father's a pig.

VALERIE: Yes.

DOROTHY: A girl can do anything she wants. And you know I love you.

VALERIE: Yes.

DOROTHY: Good. Eat up now. Watch out for that fly.

Electric light in the desert. Dorothy on the porch with peroxide on her hair, the tinfoil reflecting in the sun, a women's magazine in her hand, glossy pages, daydreams. You walk under the trees with skyscraper thoughts. Huge American trees, blind, bloodied shadows between the trunks, in your memory Louis's blond hair covering your hands, the sunlight, gasoline fumes, pins and needles in your arms. You dream of a typewriter, of Dorothy giving you a typewriter at last, you dream about moving away from the desert and your filthy little life in Ventor. Your hands are sparks flying over the black keys taking you onto the highway out of there.

Dorothy dreams of being a housewife, but has no one left to look after. She plays housewife some days to whoever passes through. Marries on a drinking spree and lands in trouble with the mayor when she has to settle her divorces. The long, long decade of the forties. First the war years with women in the factories, and later plasticky, unreal, with perfect curves and curls, and knee-length baby-doll dresses. *Daddy Knows Best* will soon be showing on everyone's new, flickering television sets; postwar plans, postwar prosperity. Dorothy sits and swivels on different barstools and smokes Peace cigarettes, holding forth in her overbearing, insistent way. The atom bomb has fallen on Nagasaki and Hiroshima, a hundred thousand burned to ash; the president has spoken to the nation. Dorothy has no television and no self-respect, she loves the president and the White House so much her eyes fill with tears. And in the bars she sounds off about nothing until she is thrown out and zigzags home across the desert, her handbag filled with stolen ashtrays and beer glasses.

The power lines blow down around the house and Dorothy has neither electricity nor lasting points of reference. As soon as a guy appears in the sunset Dorothy changes all her opinions. Republican, Democrat, prowar, antiwar, Dorothy changes her views like she changes her dresses and underpants. Several times a day and whenever required. Laughing in her mad-dog voice at their bad jokes, all over the house Dorothy's croaking, ingratiating cackle. The sky descends alarmingly close to the house and you tell Cosmogirl about it later:

> there were plants in her useless garden glowing like flames in the dusk and the white sheet of metal where the light poured out and there would be no vessel stranded in the desert just the huge bell jar over the blackness of her eyes and the blackness of her dresses and everything without memory or fear and a bit like childhood in which the heavens never exploded and there were only the desert trees and the orange tree I pinned pink wish notes to every time one of us had a birthday and all the wishes were still attainable and childlike and we hadn't yet been turned into silent dark exasperated desert creatures and as long as I was a birthday child as long as children still existed

Dorothy gazes into the distance when she is not scouring the bedroom for old letters and memories she has lost and some man who has already left her. She is a cloud of doom and the smell of slime and festering water cloaks every piece of furniture and every movement and every room and nothing seems to want to stay with Dorothy except you and the flies. She is no good with anything other than flypapers and gets into fights when she drinks too much sweet wine and rubs people the wrong way. And then she has to write long pink letters and race across the desert asking forgiveness, you and a stolen bunch of dying roses strapped to the bike rack.

The horizon is still sharp and beautiful, a fence and a boundary at the point where the world begins and ends. And the mountains are high and warm and friendly beasts now that Louis is not here. You will always be fearful of his yellow Ford appearing on the skyline of sand.

Time passes so slowly in the desert. Childhood an eternity of dazzling, blazing dragonflies as they rustle through the trees, trucks moving on the horizon, the howling of desert dogs in the distance. You are at the back of the house with the hoses and gasoline looking for snakes and giant insects. Dorothy fell asleep in the sun for too long, her hair is ruined under the peroxide and the brush pulls out her pride and joy in sorry puke-green clumps when she tries to untangle it, crying in front of the makeup mirror in the bedroom.

DOROTHY (*chunks of hair in her hand*): My hair, Valerie!

VALERIE: You little calamity.

DOROTHY: I'm nothing without my hair . . .

VALERIE: You look like a little soldier with that hair. Or without it. My brave soldier. I'll help you get rid of that mess.

DOROTHY: Waaah! I don't want to look like a little soldier. Definitively not like a filthy little soldier.

VALERIE: Your eyes make you look like a film star. With the blue on your eyelids.

DOROTHY: Louis is going to turn up at the door.

VALERIE: You've got to stop hankering after Louis.

DOROTHY: It's called eye shadow. Your father, Valerie. I'm talking about your father.

VALERIE: I don't remember him. I just remember he was a small, fat, blond guy with bad breath and ugly teeth.

DOROTHY: He was a very handsome man.

VALERIE: I think he's dead, Dolly. I think he's been electrocuted by a power line. It doesn't matter, Dolly. Only God can love you for yourself alone and not your blond hair. You'll be glad you didn't color your bush like you wanted to.

DOROTHY: I'm lucky it's not my bush.

VALERIE: Dorothy.

DOROTHY: Yes?

VALERIE: I think you're beautiful.

Dorothy's cool hands on your face and shoulders, her wine-smelling breath warm and moist, a cigarette balanced precariously on the edge of the table, the smell of soot on the sleeves of her dress. For a fraction of a second you can still hold her in your arms, her menthol scent and her smooth freckled skin. Her laugh a broken mirror.

Dorothy roams between bars with a scarf over her bleach-damaged hair. Blackened ends of green-blond debris. Scraping along in her high heels, asking for a little help with the essentials. The electricity does not come back on. Dorothy has kept on paying and ringing and complaining and bad-mouthing on the telephone; still the electricity does not come back on. No lover wants to come and climb up to the lines; at the electricity company they tire of her ranting. Dorothy cycles back and forth to the phone booth, imploring everybody in her hot, impassioned voice.

And they always come back once or twice before they disappear for good, until the day they leave with a screech of tires and never return. A few rounds of silky contrition, their hands deep in her hair, before they take their warm bellies from Dorothy forever and she starts again, painstakingly burning herself with candles and writing long pink letters and chasing across the desert with you on the rack.

There is no more money in the house, only the sun outside, white and hot and shimmering, and the gasoline drums where Dorothy sets fire to her memories. The radio is permanently on in the kitchen and Dorothy brushes her dishwater-hair over the food and traces her lipstick always slightly outside her lips. Much later in Maryland you and Cosmo decide that wearing lipstick outside your lipline at all times is a political act. Dorothy knows nothing about politics, but she knows all about lipstick and all about the future. She continues to swat at bluebottles, continues to have those depth-plunging eyes. The president is speaking on the radio and Dorothy foretells a brilliant future for you. *Valerie Jean Solanas will become president of America* and she dreams of being electric with happiness again, and the exhilarating smell of underwear will rule her household as before. She cannot stop thinking about the days at the river when the sun was high and quivering and the water smelled of iron and rotting plankton and no one knew it was poisoned yet and she and Louis lay on the grass so deep in beery kisses she nearly drowned and she imagined being a woman with her house and her refrigerator full of roses.

VALERIE: This soup just tastes like water.
DOROTHY: Shh! I'm listening.
VALERIE: What are they saying on the radio?
DOROTHY: The president's dropped another atom bomb. A

nuclear bomb on the Bikini islands. In the middle of god-damn nowhere.

VALERIE: Why?

DOROTHY: I don't know. Last year they dropped an atom bomb on the sixth of August. The war was practically over.

VALERIE: Did the animals die too?

DOROTHY: Everything died. The trees. All the flowers, all the grass, all the children.

VALERIE: What's the president's name?

DOROTHY: Harry.

VALERIE: I can just imagine his fat butt when he sits down for a crap. What does he look like?

DOROTHY: Beard, glasses, and shit on his ass.

VALERIE: Right.

DOROTHY: You're my little president. My little Miss President.

VALERIE: I want pie, not water soup.

DOROTHY: I'll have some money soon. When Louis comes back.

VALERIE: Louis isn't coming back. Is there a war happening now?

DOROTHY: There's no war.

VALERIE: None at all?

DOROTHY: Far away, there might be. A minor war. But not here. Not in America. Last year there was a war. Do you remember we were sitting in the bar all night and I was wearing my white dress? Louis was there. The war was over. That night . . . We found out in the afternoon. No one wanted to stay at home that night. Louis bought me roses. He kissed me where everyone could see. He kissed us all.

VALERIE: Why are we eating war soup if there isn't a war? I have got to be president of America.

DOROTHY: I think you will be. A nasty little president. Don't forget you're going to be a writer as well.

VALERIE: I already am a writer.

Cosmogirl dances by amid small mushrooming clouds of forgotten places and words, the hotel bed a blazing desert of everything you left undone and everything done wrong, an ocean ten thousand fathoms deep with everything you forgot and all the times you failed to say goodbye. You have forgotten her breath was luminous blue, forgotten the way she kissed your back in her sleep before she woke, the way she dreamily mumbled your favorite sentence. *The nicest women in our society are raving sex maniacs.*

And you sleep and dream of Maryland and are woken again by the dark and the presence of death, a swirling, blistering abyss of black trees and black snow falling. There is no organization called SCUM, there never has been. All that is left is the Society for Cutting Up Myself, a global organization with countless members. An organization that will never cease or disappear.

You look in your little pocket mirror (Cosmo kissed your mirrors and your lips, she pressed lipstick kisses on all the pages of your books, wrote your name in blood beside her own on the bath-room mirror that last time in Maryland) and in the mirror is a foul-smelling stranger. *Remember to write, Valerie. Don't forget to write.* It is so long since you gave up writing, slaying promises and utopian visions, decades since the turquoise portable type-writer accompanied you everywhere, since your promise to yourself never to sell the typewriter.

If you have forgiven Valerie...

...how come you have not been to see her?

When you cough, you get blood on your hand. Beneath the sil-ver coat is a screaming deep-sea creature wanting out, a birdlike monster with no feathers or skin, champing and chawing and flailing about. Your abdomen aches and weeps and the silver coat is wet and cold with urine, but you love it, and if you are going to die now anyway, you want to die in silver with silver buttons. If you are going to die anyway, you want to die with Cosmo's hand in yours. The last thing she said to you was "Don't leave me here," and the sky was heavy and oppressive and your leopard-skin fur coat was wet with fear when you took the train back to Maryland that last time.

Robert Brush called and wept on the telephone and you ran through the laboratory, setting all the animals free. You know they will not survive for long out there; the albino rabbits are going to die right away, they will hide in the trees and under the snow and form strange shapes in the park outside the lab.

Someone calls your name, someone touches your arm, in slow motion you walk across University Park, the wind gusting slightly, the smell of flowers and newly fallen snow, the sky made of dead faces, and all you want is a hole to open up in the snow and swallow you. *What is the point of forgiveness, if death treads on its heels?*

Cosmo?

Cosmogirl?

Feathery veils of light trail across the room; April is the maddest month of all with its sleet and lifeless fields. And when you open your eyes again, a lustrous bouquet of white lilies is over by the window and you cannot understand who has brought you such expensive flowers. It is a long time since anyone knocked at your door and there is no longer anyone who knows you love lilies. *I do not want to die and if I have to die now I do not want any man to touch my dead body.*

The ceiling is a swimming canvas of eyes and hands wanting to devour you, and as you stretch out your hands to the flowers in the window, you remember the scent of lilies and happiness, the faint smell of burning and lilies on her coats and dresses. The bed is a whirling chasm of unfamiliar voices and places and you long so much to hear her voice again, Cosmogirl, the most brilliant whore in the whole world, ruler of the universe, beloved. You long for snow and the sound of a typewriter, and when you open your eyes, she is sitting over by the window with a book in her hand and the sun on her hair. A cloud of smoke around her face as she smokes her strong cigarillos again, always with something to celebrate.

COSMO: What did you say?

VALERIE: Are the flowers from you? Are they for me?

COSMO: There aren't any flowers. It's your old sheets you can see. I helped you change them. There was blood and piss all over them.

VALERIE: Oh well. Have you read any of the manifesto?

COSMO (*stubs out her cigarillo on the windowsill*): I love it.

VALERIE: Do you?

COSMO: You know I do.

VALERIE: It doesn't matter if it's only the sheets, you smell like flowers. Did you know Olympia Press published the manifesto after the shooting without asking?

COSMO: I thought you wanted them to publish it.

VALERIE: Maurice and Paul made big money from the manifesto. Everybody wanted to read it because I was in the asylum over that business with Andy. Ten years later I published it myself but no one was interested then.

COSMO: Do you want me to read some of it to you?

VALERIE: Read to me while I fade away.

COSMO (*opens the manifesto*): Life in this society being, at best, an utter bore and no aspect of society being at all relevant to women, there remains to civic-minded, responsible, thrill-seeking females only to overthrow the government, eliminate the money system, institute complete automation and destroy the male sex.

VALERIE: And destroy the male sex.

COSMO: It is now technically feasible to reproduce without the aid of males (or, for that matter, females) and to produce only females. We must begin immediately to do so.

VALERIE: We must begin immediately to do so.

COSMO: Immediately. Retaining the male has not even the dubious purpose of reproduction. The male is a biological accident: the Y gene is an incomplete X gene, that is, it has an incomplete set of chromosomes. In other words, the male is an incomplete female, a walking abortion, aborted at the gene stage. To be male is to be deficient, emotionally limited; maleness is a deficiency disease and males are emotional cripples.

VALERIE: Further on. Read from further on. The end. The waves.

COSMO: Men who are rational, however, won't kick or struggle or raise a distressing fuss, but will just sit back, relax, enjoy the show and ride the waves to their demise.

VALERIE: I liked surfing so much, Cosmo.

COSMO: Shh . . .

THE NARRATORS

A. A heart full of black flies. The loneliness of a desert. Landscape of stones. Cowboys. Wild mustangs. An alphabet of bad experiences.

B. Blue smoke on the mountains. I am the only sane one here. There were no real cowboys. There were no real pictures. I vacuumed all the rooms; the dust was still there. I cleaned all the windows; I still could not breathe. It had something to do with the construction. The sun burned through the umbrellas.

C. The American film. The camera's lies. World literature's. America was a big adventure with its unreal blue mountains, its desert landscape.

D. They were filming in the desert. Wild horses chased by helicopters. She never understood what was in the script; she could never remember her lines. They were always covered by something plastic. Men had a tendency to be sucked into her mother. Men are happy in my company. It does not mean that I am happy.

E. *I, a Man* and *Bike Boy* by Andy Warhol. The story of the dissident, of frontier language, of the scream, of suicide. All these compelling mutations and machinations, without being regarded in retrospect as a tragic fate. She vented her heart between the high-rise blocks. Death's field was hers.

F. There should be a story set in the desert. There was no electricity. There were no telephone lines. How might the story be told? There would be endless dead blondes.

G. Stories. Overdoses. Sleeping tablets. Everything reaches its end.

H. Dead trees. Dead stories. Hold your horses. You must hold your horses, darling.

I. Valerie. Marilyn. Roslyn. Ulrike. Sylvia. Dorothy. Cosmogirl. A kind of insane genius. She has lost her marbles. That means we will wipe out her memories. Electroshock, injections, straitjackets, Elmhurst.

J. Remember, I am ill and I am waiting to die. Remember, I am the only sane woman here. Remember, he took my plays and killed them. They were already dead, miss. My plays were not dead. Your plays were already dead, miss. I want it added to the record of proceedings that he has killed my plays. What record, miss?

K. They had waited for hours. The harsh light over the set. That little white polka-dot dress. It was quite epic, timeless. I could have told you from the start how it would end. It could have had a different ending. There are other narrators. There are happy endings.

L. Experiments. Horses. Sunset.

M. I think you are the saddest girl I have ever met. There are no paths in the dark. There is nothing to tell. I cannot tell you how sad I am. I cannot talk about it. It is not possible to think outside your thoughts.

N. The compulsive calling forth of fragments of text and body tissue. Pain's sickness. Defense and defeat. Smiles and tears. The blues. Trying to relate to the matter then was like relating to fresh snow on an August day in New York.

O. If we called the text *The Snow*, it would not be censored. It could happily be sentimental and dirty. That was actually an ideal. What was the point? There were only filthy texts. What was the point? There were only filthy girls. Unclean, overblown, much too rhythmic. I dreamed of spotless white paper and clean unblemished people.

P. The story's flight response. A demonstration of pain. The sentences are blank. Rhetorical clumsiness. Contagious universes.

Q. Everyone else in the world would have loved me by now. Take everything from me, do it, that's what I want. When I have got what I want, I never want it again. How many times can my heart break? I am the only one here without a soul. I could have told you from the start how it would end. Take everything from me, do it, that's what I want.

R. I write for the dead. What does it matter if everyone is dead?

S. She keeps on being dead. She will always be dead. She is the only one I think about. A lie. All I want is to be with her. Rubbish. What does it matter if the narrator lies? What does it matter who tells the story?

T. Black-clad female grasshoppers and screaming fetuses. You cannot write yourself out of patriarchy. You cannot film yourself out. You stand in a desert, alone, frightened, weeping. You cannot think outside your thoughts. It is not the character's structure. Massive hegemony. The death of languages in exile.

U. Daddy's Girls unite. Isn't that American white-trash girl far too violent and naïve? You mean that dreadful woman with the manifesto, shrilling hysterically? What is she trying to say anyway? No, I really cannot hear what she is trying to say in that deep, animal voice.

V. She is saying: I dream that you will never stop searching for me.

W. How will I find my way back in the dark?

X. Darkness. Silence. The desert does not reply.

Y. She says: Follow the star. The lost highway.

Z. Follow it to the end.

Dorothy and Valerie in the desert kitchen again. Dorothy is cleaning the floor and the cupboards and everything in her path. Wearing her big black scarves and newly pressed skirts, she is washing away all her woes so that Red Moran cannot sniff them out, she says. In character, Red Moran is something of a disaster, but Dorothy is happy once more, lighting candles in all the rooms without burning her sleeves, stuffing desert animals and nailing them up on the wall, selling fox boas and having her handbag full of dollar bills, playing music on the radio without drinking wine; and all the time freckled hands swarm around your face. Never quieting, liable to come back later in your dreams.

DOROTHY: Housewives all love using soap.
VALERIE: Oh.
DOROTHY: Housewives clean away old misery and they love their daughters.
VALERIE: But you're no housewife. You're a barmaid. A working girl.

DOROTHY: You shouldn't be so smart and split hairs, Valerie. Splitting hairs is just a fool's way of making a point. I may not be a housewife on paper, but I feel like one. Happily married. Happy for my daughter. Flypaper and flyswatters to keep the shit away. Soap. Hydrogen superoxide. Soap flakes. You know you have a standing offer from Moran, Valerie?

VALERIE: I intend to carry on without a father.

DOROTHY: It's a nice offer to a nice girl.

VALERIE: There are no nice girls.

DOROTHY: You're a nice girl.

VALERIE: There are *only* nice girls.

DOROTHY: Well, it's a nice offer anyway.

VALERIE: It's a shit offer, Dorothy.

DOROTHY: I made some soap bubbles. Run and have a look in the kitchen.

VALERIE: I'm too old for soap bubbles. And you're definitely too old.

The soap bubbles float in and out of the window and Dorothy tries to catch them with the flyswatter. She is obsessed with cleaning the house, as if she were under a spell. Then she chases you with soap bubbles through the junk and rubbish in the backyard until you both crash onto the sand among the fallen dragonflies and quenched bubbles and she laughs and smokes and waves the swarms of flies from your face and foretells a happy ending for everything. You hopeless, feral creature. You burning paradise.

Dorothy has remarried, to Red Moran. Moran is dark and obese, he pops sleeping pills like sweets and takes pride in never drinking anything other than whisky. He puts you into a Catholic school and wants you to call him Daddy and he sits napping at the filling station instead of selling gasoline and papers. The fans go like planes above his head and there he sprawls, slumped over the counter, letting the customers drive past. You take some boys back after school and steal cigarettes and piss in his hip flask. He and Dorothy are closeted for hours in the bedroom with the blinds down and it is dark and draughty and cramped in the house and at any moment Moran could be standing in the middle of the kitchen floor, naked, rooting in the refrigerator. Dorothy is known for her bad taste and her bad judgment.

Dorothy groans from the next room. Red Moran and she are wrapped in sheets and sunlight and only you and the rose wall-paper can see them. Moran is on his knees, his huge body rocking. His stomach is tense and hairy and Dorothy loves it so much she almost bursts and he bends like a swaying baton over her as she lies there gazing at the cream-colored curtains billowing out of the window. Then he is on his knees in the bed and Dorothy is on all fours tensed like a desert dog; her thin, glowing body trembling in ecstasy. Her mouth is a gash on her face that you wish you could mend instead of standing there with the flies, staring into their pulsating pit of sweat and glassy eyes. And their smell that will follow you through the forest. A smell of something sour and sweet, like old fish or hamburgers.

VALERIE: I intend to keep the name Solanas.
DOROTHY: A father's name is beautiful on a girl.
VALERIE: I'm going to keep it because it means ocean bird.
DOROTHY: Your father will always be able to find you.
VALERIE: I have no father.
DOROTHY: You know I love you?
VALERIE: I know.

When you wake again patches of sunlight are spreading over the hotel room; you are not sure if the shimmering and flickering by the window are disco lights, or minuscule neon cities or only little fairgrounds on the wallpaper. For once there is silence in the corridor and on the street, just a gently buzzing light, the sound of overstrained electricity and a hazy strip of sky behind the curtains. By the window it looks as though someone has left a silver fox fur or a fox boa, and her perpetual cloud of menthol smoke obscures the view of the room. A silver thread flashing in her hand.

Dorothy?

DOROTHY: My little sugar lump.
VALERIE: What are you doing?
DOROTHY: Sewing lucky threads.
VALERIE: In what?
DOROTHY: In your silver coat.

VALERIE: It's too late.

DOROTHY: Threads of gold and silver. Lucky threads in your clothes at all times.

VALERIE: It's too late and they've never worked. Like your fortune-telling cards.

DOROTHY: Sometimes my predictions were right.

VALERIE: Bullshit. What do the cards say now?

DOROTHY: They say that you're not going to die. That love is eternal. That by May or June you'll be out again in your silver coat. And I've been sewing lucky threads in it. It will all be all right. You have to believe that.

VALERIE: Your predictions have never come true.

DOROTHY: They did sometimes.

VALERIE: Put your cigarette out and name one occasion when they did.

DOROTHY: Lots of men thought I was beautiful and I predicted they would carry on thinking that.

VALERIE: And now you're an ugly, hunched old hag with rustling skin and bad teeth and nicotine hands.

DOROTHY (*looks at her hands as she splays her fingers*): Red Moran said I was beautiful. Mr. Emin said I was beautiful . . . Everybody said it . . . By the way, did I tell you Moran died of that terrible lung disease?

VALERIE: You told me, yes.

DOROTHY: I thought everything was all right. That we were doing fine. And then he went and got that cough keeping me awake at night. I went to see him in the hospital every day. He should never have taken the job at the filling station. I said all along it was full of poisonous fumes and gases and shit.

VALERIE: He cut up all your clothes and pulled huge chunks of your hair out.

DOROTHY: What did you say?

VALERIE: You've got a memory like a sieve, Dorothy. All you've got in your head is sweet wine.

DOROTHY: I can't remember anything anymore, Valerie.

VALERIE: I remember everything.

DOROTHY: I know, thank you very much. It's like a photograph being developed inside that sharp little brain of yours. I have always chosen to remember only the wonderful things . . . clouds of pink flamingos flying low over the house . . . those skies that never return . . . kites and soap bubbles . . . a petticoat of the Stars and Stripes that I sewed for Independence Day . . . I looked fantastic in that cretion.

VALERIE: Cre-a-tion, Dorothy.

DOROTHY: Oh yeah. You've always thought words were important. I've always had so much else to think about.

VALERIE: I can remember Alligator Reef, for instance, and the ocean . . .

DOROTHY: That's right. I could see it in my cards. You and I on that beach. The umbrellas. The miles of sand.

VALERIE (*emits a laugh edged with steel*): And then what, Dorothy? What happened then, Dorothy?

DOROTHY (*her needle moving faster and faster, up and down*): I don't remember. There are lots of things I don't remember. I haven't thought about my hands before. It's true, Valerie. Completely yellow with smoke and nighttime. But it's nighttime now. You're going to go to sleep now, my baby.

VALERIE: I'm not a baby. And there is a very literal beach. There are a number of unanswered letters. Did we stay on the beach? You have to answer my questions.

DOROTHY: I'm going to concentrate on sewing now. And you're going to concentrate on sleeping now. Goodnight, little Valerie.

VALERIE: Fuck you, Dolly.

THE OCEANS

THE NARRATOR: I can help you sort out your papers. I can change the light bulbs so you don't have to lie in the dark. I can help you get up for a while.

VALERIE: Thank you, but I'm fine like this. And I prefer lying alone. But you go ahead. Knock yourself out. I'll sleep for the time being.

NARRATOR: We need to talk some more about prostitution, talk some more about the American women's movement. You have to tell me more about your relationship with the emancipation project.

VALERIE: I don't have to do anything. I need to lie here and wait and see if I opt for life or death. My heart is still beating. I am still full of hate. I can still see you. And all your papers. That means I'm not dead yet.

NARRATOR: Being close to authentic material.

VALERIE: Am I the material?

NARRATOR: There's more than one kind . . . You are the subject of this novel. I admire your work. I admire your courage.

I'm interested in the manifesto's context. Your life. The American women's movement. The sixties.

VALERIE: Whore material. Screwing material.

NARRATOR: The context—

VALERIE: —there's no such thing as context. Everything has to be wrenched out of its setting. Frames of reference can always explain away the most obvious causal connections. Buyers, sellers, slack dicks, slack pussies. It's a question of phenomena that can be totally taken apart.

NARRATOR: I'm interested in your world.

VALERIE: This is not a world I want to live in. Marilyn Monroe. Sylvia Plath. Cinderella. Lying raped and murdered on the beach. I ran home to Dorothy across the desert with dying creatures in my arms. I waited for the animal to decide on life or death. Sometimes it chose death, sometimes life. Sometimes it was a giant dragonfly that would die before nightfall anyway. It has always been like that with me, I've always found it hard to decide. It's been neither life nor death. And it seems from now on it will just be death. Well, at least it's a decision to abide by. Something of a lasting nature.

NARRATOR: Tell me about the manifesto, about SCUM.

VALERIE: A worldwide antiviolence organization. A utopia, a mass movement, a raucous slather slowly spreading across the globe. A condition, an attitude, a way of moving across the city. Always filthy thoughts, filthy dress, filthy low intentions.

NARRATOR: Number of members?

VALERIE: Unknown.

NARRATOR: Which members?

VALERIE: Arrogant, selfish women in the whole wide world too impatient to hope and wait for the de-brainwashing of millions of assholes. Rulers of the universe in every country . . . Women of the whole world, or just Valerie . . .

NARRATOR: And you?

VALERIE: The loneliness of a desert.

NARRATOR: May I hold your hand?

VALERIE: No.

NARRATOR: May I sit with you while you sleep?

VALERIE: Remember that I'm ill and I'm waiting to die. Remember, I'm the only sane woman here.

NARRATOR: I love you.

VALERIE: Fuck you.

The glint of the sun as it shines on a summer that has been fe-
verish with desertions and reconciliations. Dorothy has chased
through the nights across Bambiland. The trees are dark and
somber, and her dead desert animals rot at the back of the house.
Moran drifts aimlessly through the rooms when she disappears
into the darkness; longing for her return, he weeps, and then sits
for days on end, looking through her farewell letters. There is a
smell of unwashed underwear and old tinned food and corpses
and finally Dorothy calls you, her voice quavering, the crackling
line from the city breaking up. This time he has tried to smash
her face into an oil drum.

DOROTHY: I'm so stupid, darling. I should have realized ages
    ago that he's a jerk. I look awful. My whole face is blue. My
    eyes. He cut my dress up, my white one.
VALERIE: Hello, Dorothy.
DOROTHY: I'm so stupid. I'm so naïve.
VALERIE: Yes, you are.

DOROTHY: I'm going to go away. And I'm going to take you with me.

VALERIE: I don't want to stay here.

DOROTHY: Can you look for my white dress? I don't want to go around in my nightdress. It makes me look like a mental patient.

VALERIE: You said it's been cut up, the white one.

DOROTHY: Fuck. I forgot. I hate him. I'm useless.

VALERIE: You're smarter than Moran.

DOROTHY: Yes.

VALERIE: It's not difficult to be smarter than Moran.

DOROTHY: Come to the ocean, darling.

VALERIE: When am I leaving?

DOROTHY: The dress. You can bring another dress. And shampoo.

VALERIE: You crazy cow. Are you wearing only your nightdress now?

DOROTHY (*giggles and sniffs*): I think so . . . I look ridiculous. Nightdress and boots. No handbag, nothing. Sweetie. My little sugar lump. Bring things for yourself as well. Bring a book. Bring lots to read. I'll buy you new books. I'll buy whatever you like. I'll sort money out when we get to the ocean.

At Alligator Reef the skies have a sparkling, healing light that gets into your dresses and handbags and hair. Helicopters circle above the beach and all the time you keep close to the pink lifeguard tower below the flamingo park. Dorothy builds a night shelter under the tower every evening when darkness falls and the beach empties of bathers and the starry sky sinks slowly down over you like a dark blanket.

The bruises on Dorothy's arms fade and she is far out in the waves; as she dips under, she longs to be transfigured by the ocean. When she comes back to the shore she is covered in freckles and happy. The white dress has been mended and is lying at the water's edge, being bleached. There is sand in your sandwiches and Dorothy's chief occupation is directing her eyes like radar beams scanning for attractive strangers and yours is eavesdropping on picnics on the blankets nearby, when you are not hunting for crocodiles and sharks and giant snakes.

Dorothy is her most beautiful on the beach and your books crunch with sand and curl with salt water when Dorothy leaves them at the edge of the sea. Sand blows in your eyes and your hair is matted with salt. But the only sharks you find have polo shirts and black cars and glide slowly down the promenade. Dorothy looks at you with fire in her eyes.

DOROTHY: Tell me a story.

VALERIE: I'm reading.

DOROTHY: Tell me a story about Ventor, Valerie.

VALERIE: If you take your sunglasses off, I'll tell you a story. You look like a giant fly in those glasses.

DOROTHY (*lays her head on your lap, the umbrellas rattle in the wind*): You know what I think about flies, darling.

VALERIE: Once upon a time there was a filthy little hole full of dickheads, gangsters and crooks and small-town whores with small-town pimps. And along came a little girl called Dorothy. And another little girl called Valerie. The sun was always shining and they laughed and smoked cigarettes. Dorothy worked with her fox boas. Valerie wrote her books. The men in Ventor were a mob of hairy apes who hung out at bars and took care of their egos and their fists and their tiny penises. Their tiny, tiny pet penises. There was a desert and a little house and a bathtub. The desert was full of girls. Or rather, they wished the desert were full of girls. There was Dorothy and Valerie . . .

(*Silence.*)

VALERIE (*pulls her hand through Dorothy's hair*): Are you asleep?

DOROTHY: I'm listening.

VALERIE: You've got blood in your hair again.

DOROTHY: I'm asleep.

The ocean thunders around you, words drown in the waves and the blinding white light shifts into something softer. The sky and the sand turn to muted pink and the beach will soon be empty of bathers again. Dorothy opens her eyes.

DOROTHY: Then what?

VALERIE: Then all the villains disappear. Someone removes their brains and nervous systems and their penises. Dorothy and Valerie and all the girls and the foxes and the books and the typewriters go to Alligator Reef. And they live happily ever after. They never go back.

DOROTHY: I love you, Valerie. I love you so much my heart is bursting.

VALERIE: And Moran?

DOROTHY (*her empty gaze rests on the horizon*): I'll never go back to him.

VALERIE: Okay.

DOROTHY: I swear on my mother's grave that I'll never go back.

VALERIE: You don't have a mother, Dorothy. You can't swear on something you don't have.

Beneath the glare of the sun, beneath the cries of looping gulls, you walk along the beaches, seeking pieces of glass and shells while Dorothy is out for a drive in one of her many lunatic dresses. Outside the flamingo park there is a silken boy, selling photographs of sharks. You get a picture of a dead tiger shark and a Polaroid of his sandy shin. The stones in the sand look like birthmarks and there are new kinds of clouds over the ocean every day. One morning when you wake up there is a package on the sand.

VALERIE: What is it?
DOROTHY: Open it and see.
VALERIE: For me?
DOROTHY: Open it now. Or else I will.
VALERIE: What is this?
DOROTHY: A ribbon for the typewriter.
VALERIE: What typewriter?
DOROTHY: I'm going to give you a typewriter.
VALERIE: When?
DOROTHY: As soon as I can afford it. Rich men in rich cars.
VALERIE: I don't want a typewriter from any rich cars.
DOROTHY: But I've nurtured a little author at my freckled bosom. And for that I have to take some responsibility.

Dorothy has never read a proper book. She reads magazines and cake recipes in cookbooks, though she does not like baking and is useless at any kind of cooking. She celebrates another birthday at Alligator Reef. It could have been a black day, but her lies about her age get wilder all the time. Officially she is just under thirty and at every birthday it goes down. On her birthday by the ocean you go to a bookshop where Dorothy is going to choose a birthday book. The pale shadows of palm trees and clouds pursue you along the promenade like huge, unsettled animals. The salt-filled winds turn at the beach's end and on their way back they are hotter and saltier, and it has to be something simple, Dorothy says, like a film, like a lipstick, like Marilyn.

The book is thick and pink and Dorothy bears it like a jewel across the sea, the promenade, and the hotel complex. Then she lies for days on end on the beach looking through it, but she does not read. The loud ocean sounds are soporific and the Atlantic bewitches her, the ocean a deep blue solace. She moves restlessly on the sand, her hand searching in her handbag despairingly and time after time she empties it onto the sand to go through her belongings.

DOROTHY: What are you reading?
VALERIE: I don't know. Mine didn't have a dust jacket.

DOROTHY: I'm going to take my book to the bar for a while. It might be easier to read there.

VALERIE (*with her eyes on the book*): Do that, Dorothy.

DOROTHY: I'm not going to the phone booth today. I've got nothing to say to him. We're not going back. Period.

VALERIE: You've sworn on your breasts.

DOROTHY (*squints at her neckline*): I know.

VALERIE: All or nothing.

DOROTHY (*her eyes and eyelashes twitching in the sun*): All. I choose all. I mean I choose you. Period. Absolute period. The end of the book. I'm going to the bar now. I like this book. I think this whole books thing is interesting, truly important. Even if it doesn't seem like it. Maybe it doesn't look as though I'm interested in books, but I am. I'm going to concentrate. Everything isn't what it seems. Valerie . . . Valerie?

VALERIE: I know, Dolly. Go. I'm reading.

You keep on reading your seawater-warped books and Dorothy keeps on vanishing behind her sunglasses, keeps on forgetting. Her cigarettes always burn out on the sand as she falls asleep, her dreams invaded by black underwater trees and black luminescence, constantly descending. When she falls asleep on the beaches of Alligator Reef she dreams about someone no longer wanting to be a mother, and she wakes every time with suffocating heart and salty wet globs in her mouth. Her hand moves on the sand and in her dream and the underwater world there is no shriveled foal, knowing it is going to die, but persisting, still a sticky mucilage around its mother, constantly letting itself be kicked away, for the warm taste of her milk like a watermark on its fur, its mouth filled with black ants. She picks up her book and tries to read, but she is robbed of concentration by the ocean, and still more by her pocket mirror, nail file, and cigarette, and most of all by her way of looking furtively over your shoulder at your book.

DOROTHY: You just read and read. You must be very well informed by now.

VALERIE: Dorothy, it's only a novel.

DOROTHY: I wish I could concentrate like you. I'm always thinking about something else. The letters start swimming on the page. My heart beats weirdly somehow in my chest.

VALERIE: You'll never go back to him?

DOROTHY: Never.

VALERIE: Sure?

DOROTHY: I swear on my mother's . . .

VALERIE: You have no mother, Dorothy. She abandoned you in the desert.

DOROTHY: I promise, darling. I'm not a stupid cow.

VALERIE (*laughs and strokes Dorothy's hair*): Yes, you are.

DOROTHY: Yes, I am. But I swear on my hair and my breasts and my legs.

VALERIE: I'm not going back to him.

DOROTHY (*a small, smiling sun*): Nor me. Wherever you go, I'll go too.

Her hair blows into her eyes all the time. Soon she is over at the bar again. The wind does not subside and there are reports on the news of typhoons and hurricanes and shark attacks. At night Dorothy sits glued to the television sets in the beach bars. The wind wrecks her hairdo and her good intentions; the sand, salt, and sun both soothe and excite and in the end the ocean will have ruined all her makeup.

STATE SUPREME COURT, NEW YORK, JUNE 13, 1968
MARTIN LUTHER KING, JR., ASSASSINATED IN MEMPHIS,
ROBERT KENNEDY ASSASSINATED IN LOS ANGELES

The State of New York and Thomas Dickens give notice of a hearing in the case of *New York State vs. Valerie Solanas*. You are traveling across New York's suburbs in a police car, a beautiful drive, the sky showing no self-respect and convulsing with blood-stained clouds and you offer to pay for the ride, you are used to paying for yourself, *ten for a fuck five for a blow job two for a hand job*. But it is New York State paying for the sightseeing tour this time, *thank you most humbly, mister, a fantastic return trip to hell*.

STATE SUPREME COURT: Description of the offense: The plaintiff Andy Warhol is reported to have implored on his knees, *No, no, Valerie! Don't do it! Please, Valerie.* The defendant also shot Mr. Warhol's colleague Paul Morrissey. After several appeals by witness Viva Ronaldo, Solanas left the premises in the elevator without a word. Several hours later she handed herself in to William Schmalix, a traffic officer on Fifth Avenue. Andy Warhol is currently on an artificial respirator in the Columbus–Mother Cabrini Hospital. It is as yet unclear whether he will regain consciousness, and if so, how, and in what condition; it is still unclear whether the offense charged is attempted homicide or homicide. Attorney Miss Florynce Kennedy will represent the defendant, instead of the attorney previously appointed by New York State. Miss Kennedy is defending Miss Solanas for no fee. Miss Solanas neither denies nor admits the charge.

(*Silence.*)

STATE SUPREME COURT: Will the defense call the accused to testify?

FLORYNCE KENNEDY: No. The defendant is not *of sound mind.*

VALERIE: I am of sound mind. My mind has never felt more fully sound.

FLORYNCE KENNEDY (*whispers*): I know you're of sound mind, but you have nothing to gain from it in court.

VALERIE: Win, or vanish from history.

FLORYNCE KENNEDY (*to the court*): Would you please just give us a moment, Mr. Dickens?

VALERIE: Did you call him a dick, that judge?

FLORYNCE KENNEDY: He's called Dickens, Valerie. In court he's called Dickens, and nothing else.

VALERIE: In my court he's called a dick.

FLORYNCE KENNEDY: I've asked you not to speak in court. Call him Thomas Dickens from now on, Valerie.

VALERIE: Remember, I'm the only sane woman here.

FLORYNCE KENNEDY: I know, Valerie. You're one of the most important spokeswomen of the feminist movement.

VALERIE: Are you related to *that* Kennedy, Kennedy? Marilyn's Kennedy?

FLORYNCE KENNEDY: Shush now, Valerie.

VALERIE (*whispers*): —d-ick, d-ick, d-ick—

(*Silence.*)

FLORYNCE KENNEDY: I request that Valerie Jean Solanas, born 1936 in Ventor, Georgia, be declared medically unfit.

(*Silence.*)

VALERIE: I'm not unfit, Kennedy.

FLORYNCE KENNEDY: I know, Valerie.

VALERIE: Then why would you tell him to say so?

FLORYNCE KENNEDY: Because I want you to be free, Valerie.

VALERIE: Unfit isn't free. The hospital isn't free.

FLORYNCE KENNEDY: The hospital is better than prison.

VALERIE: But it's not an illness.

FLORYNCE KENNEDY: This is the law, not justice.

VALERIE: Laws are all over, everywhere but on my side.

(*Silence.*)

STATE SUPREME COURT: Upheld, Miss Kennedy.

(*Silence.*)

STATE SUPREME COURT: Hearing adjourned.

The State of New York and Judge Thomas Dickens declare you to be of unsound mind. Henceforth you will be regarded as incapable of making your own legal decisions and you are transferred to Elmhurst Psychiatric Hospital while you await trial. Later you will stand trial for attempted homicide, harassment, and illegal possession of weapons.

ALLIGATOR REEF, APRIL 1951
DOROTHY'S BOOK CONTINUES, THE ATLANTIC CARRIES ON WORKING

An ocean of dark mirrors. Dorothy holds your hand while she sleeps in the shade of the umbrellas. Salt waves sweep down the beaches, seabirds screech their hollow cries, ten thousand fathoms of ocean water seethe and sigh. The beach book (the pink one) lies open, filling with sand and wind and seawater. The pages are curled and sun-bleached and on some of them the water has erased the text. Dorothy is still only on page eleven. She read the end first and finds out that the lovers separate on a misunderstanding; she is inconsolable, thinking the book is about her, and then she cannot read any more. Instead she tosses her hair and flips her scarf and her eyes dart ever faster between sea and sky.

Down by the water's edge Silk Boy passes and inside his sweatshirt is a baby flamingo that has escaped from the flamingo park. He spends a long, chilly afternoon sitting beside your beach towel, listening to you as you read from your notes. Afterward your clothes are covered with flamingo feathers. Rotten seaweed and shimmering green seashells float ashore; some days the effluent from the textile mills makes bathing impossible. Swim-suits smell of chemicals and decaying algae. For several weeks now Dorothy has been running back and forth between the telephone kiosk and the beach bar. She stands for hours arguing with Moran, slamming down the receiver and calling him back, weeping loudly into the sleeve of her bathrobe, the phone booth steamed up with desperation. Once again she starts burning herself on candles. The sleeves of her dresses are always edged with black. Once again she is thrown out of cars, bruises on her arms, underwear ripped. Your skin is pink and blistered after all those hours in the sun.

Dorothy keeps on forgetting things. First she forgets her promises, then she forgets her child; her angry, sunburned child who only thinks about books, and in the end she forgets herself. Moran drives to Alligator Reef in a stolen Mercedes and his hands are wild animals again, chasing around in Dorothy's hair. She runs like a deer along the promenade. She forgets her name, she forgets the long happy spring spent by the ocean; all she remembers is their submerged screams from Ventor, all she remembers is his dead roses, his tongue and his hot stomach against hers. And she forgets her book in the sand, a forsaken scrap of pink paper about lost love by the ocean's edge. The wind turns the pages a couple of times and the stars read it one night before it disappears into the sea.

Moran has a suit and bright eyes, he is drenched in cheap aftershave and his hand shakes when he greets you. Dorothy gets a new ivory-colored dress and on the backseat is a parcel wrapped in shiny paper and done up with silk ribbon; it is a light blue typewriter. A Japanese-made Royal 100. And as the stolen Mercedes drives along empty roads, through forests and deserts, the sky is pale and calm between the treetops. The seats are hot and cracked by the sun, and Dorothy tosses her hair and laughs her desperado laugh into the cigarette smoke, as if no dangers exist. You type on your typewriter; the sound is a sound of joy and the pages are pages of mysterious beauty lying like fans on the parcel shelf at the back and you love that typewriter far too much to give it back. It is April 9, 1951. It is your fifteenth birthday.

Happy birthday, little Valerie.

Dr. Ruth Cooper sits lost in thought behind her white lace curtains in the therapy room at Elmhurst Psychiatric Hospital. She fantasizes about Andy Warhol and his unconscious, hairless body on the respirator and she dreams of a world without clamoring, sobbing patients. Her hair lies in impeccable blond waves on her head and in her cool, ringless hand she takes yours, and she holds it awhile as you speak. And there are so many questions when you are in Dr. Ruth Cooper's presence; all the silence you have swathed around you for the last few weeks surrenders in your conversations, and you assume that this is her intention. Why did you do it, Valerie? What were you thinking, Valerie? Do you realize Andy Warhol is dying?

Your answers:

One. Don't know.

Two. Don't know.

Three. I don't know what dying means. We're all dying, you know.

The patients who sit and wait in the hospital corridors all look as though they are already dead—pallid, bloated beings with darting eyes, drowning people who masturbate with the aid of hospital fixtures, old women who stink of urine and excrement—you could tell all these lost individuals that nothing else will ever happen to them, that their turn will never come, that the doctor will never have time, their visitors will forget when visiting time is, you could tell them the mental hospital is their last stop, their final repository.

And while you all wait in hope, those who are drowning hoping that it will be their turn soon, and you hoping it will *not* be yours, you recite aloud from *Up Your Ass* to a small group of castaways outside Dr. Ruth's office. The only one who listens properly and whose glance does not flicker is a new arrival with blue eyes and freshly washed hair and your heart bleeds with your desire for them to grasp that the doctor's office is not the way out, that the road from Elmhurst is not via the Therapy Room, Diagnosis, and Doctors.

VALERIE (*on her way in to see Dr. Cooper*): Now you have to get your asses in gear. You over there with the bird's-nest hairdo, stop humping the decor. Yes, I understand it's more exciting than screwing one of these guys, but stop it anyway if you ever want to get out. And you over there, you have to stop stinking of piss and puke, it's a goddamn awful strategy if you want to get out of here. Get yourself some soap and some self-respect. Remember, girls, sex is just a hang-up and we don't have time to waste on meaningless sex. Remember that SCUM is the future. Remember the future's already here.

DR. RUTH COOPER: Hello, Valerie.

VALERIE: Giving up isn't the answer, fucking up is.

DR. RUTH COOPER: Take a seat.

VALERIE: I congratulate you on wangling a lovely room, Dr. Ruth Cooper. But you don't seem totally abreast of the situation outside in the waiting area. I don't know if you've been out there—I assume you take the back exit, or you prefer to lower yourself down by the curtains rather than be confronted with the wreckage out there. All they want is to come in here and receive your blessing and forgiveness and your permission to go on being ill. I don't know how you define clinically dead, it's something you must have considered in detail during your training. Living dead, apparently dead, brain-dead, et cetera, et cetera.

DR. RUTH COOPER: Take a seat, Valerie.

VALERIE: Have you been out and looked at the patients? Perhaps you ought to schedule a study visit into your calendar.

DR. RUTH COOPER: My name is Dr. Ruth Cooper and I will be responsible for you here at this hospital.

VALERIE: Thanks very much for nothing. *Up Your Ass* makes them laugh, anyway.

DR. RUTH COOPER: *Up Your Ass*?

VALERIE: My play.

DR. RUTH COOPER: I understand. What's it about?

VALERIE: It's about Bongi, a man-hating panhandler.

DR. RUTH COOPER: Is the play about you, Valerie?

VALERIE: Is the medical report about me?

DR. RUTH COOPER: Tell me about your play.

VALERIE: It's not bad art, it's just my brain bleeding. I don't think she'll ever come back.

DR. RUTH COOPER: Who?

VALERIE: Bongi. My text. My play. My life.

DR. RUTH COOPER: Okay, Valerie. Let's talk about why you're here. You know that Andy Warhol is still unconscious at Mother Cabrini Hospital. It's still not clear whether he will survive. As far as I understand, you hit his chest, stomach, liver, spleen, esophagus, and lungs.

VALERIE: I'm sorry I missed. It was immoral to miss. I should have done more target practice.

DR. RUTH COOPER: We're talking about a person. We're talking about a person who's dying. Why did you do it? Why did you try to murder Andy Warhol?

VALERIE: We're all dying. Mortality in this country is one hundred percent. We're all sentenced to death, the only lasting thing is annihilation, we're all going to disappear, death is the end of every story. Death will triumph over you too, Doctor.

There are new meetings with Dr. Cooper all the time to get the Diagnosis the court in Manhattan is awaiting. *I don't want any diagnosis, I have my own qualifications from Maryland. I apply my own diagnoses. This is my diagnosis: Goddamn pissed off. Fucking angry. Hustler. Panhandler. Man hater. It's a nightmare to wake up in hell every day.*

DR. RUTH COOPER: Why did you try to murder Andy Warhol?

VALERIE: Is Andy still in the hospital playing dead?

DR. RUTH COOPER: His condition is still critical, which makes your own situation critical, to say the least. It doesn't look good for you, Valerie.

VALERIE: I was a pretty child. I was the prettiest nine-year-old in America. The fastest surfer at Alligator Reef. I was the star student from Maryland.

DR. RUTH COOPER: And why did you shoot Andy Warhol?

VALERIE: Have you never shot anyone, Dr. Cooper?

DR. RUTH COOPER: No.

VALERIE: Never wanted to shoot anyone?

(*Silence.*)

DR. RUTH COOPER: No, never.

VALERIE: I don't believe you.

DR. RUTH COOPER: This conversation is not about me. Why did you shoot Andy Warhol?

VALERIE: And they continue to ask her: *Why doesn't she just go right away when he has repeatedly crushed her hopes and cut up her favorite dresses?* A more appropriate question is: *Why is she going?* If there are women who step out of their shredded dresses instead of trying to mend them, they are the ones you should study. Study the refugee species. Study the laboratory mice who time after time fall outside the scope of the experiment. The laboratory animal that leaves its species owing to a belief in non-affinity or alternative affinity as a matter of choice. The mammal transformed into alien. Creature of the future. The possibilities for transcendence are endless.

DR. RUTH COOPER: I think we are getting off topic. We were talking about Andy Warhol. We were talking about why you shot him. I'd like us to keep to that for now. Later there will be a chance for you to tell me about yourself and your childhood.

VALERIE: I'm talking about Andy Warhol and his way of pretending he has gunshot wounds to attract yet more attention. It's the wrong question. It ought to be: *Why doesn't she shoot? Why in hell's name doesn't she shoot?* All her rights were under attack. A state of raped she-babies and raped she-animals. And why don't they shoot? I don't actually know, Dr. Cooper. If I knew, we wouldn't be sitting here. Half a civilization on its knees and an arms industry that turns over more every month to the corrupt world than the third world's combined debt. And that's not including the porn industry.

NARRATOR: What sort of material do we have?

VALERIE: Motorways. Trucks. America.

NARRATOR: And what else?

VALERIE: Ocean material.

NARRATOR: Tell me about the ocean.

VALERIE: Alligator Reef. The Atlantic. White sand, white stones. The all-bright water surface of steel and brume. Bladder wrack. Beach umbrellas. Tourists. Mine and Dorothy's beach. Later, Dorothy in the desert. She never finishes the book.

NARRATOR: And then?

VALERIE: The little male seahorse roaming across the beaches with his flashing camera. There's him and me and the pounding of the waves.

NARRATOR: Tell me more about the material.

VALERIE: The material is called SHE'S NOT COMING.

Dorothy and Moran lie exhausted in the flowery bedroom. Dorothy sleeps her deep, wine-induced slumber, chewing her way through the nights as though her dreams were always about food; her nightdress has ridden up to expose her private parts, which are dark and swollen. Moran has placed his hamburger-hand on her stomach like a stone. Her liver-spotted skin is a curtain across the sky and the trees. You take all the money you can find, a few clothes and some photographs, a bottle of wine, a packet of cigarettes, your notebooks, a dress that belongs to Dorothy, the transistor radio. And your Royal 100.

The wallpaper is yellow with age and sun, with desperate, joyful days of dirty windows and bad food, with all the years, all the flies. Dorothy's warm hands on your face. Dorothy's face between the huge shadows of the trees. Dorothy, full of sweet wine, lying in your bed in the afternoons when you come home from school. Dorothy with the flypapers and soap and desperado voice: *I don't want to choose, Valerie. I don't want All or Nothing.*

If I have to choose, I choose All. I choose you, Valerie. And I choose Moran, Valerie.

The stink of wine and sweat and their horror-film love, pounding with passion, is like a foul-smelling wall around them when you take your things and flee. The sky outside is flaming pink, faint stars in the garden everywhere. Glasses and bottles by the porch seat, the veranda drenched in morning sun. You slam the door to the house one last time for a final walk across the desert. The desert where Louis cleared off, where the river was poisoned and Dorothy chased around and burned the sleeves of her dresses, where you both meandered hand in hand beneath the heavens. You tell Sister White about it later:

> *I ran away in the desert. I never found my way home. Everything was cold blue sharks. I was a sick child. I missed Louis. Missed the electricity, the tingling sensation in my legs and arms. I was impossible to love. I walked through the desert. It was bright and white and lonely and I took my things and left. Everything inside me screamed, my heart, Dorothy, the light flickering. The soup bowls and bottles from the night before were still on the table, wine stains, a filthy cloth, Dorothy's pink letters, insects chasing each other across the plastic tablecloth. There was a smell of rain and water and gasoline and old wine. A lizard was standing in Moran's old whisky glass, looking at me. It was windy that day. I put the lizard inside my jumper and ran.*

The sky is a skin-colored curtain descending over you and Georgia.

You are on your way to nowhere in particular, just away. Motorways, deserts, trucks, and forests. After Georgia there is Alabama, Virginia, Florida, and Philadelphia and you walk between the trucks begging for a lift and money and hamburgers. Exhaust-fume flowers dance along at the side of the roads and sometimes Ventor flickers past with its shacks, its car wrecks and dirt roads and the reek of gasoline and motorway. Outside, the winds spiral, your jeans are dirty and you try to concentrate on the typewriter instead of America passing by with its blacked-out towns, housewives and churchgoers all behind their lace curtains. Atlantic City. Baltimore. Washington. Richmond. Norfolk. Portsmouth. Wilmington. Charleston. Jacksonville. Key West.

In the White House new wars are planned, new family programs, the president sitting at his great desk, musing about America. Dorothy continues to send him fan letters from the desert. The sky is cold and flashing and when you wake in the mornings at filling stations, service areas, and motels someone has always placed a soda or a sandwich in your hand. The drivers want nothing special from you, they like your company and do not care where you come from. They let you sleep and work in peace for hundreds of miles and hundreds of versions of America. Sometimes you jerk someone off, sometimes you let someone jerk off onto your panties or on your jeans. It never goes further than that and so it is of no account. The best time is when you are waiting in roadside cafés, before you are thrown out. There you can organize your papers and use your wash machine, which is a can with detergent and hot tea-water, and you make sure your hair is always clean. And when you fall asleep in the cargo space at night, your dreams are full of sand and rose wallpaper. Dorothy is carrying you through the desert, Dorothy in tears chasing you across America, Dorothy finding you and taking you home. The most beautiful dream of all is where Dorothy has tattooed her old surname on her arm like a bumper sticker and your name on her left breast like a cry for help inside her dress. Valerie. Ocean bird. Solanas.

THE ARCHITECTS

A. The body is a part of the building. Buildings create people. The body, the surface, America.

B. You cannot imagine a text without people. A building does not exist before the building is inhabited. The apparel, lower forms of art, the architect's genesis. The architects. The narrators. I fix my attention on the surface. On the text. All text is fiction.

C. Surface, clothes, femininity. Flocks of girls moving through the cities. Public women, public relations. Street love. Happy, sunny streets. Regulated prostitution.

D. Don't hang about in windows. Don't wander up and down a street. Don't walk around in a group of girls. Don't address strange men in the street. When can a woman spend time outdoors? Never. The winds of rape are blowing across America.

E. Heterosexual neurosis. Postmodern parasites. You have to go through a lot of sex to get to anti-sex. Martin Luther King, Jr., speaks to the darkness. The Black Panthers sit and wait. In his last speech he is mild and tender and he is no longer afraid. You will not miss me when I am gone. It will be better for you when I am no longer here. An Amazon's odyssey.

F. The interior consists of femininity and sexuality. Roses and pussies. Embellishment is removed from the male. He is the black suit. He is black cars in the city.

G. She was dressed in a fantastic white fur. She wanted to take part in a beauty contest. She wanted to look like a sculpture. Miss America. The history of the blonde. Of the whore. The world's finest, oldest profession.

H. Miss America contests were introduced the same year as electoral reform. In 1952 Colleen Hutchins from Salt Lake City was the tallest, heaviest, blondest girl in the history of Miss America. Electoral reform was implemented, men returned to the factories, new world wars began, the first wave was swallowed up by the oceans.

I. The mythical essence of drives and instincts, the monumentality of their indeterminateness. Neurosis, culture, apathy, linguistic style, perversion, immensely infantile child sexuality. Many degenerate phenomena and pathological perversions have their basis in childhood. It is no longer possible to record and catalogue sexual phenomena without the need to create an overarching theory. The life-threatening bond between children and mothers, between babies and breastfeeders. Amendment to the theory of sexuality. Hey, wait, mister.

J. There is no sun in the house. No light. I have an artificial body, an artificial longing. The doctors say to me: It is a physical disorder, not a condition. Your hatred of men is going to destroy you. You have no reflexes, you are malnourished and in trouble. Hatred of men equals trouble.

K. The ocean's influence on your plans for the future. He became obsessed with her and wanted to paint her and photograph her all the time. It was a struggle, an ongoing contract. He was there, pawing at her house. Discreet battles. He dreamed of dying of a heart attack in the ocean. Or a shark attack. Like a warrior.

L. She has so much time in her eyes. An army of men in black. How many has she screwed? I don't know. How many have you screwed? One thousand and one nights.

M. My sexiest quality is that I'm always game. I never tire. I love semen. I love dicks. It does not matter who it is, what it is, where, or how. I just love it. My sexiest quality is that I'm always game. I never tire.

N. The evil structure of language. It was an illness, a deranged, totally inappropriate grief response. I laughed and flew straight into the light. There was nothing to respond appropriately to. Everything but her voice was sucked into a black hole and vanished. What difference does it make if you have regrets?

O. Call me what you will. You are never going to know my real name. Theatricality. Setting the stage. Annihilation.

P. You want a ride? I am a death machine. There is a group of people in the city who are neutral. I don't want to come out of the closet. I am discreet. It is nice in here in the dark. Lampshades, walls, houses, roads, the state. I work with the surface. The street is a metaphor and also quite real. Like the ocean. The deep blue yonder is always present. Death is always present. I wake at night. Alone.

Q. It was a house full of secrets. A sky full of stars. Mothers with their stars and smiles.

R. White interior. Who created it? What does the white stand for? Blond woman, women's building, World's Fair. The White House. It's the white color, the clear white thoughts.

S. The American woman. History of the beauty contest. Freak show. Angel snake girl. Come (CUM) and see her beautiful body and her ugly face. Snake face. A white circus, white presidents. America is governed by white presidents. Men trapped between being humans and apes. Fuckiefuckie.

T. Daddy's Girls and Rulers of the Universe. They were not all alike. They were not all white. Not one of them was genuine. They all ruled and destroyed things. They all loved sucking cocks.

U. Cock sucking is a fantastic thing as well. Sucking dicks all day long is something real. It tastes of salt and shit and human being and black water. You can think about something else, you can't think about nothing. Ten dollars. Nothing. White houses in your mouth. Clear white thoughts.

V. Death is black. Sleep is black. Night is black. When it's black you might as well be dead. I want to know that they will not burn my body. I want to be buried as I am. I don't want any man to touch me when I'm dead. I want to know: How many times can my heart break?

W. Some experiences are significant. Who you are screwing is significant. If you have a house is significant. If you are white if you are a woman if you are alone. Your feather fingers, please caress me with your feather fingers. Harder with your fingers. That smooth tongue you have in your mouth.

X. It just happened to be like that. Everyone has a background. Everything has a beginning. Everything reaches its end.

Y. A vision of the city. Reproduction. Machines. Now artificial reproduction is possible. Reproduction of history. Artificial historiography. Artificial bodies.

Z. It shaped an entire upbringing. It was overrun with weeds around the house in Ventor. Textile. Surface. Text. Theater. Stage sets. Fabric. It wasn't architecture; it was pure white thoughts. It wasn't real life; it was an experience. The textile character of the text. They were just fictional characters, a fictional girl, fictional figurants. It was fictional architecture and a fictional narrator. She asked me to embroider her life. I choose to believe in the one who embroiders.

In a summer of never-ceasing rain, the doctors do not halt their diagnoses. Heavy curtains of tears and time and therapy sessions outside Dr. Ruth's window. Vicious explosions of sunlight inside your hospital gown amid the summer downpours, invasions of insects into the depths of the hospital and hospital food, and all the time you light new cigarettes and leave them to balance on the edge of the desk.

DR. RUTH COOPER: We're on your side in this hospital, Valerie.

VALERIE: Yeah.

DR. RUTH COOPER: We have nothing to do with the police investigation.

VALERIE: Police faggots.

DR. RUTH COOPER: I can see you're distressed, Valerie.

VALERIE: I'm not distressed.

DR. RUTH COOPER: It's okay to cry.

VALERIE: I'm not crying.

DR. RUTH COOPER: Crying can be beautiful.

VALERIE: I'm not crying, it's my brain bleeding.

DR. RUTH COOPER: Here's a handkerchief, Valerie.

VALERIE: Thanks, but crying isn't my style.

DR. RUTH COOPER: Okay, what are you thinking about when you're not crying?

VALERIE: Regrets that I made bad art. That's the only thing I can imagine crying about.

DR. RUTH COOPER: How about you smoke one cigarette at a time, Valerie?

VALERIE: Yes, how about it? When is the trial?

DR. RUTH COOPER: Later.

VALERIE: Is Andy still playing dead in the hospital?

DR. RUTH COOPER: I want to talk about your mother.

VALERIE: I'm not ill.

DR. RUTH COOPER: I want to talk about Dorothy.

VALERIE: May I smoke a cigarette then?

DR. RUTH COOPER: Yes.

VALERIE: May I smoke two cigarettes?

DR. RUTH COOPER: You can start by smoking one cigarette. Listen to me now.

VALERIE: Dorothy always smoked two.

DR. RUTH COOPER: I understand. I'm going to tell you how I see your situation.

VALERIE: Or more.

DR. RUTH COOPER: More?

VALERIE: Cigarettes. Come on, Cooper. Tell me who I am. I'm used to fortune-tellers.

DR. RUTH COOPER (*smiles, and then looks serious*): I believe you are living in a delusion and you are currently in a schizophrenic reaction of the paranoid type.

VALERIE: Really. And I can tell you about men's flagrant inferiority. About nature's true order. There is no reason to involve male mice. Mouse girls can have mouse babies with one another. I can tell you about my laboratory research.

DR. RUTH COOPER: Even though you make strenuous efforts to appear a hard, tough, cynical misanthrope, you are actually only a frightened, depressed child.

VALERIE: Call it what you will. You will never know my real name.

DR. RUTH COOPER: That's my impression. A scared little child. Full of fear. Full of self-loathing.

VALERIE: My impression is that you are a scared little male-female. My impression is that your efforts are utterly futile. My impression is that you are a really stupid little cocksucker. But it isn't your fault. It's all a result of your unfortunate background under patriarchy.

DR. RUTH COOPER: So we are talking about a schizophrenic reaction of the paranoid type with deep depression and serious potential for destructive acts.

VALERIE: I'm not ill.

DR. RUTH COOPER: You are extremely ill, Valerie. That doesn't mean you're not a very gifted, headstrong woman.

VALERIE: This is no illness. I repeat. My condition is not a medical condition. It's more a condition of extreme clarity, of stark white operating lights illuminating all words, things, bodies, and identities. Within a stroke or a shout of you, Dr. Cooper, everything looks different. Your so-called diagnosis is an exact description of woman's place in the system of mass psychosis. Schizophrenia, paranoia, depression, and the potential for destructive acts. Every girl in patriarchy knows that schizophrenia, paranoia, and depression are in no way a description of an individual medical condition. It is a definitive diagnosis of a social structure and a form of government based on constant insults to the brain capacity of half the population, founded on rape.

DR. RUTH COOPER: I want to help you, Valerie. But to do that I need to know more about you.

VALERIE: I have my own qualifications from the Psychology Institute and Animal Laboratory in Maryland, which means that I will apply my own diagnoses.

DR. RUTH COOPER: Yes, I understand you're one of their star students.

VALERIE: I was filled with happiness that day. I whistled and sang and drank cheap wine. I tried to keep on the sunny side. I always had gold and silver threads sewn into my dresses.

DR. RUTH COOPER: Tell me about that day, Valerie.

VALERIE: No. Qualifications are just a way of separating people.

BRISTOL HOTEL, APRIL 14, 1988

The smell of dead shorebirds and prostitution permeates the hotel room and as the light slowly retreats from the window, the sounds of the night take over, sirens blot out memories, and you have given up all attempts to sit by the window making notes. To write now would be to throw yourself into an ice-cold tidal wave and drown in the searing pain of salt and self-hatred. Instead you try to sleep away an hour in the yellow sheets, to concentrate on the sound of waves from a different time, the surfboard beneath your feet, the breakers, the blue jellyfish, your childish bodies promising surf and play forever, sun and sparks of life and skin, his smile enchanted.

Surfing days, the fifties, all spiral past into your slumber, a moment of blinding light in the screaming blackness of space. Silk Boy with his salty, unkempt braids, the irresistible junkie look. A long time ago you loved to search for sea creatures and debris out where it was deepest and bluest, small sharks, crabs, and seahorses. A long time ago you dreamed of drowning in someone's arms.

There is no hotel in this whoremongering state where you have not been raped and received payment and all you wish now is that you had never entered this shark industry and that death would not come so fast, not like this, and not to you. Just before you fall asleep, your hand reaches for the dying light, the glimmering luminescence in the murky brown water.

Silky?

. . . are you there, Silly Boy? . . .

SILK BOY (*his breath moist and salty*): I'm here, Valerie. I'll sit here until you fall asleep, if you like.

VALERIE: The docks are for old thoughts.

SILK BOY: The docks are for old ladies, you mean.

VALERIE: Old ladies and surfing and death. In the swimming pool, Mrs. Cox always practiced farthest in, at the shallow end.

SILK BOY: A million-dollar mermaid, a million-dollar hooker.

VALERIE: What was it Mrs. Cox always said?

SILK BOY: When I'm wet I'm fantastic, when I'm dry I'm just a boring housewife.

VALERIE: It was so cold, the bridal bouquet froze.

SILK BOY: My little bouquet of frost.

VALERIE: It was you and me and the ocean and it was always summertime. I remember chasing you under the water. You were my underwater fantasy.

SILK BOY: Are you cold?

VALERIE: Are we still married?

SILK BOY: No.

VALERIE: Why aren't we? All my life I've believed we were married.

SILK BOY: You have holes in your memories. The drugs have blotted them out.

VALERIE (*reaches her hand out into the dying light*): Give me a kiss.

SILK BOY: Why?

VALERIE: Because I need it. Because I'm going to die. Because I'm scared of dying.

SILK BOY: You reek, Valerie. Your mouth smells of death.

VALERIE (*her hands fumble with the sheets*): Kiss me.

SILK BOY: Why did you leave me?

VALERIE: Did I?

SILK BOY: You left me.

VALERIE: Did I? I don't remember. I'm going to sleep now. I'm going to sleep and I'm going to dream it's night, and I'm alone in a hotel room in San Francisco, and you're dead, and there isn't a question about death in every grammar.

SILK BOY: There are no sharks in death. Death is just the end.

VALERIE: Death is the only happy ending.

That morning the Rosenbergs were executed at Sing Sing Correctional Facility in New York. Silk Boy had been out during the night and picked magnolias and palm leaves, sold a few wet kisses and feigned gasps outside the motel on the way home and then popped in to see Mrs. Cox's partner in the coffee bar, where he collected his birthday present: a handful of dollars and a wedding cake with pink marzipan that someone had ordered and forgotten to pick up.

Your scribbles float out into the ocean, they spill over onto your hands, onto furniture, walls, and the back of used paper. You write wherever there is room. Your Royal 100 was left with a shark in Alabama, a beautiful, dangerous territory with a lot of money and extravagant food; in the afternoons you went deep into the forest with him to practice shooting birds. From that time on you have avoided sharks with weapons.

Alligator Reef, the hot, briny coast, where frost flowers spring up on all the car windows. At night you dream about Ethel

Rosenberg in the electric chair, that she is alone in the desert wearing a bikini and she is weeping, that she writes reams of shocking-pink begging letters to the American government to be allowed to live.

THE STATE (*a priest, woken in the night, holds your hand tightly for a moment*): Valerie Jean Solanas, do you take this boy?

VALERIE: Yes . . . I take this boy, and I will always love him.

THE STATE: Do you take this girl, Valerie Solanas?

SILK BOY: Yes, I'll protect her from all that scares her. When she's with me, I'm not afraid anymore. I'll hold her hand when she cries.

(*Fuck Silly Boy.*)

(*Fuck the State.*)

(*Fuck God.*)

(*Fuck you, God, if you saw everything by the river.*)

VALERIE: No, thanks. I don't need any protection. Never have, never will. I'll protect him.

THE STATE: Do you take his declaration of love, Valerie Jean Solanas?

VALERIE: No. I've always taken care of myself. That's just it. I have need of no husband, no state, no priest, no god, no father, no money.

THE STATE: Yes, or no?

VALERIE: No.

SILK BOY: Valerie, it's not important now. I only want to be where you are, only want to hold your hand when you cry.

THE STATE: Do you take this boy's declaration of love or not?

VALERIE: No, I've told you. He has to say what I tell him if I'm going to take him.

SILK BOY (*to the priest*): Do as she says.

THE STATE: Well?

SILK BOY (*to you*): Come on, Valerie. I'll say what you want.

VALERIE: Okay . . . I, Beach Boy, take Valerie Jean Solanas to live in her shadow and love her and she will be my officer and my warrior . . . my dog against the night.

SILK BOY: Okay . . . I, Beach Boy, take Valerie Jean Solanas to live in her shadow and love her and she will be my officer and my warrior . . . and my what else?

VALERIE: I am your dog against the night.

SILK BOY: I am your dog against the night.

VALERIE: *You* . . . You've got to say *you*. Not I.

SILK BOY: You are my dog against the night, Valerie.

ALLIGATOR REEF, 1953–1954
NEW NUCLEAR TESTING ON BIKINI ATOLL

The sun sinks across the sand dunes and in the campsite kiosk the television set flickers. In flippers and goggles you are waiting for Silk Boy to appear between the beach umbrellas with a plastic bag filled with a bottle of bubbly, sweets, roll-ups, and broken goggles. Mrs. Cox has given you extra sweets and extra cigarettes. She has warned you about swimming too far out, warned you about the great white sharks, the killer whales, the gigantic tiger shark.

Mrs. Cox lights fresh cigarettes and keeps you company in a camping chair with her old shark stories and she lets you eat what you want without paying. Hamburgers with mustard and gherkins and flat Coca-Cola. *There are no sharks, Mrs. Cox, just the ocean just the stars just ten sorts of flowers just happy endings.* The surfers hurtle through the waves outside and Silk Boy is always late, always stays far too long at Mr. Biondi's.

MRS. COX: Tell me about your little brother.
VALERIE: Seahorse. Animal photographer. Happy.

MRS. COX: I can see you're brother and sister.

VALERIE: Yes. Though he was born a year after me. April ninth. Same day but exactly a year later. Dorothy wanted twins. She made sure she got knocked up good and proper. She calls us her twin boys.

MRS. COX: When is she coming back?

VALERIE: Dorothy? . . . Anytime. She's always calling the phone booth with new dates, but we say we want to stay here.

MRS. COX: And money?

VALERIE: Dorothy sends us money all the time.

MRS. COX: What's his name?

VALERIE: Silk Boy.

MRS. COX: I mean, for real. An actual boy's name, I mean.

VALERIE: He's just called Silk Boy.

When Mr. Biondi pulls down the blinds in the bedroom, the beach and the sky and the light disappear, and in the sheets Silk Boy laughs. The skin nearest his eye and on his wrists and groin is quite translucent and he is always brimming with giggles and lipstick kisses and devotion. Mr. Biondi and all that silky skin, making him weep and laugh and shout out for God and his mother and eternity. And in his large and beautiful house he groans, his hands deep in the boy's hair, and he wishes he would never need to come and the boy would never leave. And when he does finally come into that childlike mouth, he just wants to come again, to drown, to melt into the boy.

Mr. Biondi bathes in money and loneliness and he tries to hold on to those enchanted hands that are forever on their way to somewhere else and he always has more money in his pockets and always has more drugs. Later, as he stands waving from the solarium with his swollen lips, his bathrobe slips open and he stands naked and pleading before the boy and the ocean and his face is a forest of dead white trees and the boy twists out of his hands and runs off along the boardwalk.

When at last he returns, the sun has gone down and Mrs. Cox has closed the shop and you have fallen asleep on the flagstones outside.

The beaches are deserted now, the bathers have gone, the umbrellas have been cleared away. The waves crash against the shore too violently for anyone to want to vacation here and there is always a black flag flying at the lifeguard tower. Silk Boy walks over the beach with his empty bottles and you lie for days on end looking for UFOs while he keeps busy, the little collector and worker. The campsite is empty and you move between the remaining trailers. All that descends over them is a green mist of beer bottles and a shower of campfire detritus and rain. Card games and dope games no longer work and Silk Boy turns his narrow back, sits smoking a pipe, complaining, and hiding from your eyes. It is impossible to write with him in the trailer. You wish he would go and talk to Mrs. Cox. You long to be alone, to be at home in Ventor, to have money, a house, a new Royal 100. Mrs. Cox is very kind, but she is a fool like all the rest. Outside the trailer, the ocean is gray and dull, and inside, all your things are wet and smelly. Hanging from the ceiling are lines of photographs and notes and underwear drying. When the tourists come back, you will leave the trailer and return to the sea. There will be lights on in Biondi's villa again.

Silk Boy and you lie up in the reeds, as the clouds move slowly along beneath the heavens, and everything apart from the ocean is calm, and in your bags you have limitless hash, and he is not hustling anymore, just cashing in empty bottles and begging for small change in the bars, and Dorothy never comes to fetch you, and his skin is silk and streamers, and he still wishes for his own laboratory with male seahorses and photography fluids and of supporting you both with his work on the road and the beach. At night you lie in each other's arms and plan the future. When night sweeps over Alligator Reef, he wishes for another boy, another time, another beginning.

VALERIE: There isn't anything you can't decide. I wish you'd figure that out. There isn't anything that can't be redone.

SILK BOY: Death can't be redone. Your sex can't. Your background can't. Neither can your destiny. Or love. The executed don't come back. I'm an alphabet of bad experiences.

VALERIE: You don't know the alphabet.

SILK BOY: A . . . Alligator Reef. B . . . Boy. C . . . Cravings. D . . . Dead trees. Dead forests. Dead gulls. Downfall. E . . . Electric chair. F . . . Fucked up. Fucking fucked up. Forgotten. Fucked-up future. False identity. Film. Feathers. G . . . Grieving over nothing. Getting lost all the time. H . . . Hooker. Hopeless. High all the time. Happy about nothing.

Hairless. Harmless. Hacking cough. Hacking hash cough. Hash hooker. Hooker kid. Whore.

VALERIE: Whore begins with W, not H. I?

SILK BOY: Okay. I . . . Idle. Impossible. J . . . Jackass. K . . . Kisses that hit you right in the heart. L . . . Loser. M . . . Mr. Biondi. N . . . Night. O . . . Outsider. Oral sex. P . . . Problems. Q . . . I don't know any words beginning with Q. There aren't any words beginning with Q.

VALERIE: *Quoailler.*

SILK BOY: I can't speak Spanish.

VALERIE: French. To constantly flick your tail. Or *querelle.* Meaning argument.

SILK BOY: Q . . . Something French. French kisses. R . . . Real boy. S . . . Seahorses. Male seahorses. On the skids. T . . . Ten for a fuck. Thunderbird. U . . . Underwater thoughts. Unholy mess. Underworld . . . V . . . Valerie Jean Solanas. W . . . Wasteland. X . . . X gene. Y . . . Y gene. Z . . . Zebras. Zebra stripes on your skin. Zebras on TV.

VALERIE: Being obsessed with your own doom and the netherworld isn't going to make you free. You can control everything if you want to.

SILK BOY: Flowers. The sun. Half light.

VALERIE: There are so many different ways you can be in the half light. Your gender isn't a prison. It's an opportunity. There are just different ways of telling. Write your own account.

SILK BOY (*laughs*): I can't write.

VALERIE: That's not the end of the world. I'll teach you to write.

And then the calls home to Dorothy.

Just the ocean in the background, terrifying telephonic creatures twisting and straining in the wires blown to the ground and you, unable to say anything and unable to hang up. Her breath, her way of exhaling cigarette smoke into the receiver. For long moments she is silent, sometimes she whispers your name. *Is that Valerie Jean?*

The large black receiver, the hopelessness, and the sand whipping fiercely into your eyes. Her voice sounds as if it were underwater during these conversations. The smell: salt, iron, lies, and menthol.

Sometimes she weeps, sometimes she holds lengthy monologues about her life in the desert. Silk Boy sits outside the phone booth, waiting.

ALLIGATOR REEF, WINTER 1955
THE HIROSHIMA MAIDENS ARRIVE IN NEW YORK
FOR FREE PLASTIC SURGERY

Sweeping over the beaches is the cold breath of the white shark, the strong smell of cigars and dollars. The umbrellas disappeared long ago, there is frost in the reeds and it is no longer possible to sleep on the beach. You can stay as long as you want on the mattresses in Mr. Biondi's solarium. There is food in the house: bread, spaghetti, potatoes, and things in tins, and dope. All day long the boy sits in front of mirrors with salt crystals in his hair, making lipstick kisses, kissing all the mirrors, writing on the glass in lipstick, *Valerie Jean Solanas will be president of America*. On the veranda he works on his seahorse collection, small dried seahorses in different colors that he sorts and organizes. Some still have seahorse babies in their stomach pouch, some are shriveled and atrophied and it looks as though they have wept for their young.

SILK BOY: This little dad has two babies in his pouch.
VALERIE: When's Asshole coming back?
SILK BOY (*fingering the seahorses*): He's called Mr. Biondi. One small and one large baby seahorse. The mothers aren't

involved at all. They take off pronto. Water duty, water fantasies, all sorts.

VALERIE: Listen, Sherlock. We have a problem. A problem other than seahorses. Bigger than seahorses.

SILK BOY: I wish you were a little male seahorse with a tiny pouch like that and I could live in it.

VALERIE (*picks up some of the seahorses and talks to them in a seahorse voice*): Right now we're living in an asshole's house. And right now I'm wondering how we can get out of here . . . (*holds the seahorses in front of his face*) . . . This is Asshole. And this is Dope Boy . . . And this is Valerie . . . Once upon a time there was a low-down Mr. Shark who loved naïve little dope boys . . . masochistic little dickhead whoreboys . . .

SILK BOY (*pries open your hands and takes the seahorses from you*): Stop it. They break when you do that.

VALERIE: We'll have to sort out this matter of the seahorses another day. I don't want to live here anymore. And you don't, either.

SILK BOY: Without Mr. Biondi, there'll be no money for college.

VALERIE: It's not real college money. We'll just be whores there too if it's Biondi Asshole money.

There are no more temporary photo labs in the campsite toilets. He has got his own little lab at Mr. Biondi's; he generally gets what he wants from Mr. Biondi. A real room with real equipment where he can work all night in the subdued light. When you are allowed in, you usually sit with a little flashlight under a blanket, reading a book and commenting on the photographs he drops down to you. And when Mr. Biondi returns from his travels, Silk Boy moves upstairs to the large floral bedroom.

A cold spell sets in, sharks glide in and out of the bedroom, black leaves fall on the small garden and at night you lie in the porch seat wrapped in blankets, planning for the future, sending off for educational materials from every university in America.

Or recording a tape for Dorothy.

Snow falls on the beach, a thin layer of frost on the sand and the lifeguard towers and the parasols. You record the sound of the ocean and then the sound of the snow falling on the beach. It is crackly and strange, but beautiful. Silk Boy moves noiselessly at the edge of the beach, under orders to be quiet.

Afterward you pull the ribbon out of the cassette and use it as decoration for a present you are sending to Georgia. In the box, sand and marine toys; shells, seaweed, starfish, reeds.

And some of the wind, too, that chases between the blue-black palms.

BRISTOL HOTEL, APRIL 15, 1988

NARRATOR: The deceased is talking to herself again.

VALERIE: What's she saying?

NARRATOR: She's talking about various things. She's saying: It's hypothetical. She's saying: It's not hypothetical. She's saying that she doesn't like arithmetic.

VALERIE: Arithmetic . . . No credit, no discount. No credit, no discount. I don't like arithmetic. And don't have gang wars over territories. It's not nice.

NARRATOR: I'll tell them to change your sheets. I'll tell them to bring some food up for you.

VALERIE: Tell who?

NARRATOR: The staff. I'll sort out your papers and your ideas. If you want, I'll make notes for you. Or read aloud from the manifesto.

VALERIE: There's no staff in this hotel. I don't make notes anymore. Instead, tell me what you were thinking about when you were sitting there in the window before.

NARRATOR: I suppose I was thinking about you.

VALERIE: You've fallen in love with someone who doesn't exist.

NARRATOR: A virtual love affair. A girl in the sand who vanishes, my mother's childhood, my father's broken heart.

VALERIE: It's not your death material. It's not your screwing material.

NARRATOR: May I hold your hand?

VALERIE: You're romanticizing this and sentimentalizing it. The notes will go up in flames in the backyard in Ventor. The dying material is just vomit, diarrhea, phlegm, and fear. There is no point in sitting here waiting. All this is just nothing-at-all material. It will all vanish.

NARRATOR: I'm so sad you won't survive this story.

VALERIE: There's really nothing to be sad about. I'll give you some good advice if you're sad, because the story ends here. Invite home a ragged girl panhandler who needs somewhere to sleep and something to eat. Invite the girl addicts who sleep in garbage cans. Invite a crack whore, a bag lady, a maniac. Stop in the subway and talk to the psychotic hookers. Don't walk away when she starts ranting and raving about nothing. Ask where she comes from, what she needs, what you can help with, what she has in her notes, if you're so interested in dying crack whores. Visit hostels, mental hospitals, drug ghettos, red-light districts, jails. The world's out there waiting for you, baby. The material is called SHE'S EVERYWHERE.

NARRATOR: I'm not stupid.

VALERIE: And not particularly smart, either.

ALLIGATOR REEF, SUMMER 1955

The birds lie on the shore, battered by the wind and abandoned, and he patrols up and down in his tattered jeans and salt tangles and the perpetual cigarette in the corner of his mouth. White feathers flutter around him as he carries them away to bury them in the reeds, lifting them out of the sand with such care. The giant birds, the ernes and the largest gulls, look like children in his arms. The clouds consume the last of the wintering light and you have grown tired of the camping life and Mr. Biondi and the ocean's way of being merely beautiful and unconcerned. Silk Boy and you each have a place at Jacksonville College for the autumn and he weeps through the night because he thinks he will appear a fool there.

VALERIE: I don't think you should touch those disgusting creatures.
SILK BOY: I don't want them to lie there all alone.
VALERIE: Death is lonely. And they're only rubbish. Shit corpses.
SILK BOY: I can't be here and know they're lying alone all over. You don't need to stay and stare.

VALERIE: It makes no difference how many you bury. There are more all the time. They stink. They make your hands smell of death.

SILK BOY: Would you leave me lying dead here on the beach?

VALERIE (*laughs*): —Little idiot—

SILK BOY (*a gull under each arm*): Would you?

VALERIE: I'd never let you die. I'll make sure that you get to a school. We're going to be students. We're going to take on all of this.

SILK BOY: But I'm just a fool.

VALERIE: You have a research project on the coast. And you have research manager and research coach Valerie Jean Solanas by your side. I swear on my career that I wouldn't let you fall like them.

SILK BOY: My brain is full of dope and dicks.

VALERIE: Your brain is full of dead birds.

The underwater days at Alligator Reef are coming to an end; the shutters are open for the season, but the tourist beach is still empty. The water tastes of seaweed and the salt water stings your eyes. You walk along wearing a wet suit or jeans and a jumper beside Silk Boy, who has a cigarette in one hand and the little worn-out hash pipe in the other. Your clothes are salty and flecked with white. The ice crystals still keep forming in your breast and he chases you across the motorways and sand dunes in his dainty dresses with his delicate wrists. You read your books and reread them, and the pages are covered in ink scrawls, a drawing of the heart, kisses, stars, moons, and inky glosses in the margins: *wet kisses, girls, male seahorses, future.*

Silk Boy has a bad memory and bad teeth and he hides himself away in photo fluids in the campsite toilets and he forgets that you have to go to Jacksonville to register; he carries on working with the photographs of male seahorses, as if your departure were not imminent. You smoke two thousand five hundred cigarettes outside and talk to him through the toilet door. In the pink developing light he is happy, contentment glinting off him when he comes back out to hang his photographs on washing lines between the trees. The photographs are of you, the Atlantic, crabs, starfish, handbags, and the dead kitten that washed ashore.

SILK BOY: You'll have worn all those books out with reading before we start.

VALERIE: It's just reading for pleasure. I'm not learning anything.

SILK BOY: When I'm nervous, I forget what you're supposed to do when you're reading. I read bits of that book about sea-horses over and over again. Then, when I get kind of electric, I forget to concentrate and the words stop meaning anything.

VALERIE: I'll be there the whole time.

SILK BOY: But there'll be nothing left of the books after you've finished, so I won't have anything to read.

VALERIE: Have you packed your bag?

SILK BOY (*with his gaze on a saltwater photograph*): Go on your own, Valerie.

VALERIE: Why?

SILK BOY: It's better if you go and collect the papers and every-thing. I'll just get nervous and start stammering and fill something in wrong and back to front and give us away. And we need more money.

VALERIE: Sometimes I think you're in love with Asshole.

SILK BOY: I'm just scared of ruining something.

VALERIE: Nothing to be afraid of.

SILK BOY: Biondi ran down a flamingo yesterday. There was blood on the car when we got back to the house. I don't want to stay here, either.

VALERIE: Silly darling.

He stands in the doorway with an octopus over one shoulder and lipstick on his teeth. That hopeless, silky-smooth boy, the fifties boy. The summer rain keeps falling on the beach and the little trailer, the new one you broke into when you left Mr. Biondi's solarium. Together you sort out all the things you need for the journey. Pages of notes, yellow and ink-stained, books and photographs with the boy's face cut out. You have written a tale about two campsite whores in a trailer on a beach in nowhere land and Silk Boy laughs into the cigarette smoke and outside the violence of the ocean rages; and in the story the campsite whores fight back against the sharks. The sun spots move softly over his small hands as he turns the pages; his mouth tastes of dope and snow.

SILK BOY: How does it end?
VALERIE: The sharks' bodies are shooting targets.
SILK BOY: How does our story end?
VALERIE: A happy ending.
SILK BOY: You won't leave?
VALERIE: I'm going nowhere without you. Do you like it when
  I read?
SILK BOY: I think you're a true writer. I think you'll be president
  of America.

VALERIE: And you'll be the president's wife. The most beautiful first lady.

SILK BOY: I'm just a regular campsite whore.

VALERIE: You're the sweetest campsite whore in America.

When you walk to the bus, he is asleep. The little whoreboy with so much money in his pockets and so much aversion to schools and unknown cities. You kiss his warm wrists and gather up your things.

The ocean birds screech outside the trailer and when he talks to himself in his sleep he sounds like a child—*I don't want more ice cream—not the sharks—no, not more sharks—I promise—just sing a smutty little magic song for nice Mr. Biondi.* His shins are sticking out over the damp, threadbare mattress (there are hundreds of Polaroids of his shins) and he sleeps with his hand covering his dick.

This silk boy is so beautiful. So beautiful and frightened and unfettered. He loves swimming where it is deepest and darkest. He loves swimming when the warning flags are up on the beach. He spends all his nights in strange cars, but he does not dare take the bus the twenty-odd miles north to register at college. Only you can save him with your books, your schools, and your faith in the future.

Dr. Ruth Cooper appears to have unlimited time for meaning-less consultations with patients, and in the end they are prefer-able to walking around amid the ward's wreckage of girls and women. And after a couple of conversations with Dr. Cooper, you no longer remember who you are. You are Dorothy, Saman-tha, Cosmogirl, you are a hundred thousand murdered women prostitutes on the beaches. Sereena, Mona, Jacqueline, Heather, Diane, Angele, Brenda.

Hey, hey, hey, Dr. Cooper. What do you know about love?

The curtains are being sucked out of the window and are flap-ping sharply against the hospital concrete. Dr. Cooper, under her impeccable hair, sits and waits for you to start crying, but you do not cry, as there is nothing to cry about. It is the hottest sum-mer in New York in seventy years. It is 1968. Andy Warhol is dying and Cosmogirl is not there anymore. On Fifth Avenue

Daddy's Girls are marching with their ridiculous posters about abortion and the pill and date rape, moronic demands to be broodmares and cocksuckers on their own conditions. A female political agenda not even laboratory mice would accept. Daddy's Girls read aloud from the manifesto. They kiss each other and burn their middle-class underwear, while all you do is wander along asylum corridors in a secondhand dress, black with yearning for death.

After persistent requests and entreaties, Dr. Ruth Cooper has obtained permission for you to wear your own dress in the ward, not the raincoat, not the mirrored spectacles, but the dress. Your bag is still impounded and the manifesto and your notes have been confiscated indefinitely.

DR. RUTH COOPER: It's okay to cry here. Everything you say will remain in here.
VALERIE: Andy Warhol is in the hospital playing dead and I have no desire at all to die.
DR. RUTH COOPER: You can rely on me absolutely for complete confidentiality. I've spoken to the hospital administration and I've obtained permission for you to wear your own clothes in the ward.
VALERIE: And my bag? Is it still impounded?
DR. RUTH COOPER: You'll get all your things back when you leave the hospital.
VALERIE: Still confiscated then. I've got nothing good to read, just those romantic novels they bring round on their stupid little library trolley.
DR. RUTH COOPER: I think you should read *Alice in Wonderland*.
VALERIE: I bet you do. But it wasn't quite what I had in mind.

DR. RUTH COOPER: I still think you should read it. I'll get it for you. It has meant a lot to me. There are similarities between you and me. We're both women, we've both studied psychology in graduate school.

VALERIE: I won't read it.

DR. RUTH COOPER: You're extremely gifted, Valerie.

VALERIE: I'm bored.

DR. RUTH COOPER: Don't throw all that talent away. You can be whatever you want.

VALERIE: Half a nation on its knees prevents me from doing that. Millions of doormats are spoiling my view of the sea. A room of one's own is a fiction that doesn't work.

DR. RUTH COOPER: Half a nation and a million doormats are beyond your control.

VALERIE: And all those waiting outside in the corridor?

DR. RUTH COOPER: That's my responsibility. And the hospital's.

VALERIE: Then I think you should grant entrance to all those who are waiting. I have more important things to do.

DR. RUTH COOPER: Things change. Women no longer accept life as second-class citizens.

VALERIE: Thanks. I know. An army of lobotomized Barbie dolls is marching along Fifth Avenue with their ridiculous posters about abortion and the pill and date rape. I can't even remember if they're for or against date rape.

DR. RUTH COOPER: Being alone is a utopia. Two people thinking the same thing makes a reality. They might be reading from your manifesto.

VALERIE: Of course they're reading from the manifesto. That's the problem. I assume they're kissing each other. I assume they're burning their middle-class underwear. I assume they've got round-trip tickets to hell.

DR. RUTH COOPER: Next time we see each other, I'll have a book for you.

VALERIE: Absolutely, Miss Higgins. Can we consider this little consultation concluded now?

DR. RUTH COOPER: One last question. Did you finance your college education by means of prostitution?

VALERIE: You're darned right I did, Doctor.

LABORATORY PARK

BRISTOL HOTEL, APRIL 16, 1988

NARRATOR: Did you fuck up your doctorate?

VALERIE: There's more than one way to fuck up . . .

NARRATOR: Did you?

VALERIE: Is it you or I who's going to die?

NARRATOR: Did you?

VALERIE: Is it you or I who's narrating this?

NARRATOR: I'm the narrator.

VALERIE: And I'm the subject of this muddleheaded, fucked-up text. You're not a proper narrator, baby.

NARRATOR: I'm just a sentimental fool, I know. But since I'm the only narrator present and interested, maybe you could answer my questions.

(*Silence.*)

NARRATOR: Did you screw up your doctorate?

VALERIE: It's probably more the case that I always had great difficulty grasping what was in the script. I always forgot my lines.

April proceeds toward doom, and every time you fall asleep in the Tenderloin you think you will never wake again, but you always do and it is still the cruelest month. You dream of huge television sets with giant monsters inside and their arms sticking out into the room; and when you wake up, you cannot remember any names, you cannot remember if they are female mammals or male mammals, but they all had face powder for TV and wolf makeup. In your dreams you fight your way through fields of murdered prostitute girls. *She was covered in leaves and earth. She lay strangled behind the church. The john fled on a woman's bicycle. She was discovered murdered in the cellar. She was found strangled in Madison Square Park. She was the victim of rape and murder in September 1982. She was discovered on a demolition site. She disappeared from the street in June. She was suffocated in her hotel room at the Pink Flamingo Hotel.*

But just a breath away is the boy who looked like your sister, a dog-eared Polaroid of ragged clouds moving unhurriedly above the sands and the pulse of the giant waves under your surfboard.

SILK BOY: Hello, Valerie.
VALERIE: What are you doing over there?
SILK BOY: The freaks are aristocrats, they say. It was the cold white shark. That icy breath sweeping over the beach. It was

nighttime and everything was quiet. Just the white shark farthest in on the shore. Do you remember the dead orca? It had huge black wounds on its body. The smell of blood on the beach. Mr. Biondi drove over animals on the roads on purpose.

VALERIE: You cried into your little powder compact afterward. Sharks aren't personal. They never seek personal revenge. They kill indiscriminately. There's no reason to be sad about it.

SILK BOY: I wish I could help you.

VALERIE: Little crybaby. Little shark . . .

SILK BOY: You've ruined your life.

VALERIE: I liked being on drugs. I never accepted the paradigm.

SILK BOY: But it all went down the tube, Valerie.

VALERIE (*opens her silver coat, the room is hot and clammy, the stench of illness rises from the coat*): You can have sex with me, if you like. Five for a fuck, three for a blow job, one for a hand job.

SILK BOY: You've got the stink of death on you, Valerie. The stink of dead orcas and dead shark dolls. I'll help you close that coat.

VALERIE: Nasty little nancy boy . . .

When you return to Alligator Reef, the trailer is deserted. You have been away too long, arranging accommodation, course documents, registration—everything and nothing. Classes have already begun, time has passed in the student dorm, and all along you meant to go back and fetch him. In the end Mrs. Cox sent a postcard from the campsite. *The boy was full of water and drugs when he was found. A drowning accident or drug-related. I identified him at the morgue. They said he had been raped by some customers and he was not your little brother at all. Silk Boy or little brother, it doesn't matter. He was as pleased as Punch about your college acceptances. Happy with that little bag in his hand all the time. He kept reading the books from cover to cover until they fell apart. He sat at the bus stop day after day, waiting for you to come back. Why didn't you come back?*

Mrs. Cox holds your hands when you try to smash everything around you. She sorts out ice cream and hamburgers for you, gives you money and joints. The campsite smells of grilled meat and sweaty old men and the clouds hang absurdly low over the shore. Your things have gone, notes, clothes, and photographs, and Biondi's villa is empty. There are strangers sleeping in his garden and the solarium no longer has windows. The doors slam in the wind. No one knows where Mr. Biondi has gone. You stay at the campsite, waiting for him to return, but he does not come. You are down on the beach, shouting at the sea, kicking at seabirds rotting on the sand, no one to bury them now; bedraggled white feathers, eyes pecked away, forlorn corpses, the waves crushing everything around you. One more time you take the bus to Jacksonville alone, your bag full of your shared college savings, and inform them you will definitively be one instead of two; you move back in to the student room with his little duffel bag, place a tiny dried-up male seahorse in the window and a sunset photograph of Dorothy, and you start reading.

Days and nights at the desk with a view of the park. Frosty windows, candles instead of lamps, but it is still warmer than in the trailer in winter. No ocean, no beach, just page after page of American history, the presidents, the world wars, and Silk Boy's tremulous underwater voice trailing you through the books. *Valerie Jean Solanas will be president of America. Valerie Jean Solanas, you are my dog against the night.*

Sun in all the trees, white dresses and fireworks, popping corks, hamburgers. In your hand your college diploma from Jacksonville, in your bag the scholarship to Maryland. Students walking joyfully through the park, everything drowning in light, parents arriving in family cars. You sit under the huge oak trees and lecture the other girls. *Always students. Never housewives. Never wipe up a man's shit or wash his wacked-off underpants. Always study. Always read and write. Don't let boys have the last word, don't let any strange men force their way into your thoughts. Do research, become professors and writers. Keep on your toes all the time. Never take drugs.* They laugh at your jokes and your card tricks, laugh when you win their money off them, blink back when you flirt with them. Everyone is impressed with your awards. All the girls want to invite you to their graduation dinners with their families. You are the poorest, and the most parentless, and have been awarded more scholarships at Jacksonville than anyone else. You have eclipsed everyone with your scintillating mind and quick wit. The principal, Sister Hyacinth, has stroked your hair and foretold a brilliant future for you in the American education system.

Later you walk in the park with your diploma and your scholarships. You are filled with happiness and possibilities. The park is dark and deserted, champagne bottles and sandwich wrappers littering the grass, and walking around with all that optimism under your dress makes you giddy. You lie beneath the starry sky all night, imagining the future, that Silk Boy is there with you, that he is such a happy student beside you on the grass, a carefree scholarship recipient and ruler of the universe, not drowned by Mr. Biondi and Alligator Reef. *It wasn't hard, Silky. There was no competition, chicken. You would have made it too, Silly Boy.*

The whole night under a tree, smoking, looking at the grass, the buildings, the sky, and you cannot stop reading the welcome letter, twisting it, squeezing it, wondering if it is real. *Valerie Jean Solanas, born 1936 in Ventor, Georgia, is accepted into the graduate program at University of Maryland, Department of Psychology.* The phone booth is lined with condensation again, the student park transformed into a lake of rain and desolation. The other students have been taken back to the suburbs by their daddies, and there is only the rain, falling onto your hair while you attempt to call home to Dorothy.

Remote, soot-black ringing tones across the landscape of sand; you remember them so well, slicing through the kitchen and the heat, while Dorothy proudly flew through the house to answer, but the desert does not answer now, only a little desert fox scampering across the yard at home in Ventor. And when the signals drop and the rain outside falls, you see Dorothy in Red Moran's arms, immersed in a deep and dreamless sleep. Dorothy in bed under the rose wallpaper, a chubby hand protectively round her head, her nightgown drawn up to her waist. Her pubic hair is dark, matted, coarse, newly fucked, and around the two of them hangs that wretched underwear smell. And no one in Ventor answers, and the words on the welcome letter from Maryland drain away in a pale blue mist, a river of loneliness to drown in.

It is like trying to call the ocean, trying to call Silk Boy to say that you are burning with pride and prospects. No answer, no matter how long you wait, just the mass of water, the submerged sounds and the oceans of time without him. Outside the phone booth, only gray curtains of rain and in the distance people walking under their umbrellas. The student town is dark and windy and you take your bicycle down to the sandy blue beach and address all that water and the heartless skies: *There are only happy endings. There are only opportunities. There are only Silk Boys, flim-flam boys, toy boys, university places, poverty scholarships. The dashing of birds, of hopes, of power systems. Only Valerie Jean Solanas will be president of America.* The sound of rain, waves, and underwaters, the cold, translucent weight on your chest and the taste of salt in your mouth, the cold breath of the white shark sweeping over the beaches.

VALERIE: I got into graduate school.
—(*ring-ring*)—
VALERIE: I'm going to study psychology. I'm going to be a psychologist and find out why everything's made up of sharks . . . *Congratulations, Valerie, I knew you'd make it . . .* Thank you very much, but it's no big deal . . . *Congrats, congrats, congrats, my little psychologist . . .* Thank you humbly, Silky, but it's no big deal . . . *Hooray for Valerie Solanas!* Thanks, thanks, but enough now.
—(*ring-ring*)—

VALERIE: You always said I should apply to school. You said I would be president of America. Where are you now?

—(*ring-ring*)—

VALERIE: You're in the ocean, because you want to be in the ocean.

—(*ring-ring*)—

VALERIE: You said I had that crystal gaze . . . And I can see you now . . . swirls of light in the green-black density . . . your underwater laugh . . . your childlike smile . . . You never came to Jacksonville . . .

—(*ring-ring*)—

VALERIE: I'm going to hang up now. I have to get ready for school. I'm going to read Mr. Freud and everything else I can find. Do you think I'll have to wear glasses there?

—(*ring-ring*)—

VALERIE: Nah, I don't suppose you could know that, you little seahorse scientist. Seahorse scientists only work in the ocean and not on land, and none of you need glasses in the sea, just a cyclops's eye, and you all work in the ocean because you don't like living on land . . . Goodbye . . .

—(*ring-ring*)—

VALERIE: Wet kisses from Valerie . . .

—(*ring-ring*)—

ELMHURST PSYCHIATRIC HOSPITAL, SEPTEMBER 8, 1968
THE NATIONAL ORGANIZATION FOR WOMEN DEMONSTRATES AGAINST
MISS AMERICA CONTESTS IN ATLANTIC CITY,
OLYMPIA PRESS PUBLISHES *SCUM MANIFESTO*

Patients are no longer permitted to use the telephones, but everyone, other than new arrivals, is entitled to receive one call a week. You accept one from Maurice; it is unthinkable that you chose his call, as he took everything you had away from you, but all the other calls are from journalists, and there is still no call from Ventor and absolutely nothing from Cosmogirl and the netherworld.

The staff, or more precisely Dr. Ruth Cooper, got ahold of the Olympia Press version of SCUM and for a couple of afternoons has let you look through it. A study in violence, Maurice calls the book in the foreword, and in the afterword Paul Krassner has written something about his ass and many more irrelevancies. *You said you liked what I wrote. You said the manifesto was a brilliant analysis of the state of the world. You said that I spoke like an artist, that I was ingenious, that I was entertaining, but all that does not matter now. It must have been the walls you were talking to, and not me.*

Maurice has chosen a photograph of you for the front cover and on the back the headlines after the shooting: Andy Warhol Fights for His Life.

MAURICE: Valerie, hello. How are you feeling?
VALERIE: Never felt better.
MAURICE: I've been thinking about you.
VALERIE: I've been thinking about *you*.
MAURICE: Whereabouts are you?
VALERIE: In the White House. Washington, D.C.
MAURICE: I mean which hospital. Is it a hospital in New York?
VALERIE: Washington, D.C., United States of pimps and balls.
MAURICE: Can I help you?
VALERIE: You can recall your copies of the manifesto and cut out the whole foreword, afterword, fake analysis, and sham commentary. I recommend that you cut all superfluous words, which in this case in plain language means all the words that aren't mine. That is more or less exactly how you can help me.
MAURICE: Everybody's buying the manifesto. You're becoming famous, Valerie.
VALERIE: And I waited in the lobby at the Chelsea for a whole fucking day and you didn't come.
MAURICE: It's lucky for you he woke up.
VALERIE: You'll be famous, Maurice. Your little asshole is going to gleam in the spotlight. You and Andy and your so-called highbrow culture. Books about sucking cocks. Films about showing your ass. Great art. It's fantastic. I can only congratulate you.
MAURICE: I believe in your manifesto. I believe in you. The problem is that you're too intelligent for your own good.
VALERIE: Do you have a medical license too? Are you a

psychiatrist as well? Everyone seems to be a doctor here. Very practical, very pleasant. Diagnoses morning, noon, and night. Thank you ever so much, it's nice to hear someone has all his marbles. Anyway, Maurice. Things are going to be much better for you, now that I'm out of the way.

MAURICE: Sales are going well. Now, at last, there are people reading your text. We're going to be moving to a larger office. I want to help you. I don't want to see you go under.

VALERIE: Got to go now. Have to hang up. I have an afternoon meeting with the president. Twenty for a fuck, ten for a blow job, two for a hand job.

MAURICE: You're confused, Valerie.

VALERIE: I've never been clearer. I've never felt better. Mind your ass next time you're out whoring, Maurice. It was you I was waiting for. A whole afternoon. When you didn't turn up at the Chelsea, I went to the Factory. I was tired of waiting by then. But it doesn't matter who the intended target was and who actually played the target's part. When SCUM comes after your asses, you'll have to shape up fast.

MAURICE: Do I take that as a threat, Valerie?

VALERIE: You can take it how the hell you want. I suppose I'll stay here until I die. I suppose you'll get rich, Maurice. Thanks very much for nothing.

(*line cut*—)

UNIVERSITY OF MARYLAND, COLLEGE PARK, WASHINGTON, D.C., AUGUST 1958

On your first day at Maryland, death is still at an unspecified number of nautical and land miles away from you. The campus has been invaded by new students. You sit a short distance from the Psychology Institute, outside the Shiver Laboratory, waiting until it is time to go in, smoking cigarettes, assuming that, whatever happens, you are wearing the wrong attire, you have the wrong equipment, and you are made of the wrong stuff. There is a smell of war about you, a state of emergency, a siege, and something else, something wetter, more dangerous: prostitution, dead ocean birds, and spiraling loneliness. It does not matter how many times you wash yourself, it does not matter how many times you scrub your crotch, the scent of iron gloves and sun-cracked car seats will remain on your skin forever. But there are flashes of sky through the trees and you have already read all you could find by Sigmund Freud, Brücke, Mahler, Adler, Horney, and Stekel. Sister Hyacinth from Jacksonville at her severest and most starry-eyed would be pleased if she could see you now, on a campus, neatly pressed and groomed. She would glow with pride if she could see the University Park.

Remember they are only buildings, Valerie, only buildings, books, and people made of blood and tears. There is no reason to be afraid. Read all the books they tell you to read at least twice. Don't question the professors. Never show them you are scared. Never behave like an outsider. Don't let anyone know more than they need to about you. Find yourself a confidante, a girl to be your friend.

Professor Robert Brush loves lecturing to freshmen. He struts back and forth by the lectern in his dazzling white shirt and his fashionable black-framed spectacles, his face a high-voltage lamp of joy and goodwill, his faith in the American education system boundless.

I am proud to welcome the psychology students of 1958 to the University of Maryland. Intrepid young intellects from all over America. And I extend an especially warm welcome to a small number of girls as well. You are particularly welcome in our department and you must have no hesitation in taking up your place here and making use of all you need to improve your minds. Today the American education system is open to all and together we are part of something new. A new age. The future. I want you to feel welcome. And I want to offer those of you with state scholarships a very special, heartfelt welcome here at the University of Maryland. I would like to express what an honor it is for us to have you here and say that it represents a step forward for civilization, for which we should all, regardless of background, be thankful.

Outside the window the trees appear to be decked in gold paper. In your bag you have some extremely expensive psychology literature, covered in brown wrapping paper, and all you can think about is that the university has made a disastrous mistake that will be revealed at any moment; your body is an escape plan on permanent war alert. *Miss Solanas, obviously you realize this is an administrative error. You couldn't have imagined the place was yours. Please understand that something has clearly gone wrong in the mail room.* And the plan of escape: when all the students whose names begin with *S* are called, you will sneak out of the building—you have taken a seat right at the back of the room closest to the emergency exit—and never look back, *exit blue-collar girl, exit Valerie Solanas.*

They say the winds of the future are blowing across America. Later you will find out that all the girls on need-based scholarships have been given the same timetable. They are few in number, but they are there. The roll call continues and the names flash past your head like a lightning storm or an exploding sunset. *Sam Abbotsway? Harry Bottomley? Arthur Josebury? Jack McDonnell? Dino Rock? Yes, sir. Yes, sir. Yes, sir. Yes, sir. Yes, sir.* When your name is finally called you leap to your feet in a flash. *Yes, sir.*

PROFESSOR ROBERT BRUSH: State scholarship?

VALERIE: Yes.

PROFESSOR ROBERT BRUSH: A hundred percent or partially self-funded?

VALERIE: A hundred percent.

PROFESSOR ROBERT BRUSH: Welcome, Miss Solanas, to the University of Maryland. A warm welcome to the American education system.

VALERIE: Thank you very much. I'm so pleased to be here. I'll do my best, I promise.

A hand in white gloves pulls you back onto your seat, interrupting your thank-you speech. A stranger's voice, high white boots, a girl who does not look like a student, a girl who looks as though she has gone out in her underwear. Expensive dark glasses, a seductive aroma and rhythm, a smile and a way of whispering so that everyone hears her, a cigarette burning in her hand under the desk. You were so focused on your name being called, you failed to hear the clack of her high heels stop in the corridor outside, failed to see the cloud of smoke, perfume, and blond hair over by the door, you were too preoccupied with Robert Brush to notice this stranger's deep, black gaze sweeping like a radar over all the freshmen before settling on you, right at the back by the emergency exit, or to see her working her way along a row of students and sitting down next to you. She does not let go of your wrist; her breath is warm and sweet and smells of beer.

COSMOGIRL: There's no need to thank them. Rule number one. Never get down on your knees, at least not in public and at least not if it's really of no advantage to you. You have nothing to be grateful for. They should be glad you chose to set your smart little foot in here. Do you want a cigarette?

VALERIE: Are you allowed to smoke in here?

COSMOGIRL: A more appropriate question would be: Can you think in here? Do you want a cigarette or not?

VALERIE: Yes, please.

COSMOGIRL: Cosmogirl. Or Ann Duncan.

VALERIE: Be quiet now.

COSMOGIRL: Valerie?

VALERIE: Yes.

COSMOGIRL: Solanas?

VALERIE: Yes.

COSMOGIRL: What are you doing here?

VALERIE: Shhhh.

COSMOGIRL: What are you doing here?

VALERIE: I'm going to be a psychology professor.

Cosmogirl puts her hand up and interrupts Professor Robert Brush and his lecture before being asked to speak. She stands up and wafts the hidden cigarette about under the desk, signaling its whereabouts with a slender column of smoke at the side of her dress.

COSMOGIRL: Do you support abolition of the death penalty?

PROFESSOR ROBERT BRUSH: We don't take a political position in the department.

COSMOGIRL: I'm not asking what the department thinks. I'm asking what you think. Just you, up there at the lectern.

PROFESSOR ROBERT BRUSH: Personally, I take a stand neither for nor against the death penalty. As you already know.

COSMOGIRL: And students who don't receive state funding?

PROFESSOR ROBERT BRUSH: Well, that's hardly our problem. Every student does as he chooses. If funding comes from stolen goods or organized crime and prostitution, it's of no interest to us.

COSMOGIRL: And the rapes in Laboratory Park?

PROFESSOR ROBERT BRUSH: We will naturally take action. The safety of our female students is a high priority.

COSMOGIRL: I understand.

PROFESSOR ROBERT BRUSH: My advice to you, Ann Duncan—

COSMOGIRL: Cosmogirl.

PROFESSOR ROBERT BRUSH: —is to become involved in one of the university's many student societies and efforts to bring about those improvements you're always talking about. We are here today to welcome new students.

COSMOGIRL: And the allocation of scholarships and research funding based on gender?

PROFESSOR ROBERT BRUSH: The criteria are knowledge and analytical skills. Not gender.

COSMOGIRL: And the requirement for dresses in seminars?

PROFESSOR ROBERT BRUSH: New times are on their way, Miss Duncan. I can promise you that. The winds of the future are blowing here already.

COSMOGIRL: And woman's place in the system of desire?

PROFESSOR ROBERT BRUSH: We'll have to save that for another day, Miss Duncan. Today is a welcome day for new students.

This is first-time Cosmogirl, first-time Cosmogirl in a lecture hall early one morning; and the room is set alight, a field of blazing daffodils, when she turns to look at you, eyes heavy with honeyed light and hubris. You find yourselves in the most beautiful of buildings, made of books, papers, the future, science, and she holds your gaze in hers and the breeze turns again beneath your blue school dress.

COSMOGIRL: Are you going to smoke that cigarette or just hold it?

VALERIE: Outside.

COSMOGIRL: You're sweet when you're embarrassed. Where do you come from?

VALERIE: The desert.

BRISTOL HOTEL, APRIL 17, 1988
THE SOVIET UNION AND AMERICA COMBINE FORCES TO SAVE
TWO WHALES STRANDED ON THE ALASKAN COAST

It is impossible to judge whether it is day or night, but the sky out there is on fire and dark clouds of birds swarm over the buildings. Dusk, dawn, or apocalypse, in the room in Mason Street it matters not. Your guts howl again; it smells as though a lump of rotting flesh is settling in your underpants. There was someone here earlier, a few hours ago, and you ended up with a couple of dollars and half a sandwich. It might have been the man who always talks about going back to Philadelphia, or the one who once said that clients can always recognize you by the ligature marks. You wish that someone you loved long ago was with you. You miss Cosmogirl, but all you have are chaotic, meaningless memories.

Cosmo?

No Cosmo, just a blood-drenched pall of trivial recollections now, of strangers' voices, strangers' hands, your skin stretched tight between the buildings, a crowd of freezing, shaggy coats. There is always snow, glistening over the trees and the sixties, and it never stops falling; when you think about it, there is always snow on the campus.

You return repeatedly to a shark who wanted you to help him reenact executions in the turn-of-the-century electric chair he had in the bedroom of his luxury loft apartment in the East Village. He loved switching roles. Victim, killer, executed, executioner. He would come violently at the moment of death, and always gave you a ridiculous sum of money afterward. You remember other stiff dicks in your mouth, and soft, filthy lumps of meat in the palm of your hand, scrawny fingers, heavy, clammy bodies, expensive suits, tongues, nauseating aftershave, saliva, semen, tears, slobbering wet kisses, all these sewers disguised as mouths. You have always been so scared that Louis would appear in the street, that you would not recognize him. And that is why you do not pick up men in yellow Fords, and rarely blond men, and never men called Louis.

It does not matter how many sharks you have had, how many journeys you have made into the underworld, now you are just a fading consciousness, oozing, bleeding, and all you want is Cosmo's hand in yours again. Vaguely you recall the outbreak of a war you were surely too young to remember, and a green-tinged research library. The decaying walls of science collapsing around you, a catalogue of American women put to death, that last snow falling on Laboratory Park.

Cosmo?

Cosmo?

Cosmo is sitting by the window with a cocktail in her hand, flicking through some magazines, the titles of which you cannot make out. They are probably articles about executions. The only things Cosmo reads are about executions and she wakes each night submerged underwater, her mouth full of black ants, believing the American government is spraying gas into student dorms in College Park. She mumbles and whispers into the drink . . . *goodbye, Silena Gilmore . . . goodbye, Earle Dennison . . . goodbye, Rhonda Belle Martin . . . goodbye, Eva Dugan . . . goodbye, Ethel Juanita Spinelli . . . goodbye, Louise Peete . . . goodbye, Barbara Graham . . . goodbye, Marie Porter . . . goodbye, Julia Moore . . . goodbye, Mary Holmes . . . goodbye, Mildred Johnson . . . goodbye, Mary Farmer . . . goodbye, Ethel Rosenberg . . . goodbye, Rosanna Phillips . . . goodbye, Bessie Mae Smith . . . goodbye, Betty Butler . . .*

VALERIE: What are you drinking?

COSMOGIRL: Apricot cocktails.

VALERIE: What are you reading?

COSMOGIRL: Senseless farewells at the American government's expense. Subjects who no longer belong in this world.

VALERIE: Cosmo, do you know that in 1972 the Supreme Court decreed that the death penalty was incompatible with the Constitution? You would have been so happy.

COSMOGIRL: I'm not happy. My Elizabeth is falling asleep in San Quentin. The California Supreme Court won't budge. The orange overalls represent death. In the death chamber they're waiting until the very last moment for a call from the president. Thiopental causes a drop in blood pressure and induces sleep, pancuronium bromide paralyzes the muscles so that breathing ceases, and the last injection of potassium chloride stops the heart.

VALERIE: But in 1976 they decided it was compatible with the Constitution again. Your absence then felt like an eclipse of the sun.

COSMOGIRL: I've never been happy. Every night Elizabeth dreams about Ethel Rosenberg in the electric chair. On the morning of October 9, wearing her white overalls, she walks from the death cell to the death chamber. The call has come from the attorney general and the governor. *Kill that woman. Kill that bitch.* Cannulas have been attached to her arms. The government has said a prayer for her soul. White clothes, rubber gloves, catheter, diapers, drugs, nurses, chaplain. When the execution has been performed, Elizabeth is still on the table in her white clothes. She's in the desert now. She's in her bikini, crying, wondering where little Frankie and I have gone. The doctors declare her dead, they say a prayer for her soul. Then the American government draws the curtains.

VALERIE: I think about you all the time.

COSMOGIRL: And my brain is an electric chair in which innocents are always being executed.

Cosmo shuffles along in her clogs, guiding you round the experiment rooms. Cigarette in the corner of her mouth as she speaks, whisky bottle in her lab coat, she has a way of constantly delivering long monologues about everything. About the drugged mice and the cancer mice, about scientific methods. Cosmo's column of smoke forever rising above her as she gives lectures with her head in the glass cages, issuing you instructions on how to take photographs. Then she gives you a ride on her scooter along the corridors and sits you down on the sofa in Robert Brush's office; it is hard to understand where all the keys come from, and from nowhere she brings out notebooks, alcohol, cigarettes, and peanuts and carries on her lecturing, and only Cosmo can make you feel like a starchy, well-brought-up middle-class girl in a borrowed lab coat with no brain and nothing to say.

Cosmo puts on more lipstick, more mascara, ever more makeup, more of everything, smudges and shadows round her eyes; snapping away, flashing, obsessed with taking photographs of you both with her Polaroid camera, your lips and hers full with kissing and happiness, a new languor in your gaze. Pictures she sticks up on all the walls in the student dorm and later places in the pockets of your coat hanging in the corridor outside, while you sit in a lecture hall. And notes, always new notes pinned up in the dorm and the library. Her words are witches' kisses and her kisses are kisses that go straight to your heart.

You dash along the corridors, Cosmo and you, through the fluorescent lamps and the night, in and out of locked offices and laboratories, snatching organs and human fetuses, cavorting with stuffed animals and old skeletons. The laboratory director gets a new family in the gold frame on his desk: a Polaroid collage in which Daddy is a psychotic ape, his wife a dissected, bleeding heart, and the children mutants. Aborted fetuses, calf-human hybrids, cancerous lumps.

The laboratory director is in the habit of taking Cosmogirl out on nocturnal drives along the motorways and forests of the night. He and a few other members of the academic staff fund her tuition fees, her student room, her drugs, and her textbooks. Cosmogirl refuses to accept any government funds on the grounds that the government is trying to murder her mother in San Quentin. *I would rather sell my pussy than my soul. My pussy is not my soul.*

And to the state of California she writes letter after letter after letter to save Elizabeth Duncan. The walls in her student room are plastered with newspaper cuttings and photographs about the death penalty and scientific discoveries, animals tested beyond recognition. Monkeys, mice, rabbits, and murdered women.

Cosmo has decided to enter your life and she is everywhere; at first nowhere, and then everywhere. In the telephone at night, in your dresses, in your coat pockets, in your photographs; you can forget everything, but you cannot forget her. You never forget the first guided tours in the laboratory, those first crystalline nights, unending, simply continuing, the flickering feeling like a fluorescent lamp when she looks at you. And every time you touch her skin, it is a step further from your own plans, from the Future and Science. And still your hand moves on, inch by inch. A rectangle of light shines in her face when you touch her. Her hair looks like a bird's nest.

VALERIE: I'm afraid, Cosmo.
COSMOGIRL (*holds up a Polaroid photograph*): Look at this picture, Valerie.
VALERIE (*sits up*): I just want to have a degree. I'm here for the future. I don't want the future to disappear.
COSMOGIRL: You can do what you want. Someone like you isn't

going to fall apart. Your mind is like steel. What can you see in the picture, Valerie?

VALERIE: Some skin, some hair, our mouths.

COSMOGIRL: Anything else?

VALERIE: I suppose you want me to say we're laughing, we look happy. We look happy and we're laughing in these photos.

COSMOGIRL: Valerie?

VALERIE: Yes.

COSMOGIRL: We're not laughing in the pictures, we're not happy. We're invincible. We're rulers of the universe. We can do what we want. That's what's in the pictures.

VALERIE: I mean to become a professor. I have to hold back.

COSMOGIRL: I don't intend to hold anything back. We're going to remake history. Artificial intelligence, artificial insemination, artificial historiography. You and me and the future. The first intellectual whores of America.

VALERIE: Hold my hand forever. Hold me back. Hold fast to my plans. Promise me you'll never go.

COSMOGIRL: Never.

The student bed is a place of shadow and lonely swooning. Cosmo in the sheets with her yellow hair, her conviction, her desire. Her body wanting to work its way into yours and disappear inside. Yours is a target that has nothing to do with Valerie. Just the burning, throbbing, tingling sensation in your arms again, *do what you will and whatever you do let it be quick*, and everything covers its eyes and waits and rigor mortis spreads through the room. At first you are scared of everything in Maryland, of Cosmo, of her kisses, of the professors, the lecture halls, the middle-class girls, the middle-class boys. Then you fly along the corridors with Cosmo's hand in yours, invincible, your brain ablaze with desire for science and the future.

Elizabeth Duncan gets a new execution date every month. In telephone calls to Cosmogirl she is incoherent and paranoid. She is crazed with fear, convinced that they will release gas into the death cell without warning. She knits hundreds of identical girls' dresses and yearns for the desert and little Frankie. Cosmo stands in the dorm in a sea of clemency appeals and weeps into the phone. The sun rises and sets on the horizon behind the hospital grounds, while you create your own after-school experiments and scientific texts. The nights are dark and swollen.

Elizabeth Duncan loved getting married. She and Cosmo crisscrossed America in search of handsome, dark-haired men to whom she pledged large sums of money in return for marrying her. And later, when they wanted the marriage annulled, she carried on to a new state and wed again. And when the money ran out, as it always did, she sent pregnant girls to the doctor and claimed it was her, and then sued her ex-husbands for child support.

VALERIE: What's she sentenced for?
COSMOGIRL: Murdering two of her new husbands with arsenic.
VALERIE: Is she guilty?
COSMOGIRL: Very guilty, I suspect.

ELMHURST PSYCHIATRIC HOSPITAL, DECEMBER 24, 1968

The snow is melting on your head. It is a long time since you stopped waiting for a telephone call. You usually give away your weekly call to one of the drugged-up girls who always hang around in the corridor so they do not miss the calls that never come. Over Christmas all the non-new arrivals have the privilege of three conversations each. It is very generous of the hospital administration, but at present they are not able to propose any kind people the patients can contact.

The windows in the dining room are covered with frost patterns, the birds stare at the patients through the panes of glass, the snow glistens and sparkles between the hospital curtains. Andy Warhol himself answers, in his hesitant, whispering voice. Talking to Andy is like talking to yourself; his voice has changed since last time, dissolved, distorted, and everything he says sounds like a question. *H-h-h-hello?*

VALERIE: Hello, Andy, it's only me.
(*Silence.*)

VALERIE: How are you feeling, little Andy?

(*Silence.*)

VALERIE: Merry Christmas, Andy.

(*Silence.*)

VALERIE: Merry Christmas, I said.

ANDY: Merry Christmas, Valerie?

VALERIE: Why haven't you been to see me?

(*Silence.*)

VALERIE: I read in the paper that you've forgiven me.

ANDY: Yes?

VALERIE: Have you forgiven Valerie?

ANDY: Yes?

VALERIE: If you've forgiven Valerie, how come you haven't been to see her?

ANDY: I have to hang up now . . . ?

VALERIE: Are you celebrating Christmas in the Factory?

ANDY: Goodbye, Valerie?

VALERIE: I don't understand.

ANDY: I'm not angry, Valerie. But goodbye, Valerie. I can't talk anymore, Valerie. We've got to work now, Valerie . . . ?

VALERIE: Really. My next suggestion is that you exhibit your body parts in some old museum in London and we call the whole thing Haute Couture.

(*call ends—*)

CHRISTMAS EVE, CONVERSATION TWO

ANDY: Hello? . . . Mom? . . .

VALERIE (*disguises her voice*): Yes, it's only little Mama Warhola . . . I just want to know if you've taken off your bandages . . .

ANDY: M-m-mom? . . .

VALERIE: If anything happens to you, I'll never forgive you. That awful male-female will never get near my little boy again.

ANDY: No?

(*Silence.*)

ANDY: Mom?

(*Silence.*)

ANDY: Mom?

(*Silence.*)

VALERIE: Valerie, not Mom. I need twenty thousand dollars for my manuscript. I need money to defend myself in court. I need money now. Withdraw all the charges against me. And then I want you to do a new film about me. I need to be on a TV show. I have no White House to work out of. Ring that man again, Mr. Carlson, that show where you sat painting your nails and called yourself Warhola, and tell him I need him, tell him I need TV. I want you to come and see me at Elmhurst. Visiting time is every Sunday at three. I'm sorry if I hurt you, but it wasn't as bad as all that.

(*call ends*—)

CHRISTMAS EVE, CONVERSATION THREE

VIVA RONALDO: Andy Warhol's office. To whom am I speaking?

VALERIE: Ask Andy Warhol to come to the phone. I'm in a great hurry.

VIVA RONALDO: You have to stop these nuisance calls.

VALERIE: Whatever . . . Wigs. Paranoia. Fake artists. Plagiarists. Kleptomaniacs. Dracula. Bloodsuckers. Leeches.

VIVA RONALDO: We've reported your calls to the police, Valerie.

VALERIE: Okay. Exciting. But if he has really forgiven Valerie, how come he hasn't been to visit her?

VIVA RONALDO: Goodbye, Valerie.

VALERIE: I'd also add that I've reported your art and your man's faces to the police. Tell him to find my play. Tell him I'll forgive him if I get my play back. Tell him, for as long as the sun shines and the sky is blue, I'll keep my promise.

(call ends—)

It is the end of McCarthy's protracted fifties, and the sixties are on their way in. You have a part-time job as a night student in the laboratory. Dwight David Eisenhower has become the president of America. You think about Dorothy all the time, daydream about Dorothy in her flowery hat beside your graduation hat, Dorothy with shining eyes and confetti, bowing and scraping in her high heels to everyone who passes. *Dolly, that's only a student. Ah. You don't need to bow to everyone who's here. Nah. They're just ordinary people. Education is just a way of separating people, Dorothy. Ah, but I haven't been to any school at all, little Valerie, I'm so proud of you, little Valerie.* Dorothy should see you now, in your white lab coat, running along the corridors at the university. She would be frightened of everything here, of the books, the buildings, the professors. Sometimes you think you should write and tell her how you are swanning around in the sciences, with unlimited access to literature and long nights in Shiver Laboratory.

The other girls have white pearl necklaces, they have their old-lady perms, which is all wrong but all right. You have dungarees under your lab coat and you are happy and wide awake all night in Shiver Laboratory. The nights with the animals are long and humid. The pygmy monkeys are comatose in their cages, and the mice, hamsters, and rabbits never sleep, running in their wheels all night, as you walk along the corridors in your white clogs, waiting for the alarm to go off in one of the cages. Flight responses in laboratory animals are heartrending; a little colony of white mice works in unison for days on an underground escape system. Cosmogirl and you keep a log of their breakout plans.

And while you wait for morning to come, you drink coffee with the night watchman and spend a long time in the toilets washing your hands and under your arms. You love walking through the glacial light emitted by the fluorescent lamps in the animal rooms. The red-eyed mice have cancerous tumors on their backs. A human ear has been grafted onto one of them. Cosmogirl has christened her Samantha. You like her best of all. She moves slowly with the full-grown ear, waiting for death. Before she dies, you will cut the ear off her. Cosmogirl and you dream of an underwater world of female mice where Samantha rules.

Nights in the animal laboratory among the luminous cages and animal experiments are endless. The animals run around in the epileptic flicker of the lights and the strong odor of disinfectant. Their animal eyes become infected, the albino mice get cancer, the alcohol mice and drug mice degenerate in the experiments. The white mice become addicted first. After just a few weeks they stop eating and working, they stop looking after their young, and the youngsters stop playing and running in the wheel. Life in the cages turns into a desperate wait by the water bottle. Dead animals are collected in huge steel containers and burned collectively every week.

THE PSYCHOANALYSTS

A. Dr. So-and-so. All doctors eat Mogadon and turds for breakfast. I feel like a goddamn whore. When can a woman spend time outdoors? Never. Language is merely a structure, says Dr. Fuck, and breathes a wind of rape into my face.

B. The decision was taken to remove her brain. There had been years of international conferences. The speakers shook their heads. Reports and diagnoses eddied around the conference halls. Outside it was completely calm. Deserted buildings, hotel complexes, beta-blockers. They drove their cars along the prom-enades. Hotels abandoned, hearts bombarded, utopias mutilated. Death's field. They drove their cars across death's field. They shared a bed with the enemy.

C. The child's paranoid universe. Childhood as a long line of ter-rifying fields to scurry through. Light coming down from the trees onto his hands.

D. Paranoid associations. Unseemly comparisons. How should I describe it? How should the story be told? There is nothing to tell.

E. We walk through the hospital grounds. Everyone is wearing white patients' apparel and everyone's hands are shaking. The tablets do not help. Nothing helps. I do not want to go to the mental hospital. I do not like that hospital park. The signs, the alarm bells, the visiting times. All the white light on his hands.

F. All my friends are whores. They burn every bridge as soon as they have a chance. Let me know if you need a character witness. How would you like to describe that night?

G. I do not want to describe it.

H. How about giving it a try?

I. I do not want to.

J. How would you describe that night?

K. Black birds hurtling down. Mammalian fetuses, bleeding, burning. End of story.

L. The conferences continued. Erica Jong sucks a cock a mile above the Atlantic. The repulsive mile-high club. The cock in the cunt. It was so goddamn disgusting.

M. I know you like it. My heart beats red, beats blue, beats rage.

N. *The Future of an Illusion. Beyond the Pleasure Principle. The Interpretation of Dreams, Group Psychology and the Analysis of the Ego. The Ego and the Id. Inhibitions, Symptoms and Anxiety. The Future Prospects of Psycho-Analytic Therapy. "Wild" Psychoanalysis. The Dynamics of Transference. Remembering, Repeating and Working-Through. Denial. Remembering, Repeating and Working-Through. Denial. Analysis Terminable and Interminable. The Theory of Sexuality. The Psychopathology of Everyday Life. Heredity and the Aetiology of the Neuroses. Wolf Man. Seduction Theory. Screen Memories. Jokes and Their Relation to the Unconscious. Infantile Genital Organization. Amendment to the Theory of Sexuality. The Loss of Reality in Neurosis and Psychosis. Dostoevsky and Parricide.*

O. She stayed in bed all day long. She had no references, she lacked persuasion. Her heart clamored, venting its wrath. Men chased over her face.

P. I drive through town in my silver car. I drive across the sky. I arrive in my silver car. I have fluffy white hair; you can call me what you like. You will never know my real name.

Q. It was a passion. Why did I have such high heels? Why did I have such short dresses? I only wanted to get closer to the sky. I was looking for my sisters. I could not find a sister. I sat in front of the television and submitted to compulsory treatment. I seldom saw a doctor.

R. But thanks very much for your comments. I am very interested in your views on the red-light district. I am very interested in the way you call yourselves educated and then call other people white trash. You are very welcome to earn a living as prostitutes for a year in the Tenderloin and then come back and tell me what you think. In general, please deliver all your opinions concerning the red-light district, regardless of how little time you have had to consider the matter.

S. My theory is that there is no theory. I went there quite voluntarily. I visited that doctor of my own free will. I had my own training, but they said it was irrelevant in the context. They said I had no sense of time. Do you know what day it is? Rape. Rape. Rape. Rape. Rape. Rape. Do you know where you are? Fuck me harder.

T. There is a psychology for everything. Red-light psychology. Red-light theory. My theory is that there is no theory. Dough. Dames. Dicks. *That* is the right way to describe it.

U. How do you want to describe the phenomenon?

V. I do not want to describe the phenomenon.

W. How would you describe the phenomenon?

X. Sharks in all my thoughts. The taste of death. Grainy white fluid in all my dreams. Abjection.

Y. I would like to point out that I am here voluntarily. You are not here voluntarily. I would like to point out that I am attending these psych appointments of my own free will. The appointments, yes. Yes, I know you are forcing me to be here. Tell me something about your childhood. I can tell you something about my ass, if you like.

Z. Why do you have to tell the truth when it is so easy to lie? I was raped by a bird in the desert.

BRISTOL HOTEL, APRIL 18, 1988

NARRATOR: Do you have a few minutes?

VALERIE: Sorry, I'm working. Ten for a fuck. Five for a blow job. Two for a hand job. The whole repertoire. No kissing. No bullshit. No fingers. No licking. Sex is just a hang-up.

NARRATOR: I'd like to know what you think about prostitution.

VALERIE: Currently I have more practical experience than knowledge.

NARRATOR: Then tell me about it.

VALERIE: It's like that boat accident in the Pacific where hundreds of people died. The ones who survived were utterly unable to speak when they were questioned by the police and later interviewed by the newspapers. One of them said long afterward that what happened the night of the disaster was not something the living should know about. People stamping on other people's hands when they tried to get into the overcrowded lifeboats. Men kicking young children out of the way to get to the front. A man spoke about a girl who was trapped, her head pinned under a cupboard. Their eyes met, and he went out to the lifeboats. It's testimony that belongs with the dead.

NARRATOR: You're not dead.

VALERIE: It's like being dead. It's testimony that belongs with the dead.

NARRATOR: You're not dead.

VALERIE: Everything is interchangeable. Thought systems work like that, organization of flesh and mind. The logic of transportation hinges on a certain predetermined quota being filled. If someone is missing, someone else is taken out in her place. There's no point in running away.

NARRATOR: Your way of thinking is distorted by so much senseless, destructive defeatism.

VALERIE: Not defeatism. Not submission. Not masochism. There are no good victims. I just find it unworthy to save my own ass when my people are being annihilated. When pussy-souls are sent to the slaughter. Otherwise another pussy-soul will have to do the work. I might just as well do it. There will always be men who like to fuck drowning people.

NARRATOR: Selling intimacy undermines the soul and self-esteem.

VALERIE: There's more to intimacy than that. Sex organs. A whore never sells intimacy. She sells a black hole in space. She isn't there. Cosmo and I dreamed of being America's first intellectual whores. I always said to her she was the most brilliant whore in America. I sold my pussy all my life, but I never sold my soul. My pussy is not my soul. I never compromised on anything. I have never cared what happened to my cunt. I've always hated it. Everyone else has always hated it. I'm going to work now. I need cigarettes. You'll have to take your questions somewhere else.

NARRATOR: I have two hundred and fifty thousand university credits and all I dream of is a faculty like you.

VALERIE: And I dream of being able to sleep for a while instead of being subjected to these interrogation methods.

UNIVERSITY OF MARYLAND, AUGUST 1962
MARILYN MONROE IS DEAD

Inside the phone booth in the student dorm during the hot summer of 1962, you call home over and over again to tell Dorothy you have been accepted to do postgraduate research. Some middle-class boy has dropped out at the last minute and you have been given his place. Cosmo is happy and invites you onto the roof for cigars, champagne, and marshmallows.

VALERIE: Valerie Jean Solanas is going to be a university researcher.

COSMO: Did you get hold of her?

VALERIE: There's no answer.

COSMO: Come and sit here.

VALERIE: There are only happy endings.

COSMO: What do you wish for, Valerie?

VALERIE: I wish I hadn't gotten this place because a middle-class boy dropped out. I wish I had a hundred thousand Sprague Dawley white rats.

COSMO: I'm so proud of you. Now you can do what you want. No limits, no compromises.

VALERIE: It was just a waiting-list place.

COSMO: That doesn't matter. You got it because you deserve it.

VALERIE: I still have to raise my own money.

COSMO: But you're the department's shining star, just as much as ever. Everyone knows that.

VALERIE: I still have to get myself a pearl necklace for the seminars. And an oh-so-respectable frock.

The night sky floats above like a black veil. Cosmo holds your hand tightly and you have listened to the ringing tone from the desert for so long it keeps reverberating in your head after you put the receiver down. A single star shoots through the darkness. Cosmo draws her fingers over the sky, as if wanting to drag more stars down for you, but the sky remains black and the darkness arcs gently over the park. The rabbits dash between the trees like white lamps.

One day Cosmo has arranged for fireworks and a cascade of artificial stars over Laboratory Park and she has promised you a wish for every star. You have wished for the postgraduate admission. You should have wished for Dorothy to figure out how to answer the telephone.

COSMO: What do you wish for, Valerie?

VALERIE: I wish that this moment would last forever. You. Your hand. The starry night. The postgrad slot. The opportunity.

COSMO: What did you say?

VALERIE: I said, I wish for money for the experiment.

COSMO: You'll be swimming in money. The others are nothing compared to you. Everyone knows. They know that you know.

VALERIE: I'll let them know I'm there.

Telephone signals, dark, forlorn, across the desert. It is August 4, 1962, and there are headlines and radio broadcasts far and wide: Marilyn Monroe is dead. Marilyn Monroe died on Helena Drive, Brentwood, California. Moran answers, out of breath, and behind you students stamp their feet and eavesdrop while they wait for you to finish your call.

VALERIE: May I speak to Dorothy, please?
MORAN: How are you? How's it g-going at the u-u-u-u- . . .
VALERIE: U-NI-VER-SI-TY. Fine, thanks. I've just been accepted as a postgraduate. Is Dorothy there?
MORAN: Ah! P-p-postgraduate. Congratulations, Valerie. We're always rooting for you, Valerie, you know. We're always waiting for you to send us a book.
VALERIE: May I speak to Dorothy?
MORAN: Dorothy's asleep. She's been crying all day over Marilyn. She's had a sleeping tablet now.
VALERIE: Wake her up.

Dorothy, streaked with tears, is lying behind the bedroom curtains in her sleeping-pill slumber. She dreams of Marilyn's blond hair, her tragic childhood. All the letters she wrote to Miss Monroe. *Dear, dear Miss Marilyn Monroe, I admire your work, your figure, your blond curls. I'm just Dorothy. A poor babe in the desert with a tragic background. I wish we could meet sometime and have a coffee.*

In the desert house the transistor radio is on in the background, news bulletins at full volume. Students walk past all the time in the dorm. You try to stand absolutely still in your clammy summer clothes.

Then suddenly Dorothy's voice purrs into the telephone. Fuzzy, gentle. *Light me a menthol cigarette, Red. A menthol cigarette so I can concentrate.*

DOROTHY: Hello, Valerie?

VALERIE: I got a spot as a postgraduate.

DOROTHY: She died of an overdose, little Valerie. It's so sad.

VALERIE: I'm going to be a scientist.

DOROTHY (*the hint of a smile in her voice*): Ah, Valerie . . .

VALERIE: It means I've been selected. It means I'm going to do research.

DOROTHY: Ooh! Are you a professor now, Valerie?

VALERIE: No, I'm going to get a doctorate.

DOROTHY (*screams into the receiver*): RED! DID YOU HEAR? RED! OUR VALERIE HAS BEEN MADE A PROFESSOR!

VALERIE: I'm going to do my doc-tor-ate.

DOROTHY: Ah. I haven't read what you sent yet. The doc-u-ment.

VALERIE: It's called an essay.

DOROTHY (*in a sleeping-pill voice*): Right, the essay. I decided not to read it. I don't like reading those fluttery sheets of loose paper. But it looked very good. I have it around all the time. Show it to everyone who comes by. Mr. Emin, for example. I tell everybody what a genius you are.

VALERIE (*the receiver pressed hard to her ear*): A doctorate. It'll take four years. I got in. There were tons of applicants. Everyone who applied had a degree in psychology.

DOROTHY (*her mother-of-pearl nails pick at the receiver*): Well, anyway, Miss Monroe was found dead in her bed. Beauty, success, and sudden death. I've been at the kitchen table here crying all morning. I've burned myself on the candles again. Damn candles.

VALERIE: Forget Marilyn. I'm a scientist now.

DOROTHY: Otherwise everything's as usual. Mr. Emin has installed a super-aerial on the roof. Mrs. Drake saw a saucer when she was drunk. She's in town now bragging about it. And as for me, Dolly, I'm not doing anything. A bit of fortune-telling. A bit of sewing . . . Sit arguing with Moran, drinking wine . . . Nothing's changed. Apart from Marilyn.

VALERIE: So what do you predict for the future?

DOROTHY: I predict that you'll do well. That you'll be a professor. You'll be what you want to be. Love is eternal, that's what I predict. You still sew lucky threads into your petticoats, don't you, Valerie?

VALERIE: It's the sixties. I don't wear petticoats anymore. No one with any self-respect wears petticoats.

DOROTHY: Well . . . Self-respect and the sixties . . .

VALERIE: What are you sewing?

DOROTHY (*mumbles evasively*): . . . a little dress for Valerie . . . a little professor's hat for Valerie . . . a fox-fur handbag for Valerie . . . leopard-skin underpants for Valerie . . .

VALERIE: That's nice, Dorothy. I have to go now.

DOROTHY: A little space-purse for Marilyn . . . a little doctoral cap . . . for Marilyn . . . and a degree for Marilyn Monroe . . .

VALERIE: Goodbye, Dorothy.

A HOTEL SOMEWHERE IN THE TENDERLOIN, WINTER 1987, ONE YEAR BEFORE YOUR DEATH

On February 20, 1987, Andy admits himself to New York Hospital under the pseudonym Bob Roberts. He would like to register as Barbara, but is not allowed. Dr. Denton Cox operates on his gallbladder for hours. Andy keeps his wig on during the operation. The silver glints against his snow-white skin. And under the hospital gown beats his nervous, irregular heart.

Andy is dreaming about you. The hospital smell has triggered dreams of you again. He dreams you are chasing him through the snow in Central Park. He dreams about his own funeral, about having to lie beside Mama Warhola in the deluxe grave in Pittsburgh. Between the heartbeats he dreams that guests drop muscle magazines and perfume bottles (*preferably Estée Lauder*) into his grave.

Nurse Min Cho keeps an eye on him and on her knitting. Late during the night following the operation he suffers a cardiac arrest. Cause: a surge of adrenaline generated by fear.

(Is he thinking of the calamitous year of 1968? Is he think-ing of you? A memory of the hospital, the operating smell?) Afterward Min Cho fills two garbage bags with material soiled by sickness and death and she is later sued by the family for a failure in care. The hospital pays out three mil-lion dollars to the Warhol family in compensation for his death.

The Village Voice calls you in the Tenderloin to inform you of the news. You have one year left to live and you answer in your lacy undies with your persistent cough, and as you reach for the tele-phone a mug of coffee falls to the floor. *Being born is like being kidnapped and then being sold as a slave.*

ULTRA VIOLET: Valerie Solanas?

VALERIE: Yes?

ULTRA VIOLET: How's life?

VALERIE (*laughs*): Fine, thanks . . . sunny . . . Who's speaking?

ULTRA VIOLET: Ultra Violet at *The Village Voice.*

VALERIE: Right.

ULTRA VIOLET: Tell me about your life.

VALERIE: I always walk on the sunny side. I always have lucky threads of gold and silver in my coats.

ULTRA VIOLET: And how are things with SCUM? Anything going on?

VALERIE: Not much.

Not much. You are shooting heroin again, have covered every public wall with notes and jottings. SCUM never existed, never will. It was just you. It was not even you. It was a hypothesis, a dream, a fantasy; what does it matter now?

ULTRA VIOLET: How many members do you have today?

VALERIE: Don't know.

ULTRA VIOLET: Andy Warhol is dead.

Faint sunshine through the window, smeary windows, the smell of smoke and sun. The smell of the ocean, maybe, and another time. Cigarette smoke in your hand.

VALERIE: Oh . . .

ULTRA VIOLET: What do you have to say about Andy Warhol?

VALERIE: Not much . . . Pop artist . . . The Factory . . . Prints . . . I don't want to talk about him . . . I've nothing to say . . .

ULTRA VIOLET: He died during a routine operation. The Warhol family intends to sue the hospital.

VALERIE: I have nothing to add.

ULTRA VIOLET: What do you think of our president?

VALERIE: Nothing. He doesn't make much of an impression here. A ridiculous old B-list actor. A john like all the other presidents.

ULTRA VIOLET: What about you?

VALERIE: A lot of surfing and a lot of sun. Disco balls versus death. The ocean is cold, still cold, shark attacks are still being hushed up by the government. It's all right, but it's all wrong.

ULTRA VIOLET: And what's your opinion of the current women's movement? Where does the American woman stand today?

VALERIE: In the shit, I suspect.

ULTRA VIOLET: And where do you stand?

VALERIE: In the shit.

(*Silence.*)

(*Shouts from the street, traffic, hum of porn music.*)

ULTRA VIOLET: What else is happening?

VALERIE: Not much. Work. Money. Sun. I've got a visitor coming now . . . More work. I have to hang up.

ULTRA VIOLET (*quick tongued*): Are you a prostitute? Do you still hate men? Do you ever think about Andy Warhol?

The windowpane is streaked with dirt and exhaust fumes, the room is boiling and freezing, ice-blue and alien. Do you still hate men? Are you still a prostitute? Do you ever think about Andy Warhol? Is the president still an ass? Does the president still have hair in his ass?

VALERIE: I need to get off the phone now. I have nothing to say . . . I'm an author. You can write that. I'm writing a book . . . Put that . . . Sex is a hang-up . . . You can write that too.

You throw the receiver down and drag on your raincoat, no, your silver coat (*the raincoat was so long ago, it was New York, the Factory, Manhattan, black raincoat, dark glasses, waiting for rain that never came*) and put your scarf into your bag with an old plastic-wrapped sandwich, your hat, and your sunglasses. The sun rides the waves in the sky out there and you paint your lips deep pink and look at yourself in the cracked mirror. *The prettiest nine-year-old in America. The fastest surfer in Alligator Reef. Star student from the University of Maryland. The woman who failed to kill Andy Warhol.* In the distance the sound of sirens and unknown women screaming, blue lights flashing and camera bulbs, a still hand on your arm. The small, gloved hand of Officer William Schmalix, and a movement, light as a bird, shielding your head as you climb into the police car.

UNIVERSITY OF MARYLAND, 1963
BETTY FRIEDAN PUBLISHES *THE FEMININE MYSTIQUE*

It is warm and dark in the lab; the animals are sleeping or moving about slowly in their cages. You have been testing electricity on male mice since morning; everything ceases to exist around you when you are working—Cosmo, the department, hunger for money—but now your concentration is on its way out and Cosmo is on her way in. The windows are open to the night, teeming with insects and flowers that only open in the dark. Cosmo sweeps in on a scooter, her hair sparkling, with a box of sweets and a surprise packet, small and white, which you snort together. She hangs a garland round your neck, kissing you hard and, as ever, too long.

VALERIE: Your hair looks like a bird's been in it. As though you've been struck by lightning.
COSMO: You're here, that's why.
VALERIE: You've got cocaine in your hair. Where did you sleep last night? With the Lab Rat?
COSMO: Tell me about the experiment.
VALERIE: A little rich girl dreamed of killing her younger

brother. The dreams kept coming back. The younger brother sat on the beach building sandcastles that were always smashed by the waves. She had a recurring dream that he would be snatched by the waves and dragged out to sea. His subsequent drowning made her go insane. Illness as escape. Depressive obedience. Psychotic submission. Psychoanalysis, a correction facility for women. A penal colony.

COSMO: Was it your little brother?

VALERIE: When I was small I fixed a pipe in the river in Ventor, and into it I told all my secrets. The words flowed away, out into the Atlantic. I said I wanted a typewriter, that I wanted to write, I said Dorothy needed a new dress and a bit of survival instinct, I called out for someone like you.

COSMO: The problem that has no name. The histories without history.

VALERIE: At the mental hospital they permitted her family to bring a sandpit into the hospital grounds, so she could build sandcastles that would not be swallowed up by the sea. The other patients never went near the sand; they all knew the story about her younger brother. But every time there was a storm over the hospital park, she went crazy with fear and smashed all the sandcastles before the storm could swallow them up.

COSMO: I dream about you at night, Valerie.

VALERIE: The function of dreams. To fend off external or internal stimuli during sleep. To reinterpret an external threat. I daydream about our work all day long, Cosmo. I dream that we're America's first official intellectual whores.

COSMO: I make myself ill thinking about you.

VALERIE: Primary gain. Escape into illness. The sickness of pain. It's not worth swanning around in the sciences. The death of psychoanalysis.

COSMO: I'm talking about you and me, not about psycho-analysis.

VALERIE: I'm in love. I'm not planning to fall out of love. I'm talking about torture and sadism and being in prison with no prison walls, imprisoned in psychoANALysis. I'm talking about being free from all that. Asylum. Artificial historiography. Anarchic kisses outside history. You and me, Cosmo. We are not part of history, not part of any story. No history, no destiny. World history is merely a criminal gang consisting of ape-men who like playing at being police, brain police and body police.

And she lets go of your hand, takes her scooter, and leaves. She lights a cigarette, waves at you, and disappears into the darkness. You call after her.

VALERIE: Where are you going now?

COSMO: To get more cake and those infernal application forms.

VALERIE: Are we going to apply for money, after all?

COSMO: It's not state money, so it's okay. Good night.

All spring Dr. Ruth Cooper sits behind her white curtains, trying to concentrate on making diagnoses. Occasionally she loses
her train of thought during your sessions and her cool hand
touches you, and sometimes she takes off her doctor's coat and
sits in her blouse and trousers. The air-conditioning has been
turned off indefinitely and she always returns to your childhood
in the desert. You prefer to discuss America's place in history,
B-52s, napalm, Agent Orange, and to dwell a while longer on
the subject of Men's Flagrant Inferiority.

Clouds contracting in a spasm of cramp outside the window,
hospital noises, the sweet smell of shop-bought flowers obtru-
sive and nauseating, while you make a note of everything she
says, working on your own diagnosis of Dr. Cooper, an account
of her childhood, a health bulletin; things do not look very good
at all for Dr. Cooper. *Diagnosis as follows: Depressive obedience.
Diminished desire impulse, diminished aggression impulse. Patho-
logically well-developed impulse control. Abnormally high predispo-*

sition toward playing Daddy's Girl. Awareness of illness entirely lacking. The sufferer's behavior tends to scare the shit out of other patients who feel ready to rule the universe.

You spend the afternoons in the hospital attic, where Dr. Cooper lets you borrow her white coat and listens without interruption, while you expound on a variety of matters, stuffed she-animals, dead creatures in formalin, and present facts about the mouse colony from Maryland. There was a time when your Sprague Dawleys lay asleep in the pocket of your lab coat, a time when Cosmo swept past in the dorm in high boots, wearing sunglasses the laboratory animals could see their reflections in. You illustrate on a dusty slate, while Dr. Cooper listens, deep in concentration, red blotches on her neck; it is all about mice, utopias, and memories, about laboratory production of mice and people, artificial thought embryos outside the tyranny of nature and the terrorism of biology. *Listen to the doctor. Pregnancy is just a temporary and unfair deformation of the body. There are secret ways to escape biological destiny. We must take control of nature right now.*

When the sun dips into the treetops you go back to Dr. Ruth Cooper's office, where you borrow her doctor's coat; and Dr. Cooper, wearing her pink turtleneck, elegant gold chains, and dark, pressed trousers, lies on the analysis couch, shuts her eyes, and listens, forgetting to write notes in the medical record. A faint buzzing sound from the green-glowing desk lamp as Dr. Cooper closes her eyes; and the dying light gently brushing her face, her freckles, fluttering eyelashes, translucent skin. Your voice labors like a machine, a steel plant, empty factories, deserted industrial towns. Her face looks like a desert while she listens.

You lose count of how many requests you have made to the hospital administration for permission to borrow and use a typewriter. All requests rejected, but Dr. Cooper allows you to borrow hers for short periods to write your life story. You write a short essay on her wonderful Continental.

DR. RUTH COOPER: What do you think about Andy, now, Valerie?

VALERIE: He's in the hospital.

DR. RUTH COOPER: What do you think he's doing there?

VALERIE: He's in the hospital playing dead. He's making a film about the hospital and a film about death, starring himself.

DR. RUTH COOPER: Why do you think he's in the hospital?

VALERIE: Great artist. Great white backdrop.

DR. RUTH COOPER: You're immensely talented, Valerie.

VALERIE: Thanks, Doctor, I know. The big question is whether it's to my advantage or my disadvantage.

DR. RUTH COOPER: Your sense of humor is fantastic. That's the key to your survival.

VALERIE: You're not such a bore yourself, Dr. Obvious.

(*Silence.*)

VALERIE: You know men have no sense of humor?

(*Dr. Ruth Cooper smiling.*)

VALERIE: You know manhood is a deficiency disease?

(*Dr. Ruth Cooper beaming.*)

VALERIE: You're okay, Doctor. I can see you know what I'm talking about.

PROFESSOR ROBERT BRUSH: You know we're extremely pleased with your work in the department. You think like a scientist. Don't waste your talent. You can go as far as you want to. But you must keep within the framework of accepted, recognized scientific methods and premises.

VALERIE: Thanks, but there's no reason to let the male mice live. They're not contributing to anything. We should be able to produce female mice only. I'd like to investigate what happens in a research station with just females. I'm sure they can reproduce without males. I need money to do the research.

PROFESSOR ROBERT BRUSH: We're looking here at what happens to the males when they are implanted with cancer cells and other foreign cells. Cancer cells, human cells, cells from other species. Reference to females and offspring is interesting, but it isn't central here.

VALERIE: The mouse boys apparently can't relate to the other mice. For some reason they seem to lack empathy. I want to know what happens if the mouse girls get to live on their own. All the results would change.

PROFESSOR ROBERT BRUSH: You need to have higher scientific requirements than that, my dear.

VALERIE: The unmotivated upsurge of the world. If women and mouse girls don't get their asses in gear fast, we're all going to die. I spend the whole night in with the cages and I can only observe that the experiments are utterly pointless. The flagrant inferiority of the males. Why are they part of the experiments at all?

PROFESSOR ROBERT BRUSH: It's not relevant, Valerie. Dismiss that thought. It's leading you nowhere.

VALERIE: I plan to write a book.

PROFESSOR ROBERT BRUSH: I think you should do that. You're one of my best students. But you lack patience. You need to work on your patience. Research is about understanding, not about change.

VALERIE: Work records, apricot cocktails, contemporary experimental psychology, I'm not interested in your empirical images, I'm not interested in endlessly dull case definitions and disorders. The place of the phallus in the theory of sexuality is laughable. Doppelganger, toy, doll, alter ego. A preliminary outline for his whole being.

PROFESSOR ROBERT BRUSH: If you could devote all that hyperintelligence to the orthodox instead, i.e., the pathways of science already well worn and well lit, then there's no limit to how far you can go. I'd be able to recommend you to whatever position you want.

VALERIE: I'm sure you would. The trouble is, how a man perceives his genitals couldn't interest me less. In certain circumstances a turd appears to fulfill the same role as a penis. Et cetera. Et cetera. It's simply more information than I require. The interesting issue continues to be: Can we regard the turd, like the penis, as having a strange little personality all its own? The onus really does seem to be on me to write my own book.

PROFESSOR ROBERT BRUSH (*laughs*): Do that, Valerie. But watch out against the marginal. The relationship between the sexes. Biology and destiny. There's nothing to be gleaned from it.

VALERIE: Your attitude will change, you'll see.

PROFESSOR ROBERT BRUSH: You'll see that yours does. Tell Ann Duncan that we'd like to see her in the seminars again. Tell her I was asking after her mother.

VALERIE: Do you have a dollar?

PROFESSOR ROBERT BRUSH: Of course. Here, have ten.

Her eyes are black mirrors. Her heart is a bruise. At nights, in one of the parks, she keeps losing her bag with her keys and money and you will go and fetch her from some Washington suburb where she has been sitting on a sidewalk and has forgotten how to get home. She starts to carry a plastic bag for her lipstick, cash, and scientific journals, instead of a handbag, and she wears her leopard-skin coat in the middle of summer, but still she is cold. And whenever you stand in your clogs and lab coat in the bright fluorescent light, she appears and empties the contents of the bag onto the experiment and her voice sounds increasingly brittle and shrill.

The Polaroid camera has to take the place of science; she is no longer working, she misses all the seminars, forgets her assignments in the laboratory, and loses her place in the department. And it makes no difference how many times you sit in front of the departmental board and beg, and it makes no difference how much she begs on her mother's behalf, and how many Polaroid pictures of laboratory mice she sends to Elizabeth. Only the animals are her true friends, only the animals hate death as much as Cosmogirl.

VALERIE: Put the camera away. I'm working.
COSMO: You have to play with me, not work.
VALERIE: Photograph some other animals.

COSMO: I'm bored.

VALERIE: Help me clean the cages instead. Have you spoken to Elizabeth?

COSMO: California Mickey Mouse Jurisdiction. Finished, done, over and out. The end. Closing credits. Mayday fucking Mayday. Look at this little idiot. She doesn't stand a chance against the males. It's unbelievable that this system of violence doesn't lead to eradication of the species. Quite the reverse, the males' aggressiveness appears to contribute to its success.

VALERIE: There are mouse girl-boys. There are shining exceptions. Auxiliaries.

COSMO: The evaders, who stand outside it all . . . No sense of responsibility . . . What is it that makes some males rape and kill, and others glide into the glass walls like jellyfish?

VALERIE: Did you call Elizabeth?

COSMO: The constant rape by dolphin males of dolphin girls and dolphin youngsters is a system that works. The females don't flee. They keep on breeding with sadists and terrorists, they surf toward their own destruction. And always with that goddamn dolphin smile.

VALERIE: The lab director. The analyst. The seminar leader.

COSMO: I know what I'm doing.

(*Silence.*)

COSMO: I do nothing unplanned.

VALERIE: They were just metaphors. For destruction, for masochism, for self-imposed rape.

COSMO: I've tried to get the mice to exhibit alternative behavior, to communicate desire or aggression or fear, for example. It doesn't happen, or at least I'm not capable of interpreting it as language. Mice don't use metaphors and yet the species still thrives. It's not male violence that distinguishes us, species similarity is striking in that respect, it's language that separates

202 SARA STRIDSBERG

mouse boys from human males, metaphor, sublimation, translation, reinterpretation, transmission, comparison, lies.

VALERIE: And the tendency among human girls toward self-destructive dolphin behavior?

COSMO: There's only one way to raise that research money. The desire for friendly pussy. The propensity to drown in their own passive flesh. I've nothing against research without funding, without credit and dog biscuits, without being a part of science. I have no wish to swan around in the sciences anymore.

VALERIE: Kiss my ass.

COSMO: You know I'd love to do that.

VALERIE: I'm going to have that money. We deserve it. Your chances of getting research money from the lab director decrease with every blow job. The screwing machine won't give us our money. If we're lucky, we'll get gonorrhea. If we're very lucky, syphilis.

COSMO: We'll never get the money. Nobody's going to let us do research on the extermination of male mice. It's like asking for money to produce an execution machine for the president.

VALERIE (*laughs*): You're a genius, Cosmo. I'm just going to run and fetch the application forms. We're going to be wading in money when the boss hears about this. An execution machine for the president. The good old sparky. The good old fellow. They're going to love it . . . Tell me more about the execution machine.

COSMO: I have nothing against being outside history. I'd rather take fuck-money than money from a state that's trying to murder my mother.

VALERIE: And what did Elizabeth say? Tell me.

COSMO: She's crocheting baby blankets. It's like a mental illness. It's disgusting. She'll do anything to survive. A classic study in personality change. Borderline. I know how it would be diagnosed. Lunacy. The threat of execution results in a population of whores in there.

VALERIE: And makes you a whore out here.

COSMO: If I give money to you, what does it matter where it comes from?

VALERIE: You're starting to smell of war, my little idiot. One more reason I wish you only champagne and streamers and princess cake.

COSMO: I'm so scared of dying. I know they're killing her. My brain is an electric chair where innocent people are being executed all the time. What does it matter? I love you.

VALERIE: Come on.

And you drop the experiment and drop everything else, and you take her hand, remove her damp fur coat, and pull her up onto the workbench, and you stop her when she tries to sit up, and you put out her cigarettes when she tries to light them, and you hold on to her, and she smells of smoke and the netherworld, and Cosmogirl, the most beautiful girl, the most grotesque, becomes perfectly calm. She is just a little laboratory animal, easily soothed, broken by testing, insane.

VALERIE: Come on, stupid.

COSMO: There's no future. There's no God. She's going to die, I know. All this is going to disappear.

VALERIE: We're here now.

COSMO: And then it will all be gone.

VALERIE: We exist now.

COSMO: And then it will all be gone.

VALERIE: Tell me something.

COSMO: I have nothing to say.

VALERIE: Tell me about Elizabeth.

COSMO: She's going to die. That's all.

VALERIE: It just makes me frightened, Cosmo, when you resort to the doe-eyed face, when you look like an injured animal all the time.

COSMO: I love you.

VALERIE: We're going to do research, Bambi, not prostitution. We're going to wash that fur coat and cover up your bruises. We're going to stop taking drugs and take over instead.

VALERIE: Nineteenth Amendment. The right to vote. Silence. World war. Activities ceased, the liberation movement went underground.

PROFESSOR ROBERT BRUSH: A new age is coming. You and Ann Duncan are part of the future.

VALERIE: There's nothing in it for us.

PROFESSOR ROBERT BRUSH: A new world is dawning outside the department. You have your brain, and I'll see to it that you have a place, a budget, and a job in science. The only thing you need to provide is patience.

VALERIE: Definitely not for us.

PROFESSOR ROBERT BRUSH: Ann Duncan has to come back to seminars. And you must start working within a scientific framework. Your current work can be regarded as non-work. It might as well be silence.

VALERIE: A psychoanalytical perspective on all that silence. The function of projection and transference. James Dean. The war. Marilyn Monroe. The war as a super-projection onto a screen resembling the sky. Superpower. Superman.

PROFESSOR ROBERT BRUSH: I can't watch, it makes me despair, when you distance yourself from science like this, especially when it applies to yourself.

VALERIE: Margaret Mahler and Melanie Klein are sucking psychoanalytical cock in Brücke's lab. It doesn't matter how long you lie around relaxing and interpreting damp patches on the ceiling. This is not childhood, it's an aberration. Childhood is the place assigned to women in the laboratory, the system of desire, the money system. Men's childhood, perhaps, not women's. In every man sits a masturbating little infant with extremely sadistic impulses. The role of psychoanalysis is to rehabilitate the sadistic man-child.

PROFESSOR ROBERT BRUSH: As I said, I wish you'd return to the case analysis. Whatever our differences, the whole point is not to turn away from the world, it's always to go back to what we label reality.

VALERIE: Don't look at her childhood, look at her place in the system of desire, at her unhappy childhood among sadists and misogynists. No desire options in any shape or form. Thanks to truncated libido, sometimes truncated genitalia, truncated aggression. Everything stems from the allotted task, to be a screen for projections, for dreams of the Wild West. Couch, transference, and a gigantic transference neurosis. There's nothing behind the screen. Marilyn Monroe, Doris Day. Truncated desire impulse, truncated aggression impulse, all American women. The death of psychoanalysis, Professor Robert.

PROFESSOR ROBERT BRUSH: Your method of thinking is like an injection of new blood for this department. If you drop your project with female mice, I'll make sure you have funding for as long as you want.

VALERIE: If you stop fucking people who are drowning, I'll think about it.

The trees blossom late in New York and it is summer by the time the desert dragonflies invade the cities, where hairstyles are piled up and blond. Windows to the street are open and strangers wave from the balconies. You run through the crowds, holding Cosmogirl by your sweaty hand. The White House and Lyndon B. Johnson smolder in everyone's thoughts. Everyone is there. Everyone has to buy the first version of the manifesto.

Kay Clarenbach and Muriel Fox from the National Organization for Women speak into megaphones about sexual politics, about the tyranny of biology and the unhappy housewife. The unfortunate relationship between man and woman and their need for sexual love without martyrdom. They adore talking about men. Men are heartily welcomed into NOW (National Organization for Worms). You have your own movement, the Society for Cutting Up Men, and there is nothing you like more than amphetamines pumping through your head.

You pull Cosmo by the hand through the protest march, both of you yelling and chanting: ALL MARRIED WOMEN ARE PROSTITUTES, ONLY REAL WHORES ARE REAL WOMEN. And to any girl who wants to know, you say: In just a few hours we could mobilize an army of man haters. In only a few weeks we could bring down the president, take over this country and everyone's mind. The unwork force. The fuck-up force. Destroy this filthy state. The United States of Pimps and Balls. The United States of Nothing.

At the corner of a street you kiss her, a wild animal howls inside your chest, breathless, fluttering moments of deepest pink, anarchic kisses outside history. Cosmo and you run hand in hand outside the women's movement's second wave, outside the New Left and women's lib, far outside the feminine mystique, feminist glamour girls, the Vietnam movement. The American women's movement is made of you and her, you are America's first intellectual whores and you are the author of the only text worth reading, *SCUM Manifesto*.

It is New York's hottest summer and dead dragonflies lie in drifts on the sidewalks. You are wearing your white fur coat of silver fox, your nylon tights, your smelly high-heeled boots, and you take pride in always having lipstick on your teeth and gigantic mirrored sunglasses that Cosmo can see her reflection in as she layers on more makeup, more glitter, more cocaine. And every manifesto gets a lipstick kiss before you sell it for a dollar or a few cents. The sun blinds your eyes, oil drums and placards burn on street corners; and this is your time, a parenthesis of fast-igniting flames and sudden heat. Sparks of skin and flaring magnesium.

NARRATOR: I keep thinking of your wild-animal language, of your time at the university. Then I think about New York and the Factory. Questions central to this novel. Why did you stop writing? Why did you leave Maryland? Why did you shoot Andy Warhol?

VALERIE: Mirror, mirror on the wall. These are all the wrong questions. The right question is: Why did she carry on writing; why did anyone carry on writing? Why didn't she leave the university; why did any girl stay in the faculty? Why didn't she shoot; why did so many of her kind have no access to weapons? All her rights were under constant attack. Idle and beautiful, they walked around their gardens on Long Island. Why didn't they just destroy their gardens? The feminine mystique.

NARRATOR: In an interview with Howard Smith in *The Village Voice* in 1977 you say . . . It's after the women's prison, after the mental hospitals, and you've just published the manifesto yourself—

VALERIE: —Thanks. If you want to give a lecture about my life, then maybe I'm the wrong audience. I'm not terribly interested. I fucked everything up, that's the answer to all your questions. I couldn't take living like a lobotomized brood cow, and the world around me couldn't take that.

NARRATOR: In the interview with Howard Smith—

VALERIE: Imbecile. Infantile. Irritating. I remember he volunteered himself for a blow job after the interview.

NARRATOR: —you say of the manifesto that it's hypothetical. Later you retract that. I'd like to know what you mean by hypothetical. You also say that SCUM was a literary device, that there is no organization called SCUM.

VALERIE: There was only me. I don't like arithmetic.

NARRATOR: In my novel—

VALERIE: —You and your little novel will have to excuse me now, because I've got work to do.

NARRATOR: I have money.

VALERIE: How nice for you.

NARRATOR: I mean, I have money in case you need some, so you don't have to . . .

VALERIE: Don't have to what?

NARRATOR: I'm just saying, I have money if you need some.

VALERIE: Don't have to what?

NARRATOR: Sell your body. Be a prostitute. Capitalize on intimacy. I don't know what to call it.

VALERIE: Sexual politics. Organization of so-called love, i.e., rape. Red-light district. Special areas of the city sprang up, the women were summoned for government-funded tests every week to keep their clients, the johns, the boys, free from disease. Take everything from me. Do it. That's what I want.

NARRATOR: It reduces to something deeply tragic if you hate men and are forced to sell yourself to them all your life.

VALERIE: Charge for rape. Organized rape. Systematized rape. Rape that can be preplanned. Structured sucking-off. Formalized fucking. Charging for rape. Rape isn't free. It's impossible to rape someone who does it of her own free will. All married women are prostitutes. Only real whores are real women and revolutionaries. I don't sell my heart, I don't sell my brain, I sell a few minutes and a part of my body that isn't mine.

THE FACTORY

Dr. Cooper does not tire of getting beaten at poker. Her losses accumulate and it is lucky for her that you are not playing for money. She is far too distracted to stand a chance, and it is obvious she imagines the game of cards will lead to a mini-discourse from you on your unhappy childhood. She is obsessed with childhood and seems as devoid of tactics as she is of natural competitive instinct.

VALERIE: Do you want to get your own childhood back, Doctor?

DR. RUTH COOPER: I want you to tell me more about yours.

VALERIE: It was my childhood that made me into a feral creature.

DR. RUTH COOPER: And the relationship with your father?

VALERIE: And into a devil at poker.

DR. RUTH COOPER: And the relationship with your father?

VALERIE: I don't have a father.

DR. RUTH COOPER: And the relationship with your mother?

VALERIE: I chased after our kites across the desert. We were young and wild and free. I'm sorry, Dr. Cooper, but I have to fuck up your theories. Dorothy was a light bulb, a shiny piece of mica.

DR. RUTH COOPER: And your childhood?

VALERIE: I counted roses on the swing seat cover. I dreamed of a typewriter. I pissed in a nasty boy's juice.

DR. RUTH COOPER: Your upbringing has been described as loveless and violent. Your language and your attitude are characterized by a strong sense of abandonment.

VALERIE: Motherhood is potential for social change. Everything of value has been built by mothers. Dorothy built a house without money. She gave me food for fifteen years. And sunshine and blood.

DR. RUTH COOPER: The ability to love is directly linked to the ability of the small child to rouse tender feelings in the mother.

VALERIE: Hey, hey, Cooper! What do you know about love?

DR. RUTH COOPER: I am not the patient.

VALERIE: Cosmogirl has gone for good. That's all I know.

DR. RUTH COOPER: I know you're feeling despair.

VALERIE: Why do you always wear those ugly glasses?

DR. RUTH COOPER: I have a visual impairment. Myopia. I have to be able to see my patients in order to work.

VALERIE: Take your glasses off.

DR. RUTH COOPER: I would prefer you to sit back down on your chair.

You have climbed up onto Dr. Cooper's shiny, sexy desk (*it is strictly forbidden to climb on hospital furniture*) and removed her glasses (*it is strictly forbidden to touch hospital staff*). Through her spectacles there is mist and vague outlines, and Dr. Ruth Cooper's naked little boyish face, and Dr. Cooper waving her arms and wanting her glasses back. Without her smart, dark frames, she is no one. Dr. Ruth Cooper gives one of her West Coast laughs, a laugh of salt and beach wrack and sea anemones. She is very bad at playing Dr. Stern.

DR. RUTH COOPER: Give me my glasses.

VALERIE: Do you like girls?

DR. RUTH COOPER: No.

(*Silence.*)

DR. RUTH COOPER: Or rather, I mean, obviously I like girls. I like girls. I like boys. I like all sorts of people. Girls don't turn me on sexually, if that's what you're asking.

VALERIE: You're sweet when you're lying.

DR. RUTH COOPER: I'm not lying.

VALERIE: Do you like me?

DR. RUTH COOPER: You know I do. I like you as a patient and as a person. You could be my child.

VALERIE: Your little human baby. I don't want to be anyone's child. Children don't exist.

DR. RUTH COOPER: If you'd been my child, you wouldn't have ended up here.

VALERIE: You're beautiful without your glasses.

(*Dr. Ruth Cooper blushes and flicks through her notes.*)

DR. RUTH COOPER: The trial is fast approaching.

VALERIE: And you want us to talk about my childhood.

DR. RUTH COOPER: What do you want to talk about?

VALERIE (*gives back the glasses*): Do you know why you lose all the time?

(*Dr. Ruth Cooper laughs and puts her glasses back on.*)

VALERIE: Because I prefer being lucky at games, and you prefer being lucky at love. The concept of romantic love is just a method of keeping half the population imprisoned in suburban backyards. A devastatingly simple way of giving intelligent people the idea that dishcloths are more important than literature.

DR. RUTH COOPER: I know nothing about love.

VALERIE: Well then, Dr. Cooper, I suggest we have another round so you have a chance to recoup your losses.

(*Silence.*)

VALERIE: Dr. Ruth Cooper?

DR. RUTH COOPER: I lied before. I dream of shooting all the men I meet. I hate the way that after intercourse they ask if they can do anything for me.

VALERIE: Take your glasses off, Cooper.

DR. RUTH COOPER (*takes off her glasses*): I don't want to be a psychiatrist any longer.

VALERIE: It'll be all right, Doctor. Concentrate now so you don't lose any more money.

DR. RUTH COOPER: Ever since you arrived here, I haven't known what to do.

VALERIE: All we know is that you have an exceptionally underdeveloped poker face, Dr. Cooper. But it's okay, Dr. Cooper. There's no reason to tell the truth when it's so easy to lie.

In the elevator on the way up to the Factory, the mirror is dominated by your smile, your cherry-red lipstick and rosy-fevered cheeks, and in your coat pocket is the play, wrapped in tissue paper. Billy Name greets you in the lobby with open arms and piercing eyes and Andy Warhol appears from nowhere with kisses on the cheek and leftover streamers festooning his sweater and a Polaroid camera.

Columns of hash smoke rise above their back-combed pop-art hairstyles and Andy Warhol has that habit of gliding in and out of the wings, surfacing out of nowhere and then quietly vanishing into a sea of white walls and guests. His apparition emerges, a shimmering, glittering fagginess, only to melt away; his wonderful manner of emasculating and disarming himself.

ANDY: Hello, Valerie.
VALERIE: Andy Stupid Warhol.
BILLY: Valerie Solanas.

VALERIE: I see you've de-manned yourself in an exemplary fashion.

ANDY: Welcome to the Factory, Valerie. You haven't been here before, have you?

VALERIE: Not as I recall. We need to get on with this Turd Session right away.

BILLY: Sure, Valerie. Wouldn't you like something to drink first?

VALERIE: Some bubbly, please. And something strong to smoke. But first you have to list all the ways in which you are all turds. Say after me. I am a low-ly ab-ject t-urd.

ANDY: I am a turd, a lowly abject turd.

VALERIE (*points at Billy*): Good.

BILLY: What am I supposed to say?

VALERIE: I am a lowly abject turd.

BILLY: Oh yeah. I'm a turd, a lowly abject turd.

VALERIE: Great.

BILLY: What the hell is a Turd Session?

VALERIE: To help men in the Men's Auxiliary of SCUM, SCUM will conduct Turd Sessions, at which every man present will give a speech beginning with the sentence: "I am a turd, a lowly abject turd," and then proceed to list all the ways in which he is. His reward for doing so will be the opportunity to fraternize after the session for a whole, solid hour with the SCUM who will be present.

ANDY: That sounds fantastic.

VALERIE: I've brought my play with me, Andy. *Up Your Ass.* I had some alternative titles: *Up from the Slime*, *The Big Suck*, and a few more. I want you to read it. And you, Mr. Fat Turd (*pokes Billy in the stomach*), can run along for some bubbly. Then you can list all the ways in which you are.

ANDY: *Are* what?

VALERIE: Low-ly ab-ject t-urds.

ANDY: Sure, Valerie. Come and say hello to the others first.

VALERIE (*takes the play out and hands it to Andy*): For you, Andy. The only play worth putting on.

ANDY (*leafs through it, smoking*): Interesting, Valerie.

VALERIE: What do you think?

ANDY: Interesting, Valerie. It could be, Valerie, that we decide to produce it.

Andy's face looks like an inflamed wound, his laugh reveals his decaying teeth beneath his silver wig, his clothes smell faintly of seaweed, he stammers and giggles. People have dispersed and are sitting on the shiny white floor, whispering to one another. They look up hastily without saying hello. Paul Morrissey passes with a bouquet of roses. Andy is swallowed up by one of the large white backdrops. You tell Sister White about it later:

> *when I got an invitation to the Factory, I went with no expec-*
> *tations and left with my handbag full of promises. I didn't know*
> *much about Andy Warhol, mainly that he was a hotshot in New*
> *York, something to do with imitations and screen prints. I'd*
> *seen him on television when he was painting his nails and call-*
> *ing himself Miss Warhola and Miss World. I knew he was*
> *illiterate, he was leafing through fashion and muscle magazines*
> *without even understanding the captions and he used to spread*
> *a rumor about himself that he dressed as a bag lady and sneaked*
> *around New York at night giving out food to other bag ladies. I*
> *liked the Factory at once, there was always food and something*
> *to drink, they were all freaks and all around the walls drug*
> *addicts and prostitutes sat waiting for Andy to come and make*
> *art out of them. I decided straightaway that Andy would lead*
> *the Men's Auxiliary of SCUM, he was perfect, this sparkling*
> *little gay creature, the albino look, the silver wig*

Open arms, wide gestures, champagne fizzing and popping in your mouth. The Silver Factory is a gigantic mirror and you are not sure how many people are actually prowling around; the silver mirrors reflect tenfold and distort, and when you are high, you speak to mirrored figures as well, and you are gratified to see that you look a freak even among freaks, in your floppy, sweaty boots and dirty fur coat. And it might be rather tedious to talk to mirrors, but since everything around Andy has the same flat, smooth surface, it does not matter.

Andy's films are projected on the walls, and when you are not high, you stay close to them, instead of the mirrors. You are a black spider who loves the Factory. You tell Sister White about it afterward:

> there were shopping bags everywhere in the Factory. Andy loved shopping. He always had money. He bathed in money and grass. Shopping was part of art. He was involved in something to do with the boundaries between art and shopping. Art, my ass. The guy loved new things, he loved buying, loved having limitless money. He was a materialistic faggot, that's all. The male "artist" is a contradiction in terms. Andy slid like a shadow across the Factory, a parasite on other people's bloodstained memories. He brought me champagne and wanted to know all about my childhood and my plans for the future. I liked being there so very much, I wanted to be one of those needle junkies and fag-whores who sat along the walls, sweating and mumbling and waiting for Andy to come and make art out of them. They were very happy days. Andy laughed at everything I said. I read aloud from the manifesto. Those huge surfaces. I wanted the Factory to swallow me up forever.

"GREAT ART"

You stand in the Factory under an enormous screen on which Andy's films are shown around the clock. *Blow Job. Taylor Mead's Ass. Vinyl.* As Viva wanders around nearby, straightening pictures and vases, she casts a long look in your direction; she sounds like a reference book when she answers your questions.

VALERIE: Is that Andy's film?

VIVA: *Blow Job*, from 1964.

VALERIE: What's it about?

VIVA: A male prostitute who bleeds and snivels into the camera while he's getting a blow job.

VALERIE: Ah. What else?

VIVA: That's what it's about.

VALERIE: Why is it about that?

VIVA: Because it's art.

VALERIE: I think it's a good thing for Andy that *Up Your Ass* turned up here at the Factory.

VIVA: It's great art, Valerie.

VALERIE: Sure. It's fantastic.

ELIZABETH DUNCAN AND DEATH, SEPTEMBER 1967

It is nighttime and Cosmogirl stands beneath a fluorescent light in the laboratory, screaming, wearing her lab coat with nothing underneath. She has called you in New York and you have taken the night train back and when you eventually arrive she does not recognize you. The decision has come from San Quentin that Elizabeth is to die on October 9, 1967, and this time it is final; your decision to live in New York without Cosmo is also final and irreversible. You are tired of phony science and stuffed animals and of her habit of spending her nights in strange adventures with strange men in strange cars.

The most beautiful girl, and the most grotesque. Her skin is dead and white, clammy and unfamiliar, and there is only one thing to do: take a taxi to the Supreme Court one last time and kneel before the court, weeping and begging. You make her put on respectable clothes and you gather up all the documents on Elizabeth Duncan's hopeless case.

There is not a judicial cock in this state that Cosmo has not taken care of. For a number of years, she has kept Elizabeth alive with the help of the soft tongue in her mouth. But this time neither the tongue nor the featherlight fingers can help, nor any other form of pleasure. America murders Elizabeth Duncan with three lethal injections and Cosmo loses everything that she was, her brilliance, her impudence, her will of steel, she even stops taking payment for her services, she becomes a missing laboratory animal, sleeping under the trees in University Park.

Olympia Press, founded in Paris in 1953 (on a shoestring) by Maurice Girodias, with the function of perverting American tourists and selling pornography, published *The Story of O* in 1954, *Lolita* and *The Ginger Man* in 1955, all of de Sade's novels and most of Henry Miller's best works, *Candy* in 1958, *Naked Lunch* and Durrell's *Black Book* in 1959—not to mention dozens of other interesting authors, masterpieces, and diversions.

Today, as a consequence of the climate under de Gaulle, Maurice Girodias and Olympia Press have left Paris to make a fresh start in New York.

We are not interested in anyone famous, or half famous. Our function is to discover talent. Unknown authors are our specialty. You have been rejected by all existing publishing houses: well and good, you have a chance with us. We read everything—carefully, impartially, and optimistically. Send your masterpiece to the Editorial Department, Olympia Press, 36 Gramercy Park East, New York, N.Y. 10003—and don't forget to include a stamp for return mailing, as, after all, we **may** return your manuscript.

CHELSEA HOTEL, NEW YORK, NOVEMBER 1967

At the Chelsea Hotel you write *A Young Girl's Primer*, which you intend to publish in *The Village Voice*, and you continually produce new versions of the manifesto. All your notes from Maryland lie spread out in the hotel room, all your letters to the editor, columns in the student newspaper, essays, all the texts you wrote with Cosmo. At night you sit outside on the fire escape, working. Everything falls into place, you write without thinking and without the abyss in your soul. There is no emptiness, no loneliness, no yearning for Cosmo, only oceans of joy and the heat of the tarmac. Every day new bouquets of vivid flowers in the lobby and your handbag filled with fabulous pillboxes.

This is your place. New York, Chelsea, the sixties, political beings and paradoxes, freaks, artists, utopias. People who write and people who make art. Telephone calls down to the hotel's little desk clerk make you happy and calm. His fleeting giggle down the line and the rays of sunshine cast into the room.

LITTLE DESK CLERK: Lobby.

VALERIE: Is that the little clerk?

LITTLE DESK CLERK: How can I help you, daaarling?

VALERIE: I need a new telephone. A dry telephone with no crap on the wires.

LITTLE DESK CLERK (*laughs*): We'll change your phone immediately.

VALERIE: I'd like a black telephone. It has to be clean, you need to wash it carefully. I don't want to have other people's breath and thoughts when I make my calls.

LITTLE DESK CLERK: I'll change your telephone myself.

VALERIE: I want to have the phone disconnected up to six o'clock. I'm writing. You can put that in that logbook of yours. Put that I'm writing. Put that I'm writing the manifesto. Put that the phone has to be disconnected and clean. Listen to me.

LITTLE DESK CLERK: Yes.

VALERIE: And another thing, I need more light in the room. The ceiling light is too faint. I'm going blind writing in the dark all night.

LITTLE DESK CLERK: I'll fix it.

VALERIE: Tomorrow?

LITTLE DESK CLERK: Tomorrow, first thing.

VALERIE: And I don't want anyone going into my room when I'm not there. No cleaning. No cleaning needed here. I'm an excellent cleaner. Listen to me now, listen stupid little—

LITTLE DESK CLERK: —I'm listening . . .

VALERIE: Don't interrupt me . . . Sex . . . Sex is a refuge for the mindless. The more mindless the woman, the more deeply embedded in masculine culture. In short, the nicer she is, the more sexual. The nicest women in our society are raving sex maniacs . . . Do you follow?

LITTLE DESK CLERK: I follow.

VALERIE: To continue . . . On the other hand, women who are least embedded in masculine culture are least nice. Crass, simple souls who reduce fucking to fucking; who are too childish for the grown-up world of suburbs, mortgages, mops, and baby shit; too selfish to raise kids and husbands; too uncivilized to give a shit about anyone's opinion of them; too arrogant to respect Daddy, the Greats, or the deep wisdom of the Ancients; who trust only their own gutter instincts; who equate Culture with chicks . . .

LITTLE DESK CLERK: That's very funny . . .

VALERIE: Thanks . . . To continue . . . Unhampered by propriety, niceties, discretion, unhampered by public opinion and morals, unhampered by the respect of assholes, and always cool, lowdown, and dirty, SCUM gets around . . . and around and around . . . they've seen the whole show, every bit of it, the fucking scene, the blow-job scene, the dyke scene—they've covered the whole waterfront, been under every dock and pier, the peter pier, the pussy pier. You've got to go through a lot of sex to get to anti-sex and SCUM's been through it all, and now they're ready for a new show; SCUM wants to crawl out from under the dock, move, take off, burst out. But SCUM isn't in control yet; SCUM is still in the gutter of our society, which, if it's not deflected from its present course, and if the bomb doesn't drop, will hump itself to death . . .

LITTLE DESK CLERK: Valerie.

VALERIE: Yes?

LITTLE DESK CLERK: Everyone's going to love you.

VALERIE: I know. You can be part of SCUM's Secret Auxiliary. I mean Men's Auxiliary. You give things away, you're kind. You know the meaning of life is love. Love is like friendship. Sex is not part of a relationship. It's a very solitary experience,

not at all creative. Sex involves a gross waste of time. You have
to go through a lot of sex to get to anti-sex.

LITTLE DESK CLERK: I have to work now. I'll come up in a
while.

VALERIE: Come as soon as you can. Knock first. Otherwise you
can forget what I said about the auxiliary. Remember. As soon
as you can. Move your little ass. And no sex. Sex is a hang-
up. Write that down in that little hotel book of yours. Please
send a postcard to Cosmo Duncan and tell her that sex is just
a hang-up.

It should have been you and Cosmo and New York. It does not
matter it is only you. It makes no difference anymore that Cosmo
is in Maryland, screwing lab directors. Because everything suddenly seems to fall into your lap: an abandoned typewriter, easy
fuck-money, Andy Warhol and the Factory, lucidity in your writing. The words strike like lightning inside you. This is your city,
your land. Everything up to this point has been depression; you
decide that you have always been unhappy and now you are
sharp, unbreakable.

Early in the mornings you sit at the typewriter, working. As soon
as light breaks, you leap out of bed, run down and buy a pot of
coffee with vodka, light your cigarettes, and there is that crystal
clarity, the irritation, like masturbating for hours in vain. You
write as if the typewriter were attached to your arms, a strange
brightness in your head that keeps you awake and makes you run
between the skyscrapers in your lace nightgown to deliver new
versions of your play to the Factory.

New York is snowy, sweltering, skittish. November is a remarkable month and the skyscrapers reach for the heavens and you do not yearn for Maryland, for Alligator Reef or Ventor; for the first time you yearn for nowhere and your nights are dreamless, snow-white. At the Chelsea Hotel a male artist pays you a visit with a dildo and pays the rent for the rest of the month; your groin does not stop bleeding afterward and the killing machine keeps operating in Florida, Arkansas, Nevada, Texas, California.

Cosmogirl has stopped writing threatening letters to the state that murdered her mother. Instead she calls you in New York, rapid drowning breaths, the pounding of the sea in the background, her voice wandering and thick with smoke and too much unfamiliar skin, as if her words have spent too long underwater. The smell of car and ocean forces its way into the hotel room, her deepest, wildest doe-eyed look, a scientific rhetoric crumbling more and more. Everywhere signs of Cosmo infiltrate, inside your dirty underclothes and into the hotel room, blinding white with sunshine and promises. But increasingly Bongi from *Up Your Ass* takes over; mounds of drafts pile up around you. The typewriter, the pace, the loneliness, the conviction. The moment you replace the receiver, you forget her.

COSMO: It's me, Valerie.
VALERIE: Hello, my treasure, what are the rabbits doing?

COSMO: Larking about in the park.

VALERIE: Have they written any new novels?

COSMO: The black-and-white pudgy one did.

VALERIE: What happened?

COSMO: She finished it and then she read it through and said it was the best novel she'd ever read. Then she left it under a tree and forgot she'd written it.

VALERIE: And the mice?

COSMO: Revolution in the cages.

VALERIE: Have you wiped out the male mice yet?

COSMO: Soon.

YOUR LONG SILENCES WITH COSMO

Cosmo loves twirling the telephone cord around her while she talks. You can see her in your mind, making the cord into a dress in a student dorm that is moving further and further away from you. You cannot concentrate, her voice is a foreign, murky pool, and as she speaks, you read through the last sheet of paper in the typewriter, put in a new one, and light a cigarette. *You know, Cosmo, it's like having a lucky engine in my body when I write. I'm so tired of stuffed animals and professors. You know, Cosmo, when I write, the trees outside look as though they're clad in gold paper.* She takes long, uneven breaths, and sometimes it sounds as though she is asleep. You have time to write another page before the conversation carries on, and then she might suddenly be wide awake, electric.

COSMO: What are you doing? Do you miss me? When are you going to come? When are we going to get married?
VALERIE: Working. Soon. Already married. In our hearts. Any news?

COSMO: A New York artist was here and he planted a wish tree in the park. Visitors could fasten their wishes onto the tree on little slips of pink paper. I've been there several times and made a wish.

VALERIE: What did you wish for?

COSMO: Elizabeth. You. Most of all that she'll come back. That you'll come back. How's New York?

VALERIE: Cold. I've invited myself to various hot parties with various hotshots. I've been to Andy Warhol's at the Factory a few times. I've drunk expensive champagne and looked at his ridiculous pop art.

COSMO: Has he said anything about your play?

VALERIE: Soon. Everything's on the turn now. I know it. Soon Andy will decide he's going to produce it.

COSMO: The mice miss you. And the rabbits. All their novels are about you now.

VALERIE: And the Lab Rat. Do you see him?

COSMO: Sometimes.

VALERIE: Do you suck his cock?

COSMO: I'd rather be with you. You know that.

VALERIE: Sex is a hang-up. You know that.

COSMO: I'll be back soon. Are you keeping me a place in the Chelsea bar?

VALERIE: Sure.

COSMO: He thinks you're the most talented one in the university, Valerie.

VALERIE: I think he's an asshole. He's the supervisor of a load of incarcerated mice, that's all. If he'd been smart, he'd have given me money for the project. Smart lab directors don't stop smart projects. Smart lab directors don't shit their pants because male mice turn out to be superfluous, self-destructive, and a danger to the species. He shouldn't have taken it personally, he should have kept on riding the waves to his own demise.

COSMO: It was because you didn't want me.

VALERIE: Kiss my ass.

COSMO: You know I'd love to kiss your ass. I dream about it at night. Why don't you let me do it?

VALERIE: I don't have time for sex. I don't have time to talk any longer. There's a publisher in my sights. They advertised for new writers and it's me they're looking for. They just don't know it yet.

COSMO: Will you call?

VALERIE: I'll call.

BRISTOL HOTEL, APRIL 20, 1988

NARRATOR: Shall I light a cigarette for you?

VALERIE: I'm writing. And I can't smoke anymore because of my lungs.

NARRATOR: What are you writing?

VALERIE: It's about mice and language and loneliness.

NARRATOR: And why did you stop writing?

VALERIE: Silence of the mammal.

NARRATOR: You're a girl, not an animal.

VALERIE: A she-mammal or a female child. I was on the borderline between human being and chaos. Cosmo dreamed about filming captive animals in America and Europe and she planned to visit every zoological institution open to visitors. She loved animals, dead and living. One summer we traveled around filming stuffed animals in museums.

NARRATOR: And why did you stop writing?

VALERIE: Up to now the history of all societies has been the history of silence. Rebel, psychoanalyst, experimental writer, woman's potential as dissident. Language has become increasingly a physical substance whose only function is to underline my loneliness.

THE FACTORY, DECEMBER 1967
NEW WHITE INDUSTRIAL BUILDINGS ON UNION SQUARE

Andy's pockmarked face opens to the spotlight. A gently droning, drowsy sound from his film camera, only you and the silver wig and your wooden chairs in an orb of light, the rest of the Factory in compact darkness. Andy has red patches on his cheeks, his eyes are infected, and he has invited you for pink champagne and fried chicken. A light breeze in the room from an open window somewhere in the dark and a bouquet of flowers under your chair. Strangers move around in the blackness, it does not matter who listens, the light shines only on you and Andy Warhol.

VALERIE: May I say whatever I want in the film?
ANDY: Say what you want. We're improvising.
VALERIE: Aren't there any lines we have to use?
ANDY: You're talented enough not to need lines.
VALERIE: I've never been in a film before.
ANDY: I'm not interested in actors; I'm interested in people.
VALERIE: I don't like them.
ANDY: Who?

VALERIE: People.

ANDY: Why?

VALERIE: Because they fuck me in my face as soon as they get a chance.

ANDY (*laughs*): The camera's rolling.

VALERIE: What sort of film is it?

ANDY: Is it true you went to grad school?

VALERIE: Grad school was shitty.

ANDY: What did you study?

VALERIE: Can't remember. It was a shitty faculty.

ANDY: And your upbringing?

VALERIE: I was raised all over.

ANDY: Where?

VALERIE: In the desert. Blue-collar America.

(*Silence.*)

VALERIE: You know, I like being in the Factory.

ANDY: It's great having you here.

VALERIE: I didn't think you liked women.

ANDY: I like you.

VALERIE: Do you sleep with men?

ANDY: I suppose so.

VALERIE: I don't know what to do with my arms. Shall I look into the camera?

ANDY: It's good when you look into the camera while you're speaking. You have intense eyes; you're observing your surroundings like an artist.

VALERIE: I mean—do you sleep with men?

ANDY: If I slept with anyone it would be with men. Now tell me where you come from. Tell me about your father.

VALERIE: I have no father. Politically I'm a lesbian, politically I'm fatherless, and politically I'm a woman.

(*Silence.*)

VALERIE: I still have his name. It's incredible.

(*Silence.*)

VALERIE: Louis Solanas.

(*Silence.*)

VALERIE: Dorothy loved him, she wept a river of tears when he left. Dorothy has always had extremely bad taste.

(*Silence.*)

VALERIE: Sex is a refuge for the mindless.

(*Silence.*)

VALERIE: The nicest women in our society are raving sex maniacs.

ANDY: Tell me more, Valerie. I like it when you tell me about your childhood. You describe it like an artist.

VALERIE: There was a darkness that descended just before my seventh birthday. The darkness was called Louis Solanas and I behaved like an idiot. There was always one picnic or another by the river. Dorothy was there every time and the light was so strong and I didn't know what to do with myself. I fell asleep and dreamed I was flying over snowcapped mountains and that people were standing underneath, applauding. When I woke, Louis was lying beside me and I'm still called Solanas. It's unbelievable. My dress was snow-white, I never had a white dress after that.

ANDY: Don't stop.

VALERIE: It was the way things always are, I suppose. He had his hands inside my white dress, the desert animals were screeching in the distance, there was a smell of sausage, a smell of water. There was little more to it than me letting him. And then a darkness like any other, and then the light coming out of the trees onto his hands.

ANDY: Tell me more about Louis.

VALERIE: When it's black outside you might as well be dead.

(*Silence.*)

VALERIE: Why should I tell you about all this?

ANDY: I like listening. I have no memories myself. I like other people's memories. It connects me to other people. It makes me real. Just tell me, I'll listen, we're the only ones here.

VALERIE: It was nothing special, really. Louis used to screw me in the porch seat after Dorothy had gone into town. The fabric on the seat cover was covered with roses and I counted the roses and the stars while I rented out my little pussy for no money. And I don't know why, but some chewing gum got stuck in my hair every time. It must have fallen out of my mouth. We used to cut out the stickiest snarls afterward and he would chain-smoke. The strange thing is, I sometimes miss the electricity and that tingling sensation in my legs and arms.

ANDY: I just want to cry when you talk about it.

VALERIE: There's really nothing to cry about. All fathers want to fuck their daughters. Most of them do. A minority refrain, for some unknown reason. I've been fucked by America. It's absolutely all right and absolutely all wrong. The world is one long yearning to go back.

ANDY: Being born is like being kidnapped and then being sold as a slave.

(*Silence.*)

VALERIE: What do you look like without the wig?

ANDY: I never take it off, ever.

VALERIE: Why is it silvery gray?

ANDY: I want to fend off aging and death.

VALERIE: And how well do you think you're succeeding?

ANDY (*laughs*): So-so.

(*Silence.*)

ANDY: I agree with you that sex is vile.

VALERIE: The intimacy factory. Fucked to death in every country in the world. Alienated and aliens.

(*Andy stops filming and lets the camera slowly drop to his knee. You reach for it and continue filming.*)

ANDY: I love all that in the manifesto about sex.

VALERIE: The whole manifesto is about sex.

ANDY: About the peter pier and the pussy pier.

VALERIE: I know. Sex is a hang-up. We don't have time to waste on pointless sex. We have to make art now, little Andy.

ANDY: You have to go through a lot of sex to get to anti-sex.

VALERIE: I see you've been reading your *SCUM*.

ANDY (*holds his hand motionless over the wig*): I daren't show myself without it anymore.

VALERIE: Take it off.

ANDY: I look awful.

VALERIE: It's okay. All men do.

ANDY (*laughs and takes off the wig*): My face looks like an ulcer without it. I look like an evil doll.

(*Silence.*)

VALERIE: Why are you crying?

ANDY: I don't know.

VALERIE: It's okay not to know. What are you thinking about?

ANDY: I'm thinking that I don't have any memories. I have nothing. I'm just a blank. The wig emphasizes the anonymity in my character.

VALERIE: I think you're quite cute without the wig.

ANDY: I don't want to be Andy Warhol.

(*Silence.*)

VALERIE: I've seen your other films.

ANDY: Do you like them?

VALERIE: No.

ANDY (*laughs*): Why don't you like them?

VALERIE: Because they suck. Because they're bad art. They're just screwing art and voyeur art and nothing art.

ANDY (*laughs and cries*): I don't like being Andy Warhol.

VALERIE: It's okay to make bad art. There's no price on your head for doing it.

The television room is hot and sticky and it is deadly to linger in there. In the ward, summer increasingly holds sway. The patients are permitted to sunbathe in the hospital grounds wearing only their underwear. On the television are further reports of the murder attempt on Andy Warhol. It has nothing to do with you. You have always been in the hospital and here you will stay, letting the trees bleed to death outside your window.

Everything is in a torpor and your sheets smell of doom and nether realms, but time still evidently goes by outside. The ban on going farther than the flagpole is suddenly lifted and you are allowed to roam freely around the hospital grounds. Dorothy flickers past on the television screen and the picture sends lightning flashes of pain through your brain. And Sister White is there with her sweet voice in her persuasive nurse's uniform, circling round you like one of Dorothy's bluebottles and changing the channel every time Andy Warhol appears on the screen.

A reporter has been snooping around in Ventor with a camera team, this much you gather. *Pets? Sexual assault? Blue-collar or white-collar? Issues around impulse control as a child?* Dorothy is ravishing in sunglasses and polka dot blouse. Her eyes cut to the camera and she uses difficult words that sound foreign in her mouth, as if dealing with a massive lump of foul-tasting chewing gum. The desert rises like a wild animal behind her face as she concentrates intently on the camera. Carried away by the attention or simply desperate? Probably carried away—the reporter is very good-looking—and it is a long time since you heard anything from Ventor.

VALERIE: Where's my doctor?
SISTER WHITE: Who is your doctor?
VALERIE: Dr. Ruth Cooper.
SISTER WHITE: She's not here just now. She could be on vacation, could be leave of absence.
VALERIE: Oh.
SISTER WHITE: Would you like to go out in the park for a while?
VALERIE: No thanks. I'm going to watch a show.
SISTER WHITE: Walking in the park is good for the mind.
VALERIE: Television shows are good for the mind. Do you have *Daddy Knows Best* here?
SISTER WHITE: Of course. Shall I help you tune to the right channel?
VALERIE: Tell Dr. Cooper I'm glad she's not here anymore.
SISTER WHITE: She's probably only on vacation. Don't take it personally.
VALERIE: I definitely won't do that. I'll ring Andy and tell him it wasn't personal. Sharks are never personal. They're never after personal revenge.

Dr. Ruth Cooper does not come back. The flowers behind her curtains are left to die; her coat hangs white and abandoned somewhere in the darkness; no longer does she sit at her window, closing her eyes, smoking cigarettes, and laughing at your jokes. The sun moves back and forth across the hospital grounds and she is there no more to show you the attic and the cellar and all the formaldehyde embryos, deformed and iridescent pink, and the stuffed birds. No more of her little questions, nor the cigarette lighter always at the ready in her coat pocket. Dr. Ruth Cooper's white coat disappears from Elmhurst, her jacket drowns in sunshine as she hurries across the hospital park, and, like all the rest, she forgets to say goodbye.

Dr. Ruth Cooper liked letting you hold forth about different subjects, letting you wander at random between the stuffed animals, letting you join in the diagnoses; it did not matter that she wanted to talk about Dorothy the whole time. Sunshine streamed through the formaldehyde and all you wanted to speak about was male destructiveness, the way embryo boys swallow their girl twins, *fetus in fetu*, about the experiments in Maryland's yellow laboratories. You found an old lectern and there you stood, giving a lecture in her white coat while she sat by the window making a note of everything you said. Without her glasses she looked like a little boy.

. . . I only want to speak to Dr. Ruth Cooper . . .

VALERIE: Will someone be so kind as to fetch Dr. Ruth Cooper?

PSYCHIATRIC CLINIC: Dr. Ruth Cooper is no longer here. Today you're talking to me.

VALERIE: I can help you with your diagnoses. Dr. Ruth and I collaborated. I wore her white coat when we worked on diagnoses. Dr. Ruth Cooper let me give lectures in the attic on all sorts of subjects.

PSYCHIATRIC CLINIC: Thank you, Miss Solanas. You just need to answer my questions. You've said that Dorothy was away for entire nights. Did she hit you? Were you an unloved child?

VALERIE: I'll help you. Diagnosis: Fucking angry. Pissed off. Man-hating tigress. Hustler. All married women are whores. Are you married? Meat is murder. Sex is prostitution. Prostitution is murder. A piece of dead meat. Where's Dr. Ruth Cooper?

PSYCHIATRIC CLINIC: Tell me about Dorothy.

VALERIE: I can tell you about my ass, if you like.

PSYCHIATRIC CLINIC: Despite your energetic attempts to appear a hard, tough, and cynical misanthropist, you are in fact a terrified, depressed child. That's my impression. A terrified little child. Dorothy didn't look after you. There was no home to speak of. I would describe your early life as wretched and miserable. No money, no love, no caring to speak of, sexual abuse, assault. You're just a child. Schizophrenic reaction of the paranoid type with deep depression and serious potential for destructive acts.

VALERIE: Et cetera et cetera. Okay. Thanks very much. Cut. It's very, very interesting, but we'll cut it there. That's it for today. Thank you and goodbye.

It is stormy in the hospital garden. Dr. Ruth Cooper hurries through the trees to collect her things after office hours. You sit by the large window in the dining room and look at her bright summer jacket flailing ominously between the trees. From a distance she looks like a huge bird in distress. Everything you wish for now is connected with death. Cosmogirl, for example.

CHELSEA HOTEL, FEBRUARY 1968

Maurice Girodias of Olympia Press moves in to the Chelsea Hotel and you agree to meet in the hotel bar downstairs. You spread your texts out over the bar and smoke cigarettes in a black holder while you wait for Maurice.

VALERIE: How's it going for this little dive?

BARTENDER: It's going well, I guess, thanks.

VALERIE: Things would improve if you stopped playing Muzak.

BARTENDER: It's not Muzak.

VALERIE: Bullshit. Switch the Muzak off.

BARTENDER: It's not Muzak.

VALERIE: Whatever you call it, turn it off.

BARTENDER: It's Sammy Davis.

VALERIE: Muzak.

BARTENDER: Sammy Davis is a great artist.

VALERIE: Never heard of him. Muzak.

BARTENDER: You can pick up your papers. This isn't a garbage dump.

VALERIE: It's my peripatetic office.

BARTENDER: Call it what you want. Take the office away.

VALERIE: I'm waiting for someone. An important meeting. An important contact. A publisher. I'm a writer. You can put that in the little notebook of yours. W-R-I-T-E-R.

BARTENDER: Pick your papers up.

VALERIE: It's an important meeting. I'm nervous. You ought to offer me a couple of long cocktails instead of standing here distracting me.

BARTENDER: We don't give away free drinks here.

VALERIE: Maurice Girodias. Publisher from France. He's advertised for new talent. I telephoned him immediately. You'll regret it if you don't give me a few drinks. SCUM will come after your ass.

BARTENDER: Remove your papers now, madam.

VALERIE (*prods him in the chest with the mouth of her cigarette holder*): If you remove the Muzak, sweetheart.

BARTENDER: Okay, madam. What would you like to drink? A cocktail on the house for guests who are kind and take their papers away.

VALERIE: Thanks. I'll have vodka with ice and lemon. And you can turn that Muzak down a bit.

Maurice is elegant and pinstriped and he kisses your cheeks with lips that are cool. He is full of politesse and pleasantries and smells strongly of cologne and deep pockets. It is quite obvious he is "your man."

MAURICE: I'm happy we could meet so soon.

VALERIE: Me too.

MAURICE: What would you like to drink?

VALERIE: Spirits.

MAURICE (*to the bartender*): A whisky for the lady.

VALERIE: All right. If you're having a whisky, I'll have a vodka with ice and lemon.

MAURICE (*laughs*): Okay. A vodka for Valerie Solanas and this lady has changed her mind and will have a glass of red wine instead. A Beaujolais nouveau.

VALERIE (*knocks back her vodka when it arrives and taps the empty glass on the bar*): Very French.

MAURICE: We'll have another straightaway . . . Tell me about yourself, Valerie.

VALERIE: Will I get a dollar if I tell you something really disgusting?

MAURICE: Of course.

VALERIE: Okay . . . M-E-N.

MAURICE: What did you say?

VALERIE: Give me a dollar.

MAURICE: Let's hear it then . . .

VALERIE: Thanks. Nice handkerchief, by the way. Is it for blowing your nose into?

MAURICE: It's not *that* sort of handkerchief. Tell me now, or there won't be any money.

VALERIE: I've already said it. You'll have to give me another dollar if you want to hear it again.

MAURICE (*takes a dollar bill out of his breast pocket*): Here you are.

VALERIE: M-E-N.

(*After a moment's thought, Maurice laughs.*)

MAURICE: Tell me about yourself.

VALERIE: Man hater. Writer. Scientist. Surfer.

MAURICE: Interesting. What have you written?

VALERIE: A play. *Up Your Ass.* A manifesto. SCUM. Society for Cutting Up Men. And other works in progress.

MAURICE: Interesting. What sort of play?

VALERIE: About Bongi. About a man-hating tigress who plays around with everything and everybody. A rescue mission for world literature and world drama.

MAURICE: And the manifesto?

VALERIE: Man haters' manifesto. The only book worth buying.

MAURICE: Interesting. Tell me, why do you write?

VALERIE: Men's flagrant inferiority. Nature's true order. We need an agenda for Eternity and Utopia.

MAURICE: And men?

VALERIE: Creeps and masochists. You ride the waves to your own demise.

MAURICE: I mean—may I read the things you've written?

VALERIE: You *shall* read them. Give me another of those brown cigarettes and a few dollars and you can read straight out of my ass if you like.

MAURICE: What did you say the play was called?

VALERIE: *Up Your Ass.*

Maurice, Bongi, and you dance to the wonderful disco music of the Chelsea bar. In the music you hear the sound of plane after plane taking off. Maurice has given you an advance of six hundred dollars to write a novel based on the manifesto.

MAURICE: Where do you live?
VALERIE: Nowhere.
MAURICE: Where do you come from?
VALERIE: The desert.

Sister White keeps you company in the corridor outside Dr. Cooper's consulting room, where the notice on the door will remain the same for the rest of the summer: BACK SOON. PLEASE BE SEATED WHILE YOU WAIT. Sister White appears to have the power to walk through walls and suddenly she is there beside you; she is unlike anyone else on the staff of the hospital, the only one who is not obsessed with Andy Warhol's medical condition and the only one dressed in white who is gentle as well.

Waves of freckles swarm across her arms; she listens without interrupting and she offers you mints and ice-cold water in small white paper cups.

For the time being it is not clear whether she is an angel or a nurse, but equally, for the time being, that does not matter. There is so much that is unclear right now. All you know is that the trees have huge wounds on their trunks, and if someone asks you where you come from, the answer is that you come from your mother's hands.

VALERIE: I. Will. Only. Talk. To. Dr. Ruth. Cooper.

SISTER WHITE: Dr. Ruth Cooper isn't here at the moment, but she's written a report about you that's going to be used at the trial. A very nice report. Would you like me to read it to you?

VALERIE: You can read whatever you want. While you're at it, please read something out of the hospital administration's policy for confiscation of personal belongings and the psychiatrists' action plan for hypothetical emergencies of an acute and—from the patient's point of view—incomprehensible nature.

SISTER WHITE: Dr. Ruth Cooper writes: "Valerie Solanas is fantastic. Valerie Solanas has a fabulous use of words. Valerie Solanas has a magnificent sense of humor, black as night and idiosyncratic. Valerie Solanas is obsessed with sex. Valerie Solanas is brilliantly intelligent. Valerie Solanas turns all conversation to her favorite topic, Men's Flagrant Inferiority."

(*Silence.*)

SISTER WHITE: You've made quite an impression on Dr. Ruth Cooper.

VALERIE: It's fantastic of Dr. Ruth Cooper to have produced this piece of paper. I myself have been working on my report about Dr. Ruth Cooper all summer. If you take out the shorthand book, Sister White, perhaps we can put this in the trial too.

SISTER WHITE: I'd like to hear your report.

VALERIE: Out with the notebook . . . keep up, Sister White . . . *Valerie is fantastic.* Dr. Ruth Cooper kills time in the tedium of the psychiatric clinic. *Valerie has a fabulous use of words.* Dr. Ruth Cooper makes notes in the medical record and believes that one day they will become a novel or a collection of poetry. Foundation course in psychiatry. All psychiatrists are failed psychopaths and mental patients. *Valerie has a magnificent sense of humor.* Dr. Ruth Cooper should have paid for a ticket. Besides, she has a serious tendency to mistake tears for laughter. Foundation course in psychiatry and linguistics. Laughing is a substitute for weeping in the same way that words are a substitute for screams. *Valerie is obsessed with sex.* Dr. Ruth Cooper is obsessed with Valerie. She is obsessed with the idea there are two separate biologically based genders that determine everything from the weather to childhood. She has so much to learn. A space rocket is ready for Dr. Ruth Cooper, destination next century. Foundation course in bedside manner. Most patients prefer to project themselves toward the future, rather than their dirty, piss-soaked past. *Valerie turns all conversation to her favorite topic, Men's Flagrant Inferiority.* Dr. Ruth Cooper uses her working hours to improve her skills at the patient's expense. The patient will eventually send a bill, but at the moment lacks a current address for Dr. Ruth Cooper. The hospital administration will not cooperate. And the trees outside her window bleed to death.

SISTER WHITE: I understand you miss having a doctor.

VALERIE: No. Incidentally, forget that last part, cross out the part about the trees. It's possible they've stopped bleeding by now, it's a while since I looked out. I don't need a doctor; I need a decent life.

SISTER WHITE: When you arrived at Elmhurst your face was white and you were having epileptic fits. You said: *Well, if they could put one man on the moon, why not all of them?* I laughed and let you smoke indoors. You were electric and epileptic. You returned continually to man's flagrant inferiority.

VALERIE: I lost my way in America. I never found the road home. It was all cold, blue sharks. I was a sick child. I longed for Louis. I longed for the electricity, the tingling sensation in my legs and arms. It was impossible to love me. I raced across the desert. It was bright and white and lonely and I took my things and left. Everything inside me screamed, my heart, Dorothy, the flickering light. The soup bowls and bottles from the night before were still on the table, wine stains, a filthy cloth, Dorothy's pink letters, the insects chasing each other across the plastic tablecloth. It smelled of rain and water and gasoline and old wine. There was sun. Ventor. Desert animals. Dorothy. A lizard was standing in Moran's old whisky glass, looking at me. It was windy that day. I put the lizard inside my jumper and ran.

SISTER WHITE: I think you should sleep for a while.

VALERIE: I laughed and flew straight into the light. I'm a suicidal goddamn whore. Is this story almost over? Is Dr. Ruth Cooper coming back soon? Cosmogirl? Dorothy? Andy Warhol, is he still in the hospital, playing dead?

SISTER WHITE: It's nighttime, Valerie. You're tired. I'll hold your hand while you fall asleep.

VALERIE: I don't intend to sleep. Remember, I'm the only sane woman here.

BRISTOL HOTEL, APRIL 21, 1988

VALERIE: I think I've wet myself again.

NARRATOR: Then it's lucky I'm here.

VALERIE: Will you hold my hand when I go?

NARRATOR: I'll hold your hand.

(*Silence.*)

NARRATOR: What are you thinking about?

VALERIE: Blood oaks. Sugar maples. I dream about enormous American trees. I dream I'm under the huge blood oaks doing some target practice with Cosmogirl. I dream about her laugh.

NARRATOR: Look at the one you love. Smell her. Talk to her. Soon she'll be gone.

VALERIE: I don't want there to be any story.

NARRATOR: I'll hold your hand. There is a story.

VALERIE: What does it mean when I say there isn't a story?

NARRATOR: I don't know.

VALERIE: It means there is a story.

The Philadelphia train is cold and miserable and outside there are only lifeless fields, lifeless slip roads, lifeless birds' nests in the bare trees, and the sky has never been as vast as this. You do not weep, because you are afraid of weeping, and because you are afraid of someone seeing you weep, and because you are concentrating on the countryside and the sky outside and the walls of water that will crash over the train and drown you.

The train to Washington is even colder, the sky vaster, the light harsher, and if only there were some shade around you; and you have to masturbate in one of the toilets to stop yourself vanishing into the light. Cosmogirl walking through Manhattan with her fair hair, orgasm. Moving across the ocean, desert, and cities, orgasm. Her brain still functioning, orgasm, still with her place at the university, orgasm, still working on your agenda for Eternity and Utopia, orgasm—

The glacial skies outside the bathroom window are all the occasions you were going to fetch her from Maryland, *after, later, in a while, in the future*; the miles of farmland are all the times you were going to buy train tickets and never did, the rhythm of the train the phone calls you did not make, the other passengers the letters you did not write. New York is oblivion and America is your habit of always forgetting to say goodbye. If you forgave her, why did you not go to see her? When they have taken what they want, they never want it again. What is the point of forgiveness, if death treads on its heels?

At the university, Robert Brush has destroyed his desk and all the pretty formaldehyde jars. A havoc of water-stained papers and overturned bookcases and Robert Brush with the window open and his shirt undone. When Elizabeth went, Cosmo wrecked people's backyards, overturned garden gnomes and birdbaths and drove stolen cars across their suburban lives. Perhaps it is she, and not Robert, who has made sure the floor is covered with human embryos and Siamese calf twins.

VALERIE: Your goddamn cock.

PROFESSOR ROBERT BRUSH: Hello, Valerie. I'm so sorry.

VALERIE: You have to give me the money. It's my money. It was her money.

PROFESSOR ROBERT BRUSH: What can I do for you?

VALERIE: She's dead. She doesn't need money anymore.

PROFESSOR ROBERT BRUSH: I'm as sad as you are.

VALERIE: I need money. She doesn't need money. Not now, at any rate.

PROFESSOR ROBERT BRUSH: I didn't realize she was so unhappy. I could see she was unhappy, but not to what extent.

VALERIE: I don't know why I should listen to you. You're the supervisor of a gang of incarcerated mice. Cosmogirl has gone. I've nothing left. I don't care about science any longer. Give me Cosmo back. If you can't give her back, give me the money.

262 SARA STRIDSBERG

PROFESSOR ROBERT BRUSH: What happened?

VALERIE: She's dead now. She's not always going to be dead. She's going to carry on doing research.

PROFESSOR ROBERT BRUSH: Sit down, Valerie. Would you like something to drink?

VALERIE: There's something wrong. Her name is light as a feather. I noticed it as soon as I realized the word Cosmo doesn't work with the word dead. The weight of the words is completely different. They don't go together. It's wrong. It's a conspiracy. She'll come back. Cosmo always comes back.

PROFESSOR ROBERT BRUSH: Will you tell me what happened?

VALERIE: Only that every night she begs me to go down to the beach and hang myself in a tree. Only that I can't bear to see your crocodile tears.

Valerie.

I've changed my mind.

I want to come back.

There are no happy endings.

Elizabeth died alone in San Quentin.

She didn't recognize me in the end.

I asked you to stay.

The last thing I said to you was, don't leave me here.

The grass doubles over toward the ground, as if waiting for a storm. Cosmo has disappeared into the underworld. Her eyes are an eclipse of the sun, a black sheet pulled down over the blue. You walk away from the university buildings, the psychology department, Shiver Laboratory, the university grounds, and College Park. Robert Brush shouts after you through his open window; he wants you to stay, give him your blessing, free him from possible IOU demands from the underworld. You have your own IOUs, long and dark and impossible to honor right now.

Hordes of students cross the park, a girl who looks like Cosmo touches your arm as you pass. Over there are the trees where she kissed you the first time. There, her last call to New York. At the bottom of your coat pocket, the telephone message you forgot. There, the days she no longer called and you no longer noticed. And there, Cosmo alone in the laboratory at night, and the first snow falling outside the window (the last snow), where she talks to herself and the blackboard.

Shiver Laboratory is bathed in flickering, painful spotlights. The corridors are shiny and look as though they are underwater and the night watchman waves to you on his way home. The storm inside your head builds up, the amphetamine surges through your body, nothing will bring you down this time. You open the animals' cages and open the doors to the darkness. You leave the keys on the steps outside, kiss the front door with your lipstick, press your head against the façade until it bleeds. The lab animals vanish into the night.

Time and trees collapse in the park. The sun burns shamelessly through the foliage and the flowers in the lounge die. You continue playing the patient and Sister White continues playing whatever role she has. You sit for days and observe how the patients act as patients and the staff act as staff; it is a very entertaining pastime and at present it is difficult to distinguish the hospital from a funfair. But in the parking lot on the other side of the fence the yellow Ford is there again, staring at you with its evil headlights. The presence of the Ford means this is not a funfair.

After the Stonewall riots Allen Ginsberg says: "The guys there were so beautiful—they've lost the wounded look fags all had ten years ago." You are still waiting for the trial and Dr. Ruth Cooper and all your confiscated belongings.

VALERIE: How do people know whether they have to play the part of staff or patients?
SISTER WHITE: They just know.

VALERIE: Is it the hospital director who does the casting?

SISTER WHITE: You could say that.

VALERIE: With all respect, Sister White, what part do you play?

SISTER WHITE: Nurse, bordering on an angel.

VALERIE: Nurse and angel, bordering on my mother. Bordering on a dark embrace, or a sleep.

SISTER WHITE: That was nicely put.

VALERIE: Why is that car there all the time?

SISTER WHITE: The parking lot is full of cars. Which car do you mean?

VALERIE: The one that's been standing there for a week. The Ford. The yellow one.

SISTER WHITE: There are different cars every day. Some of them are the staff's cars. Others belong to visitors. There are different cars every day.

VALERIE: No one ever has any visitors here. This is not a place sensible people visit of their own accord.

SISTER WHITE: Are you hoping someone will visit you?

VALERIE: The answer is no.

SISTER WHITE: I can call Dorothy.

VALERIE: The answer is: definitely not.

COSMOGIRL MY LOVE

The sun rises and sets between the skyscrapers. Demonstrations in Harlem continue. In Hiroshima the soot-blackened shadows of burning people will remain forever on the walls. At night she wandered around in the laboratory, talking to the animals and the night watchmen. When they took her keys from her she broke an office window and let the magpies build a nest inside the lab. A keen March wind and Cosmo lectures to herself and to the auditorium, all lit up. Only a few mouse girls sit and listen in the rows at the front.

She walks back and forth writing her formulae on the blackboard, laughing and smoking, twirling her pointer, chanting, chiding: *no Y genes only X genes, no walking abortions—the X gene's obvious potential to fuse with an X gene a scientifically well-hidden well-kept secret—send chimps into space, send humans into space, manufacture nuclear weapons, teach mice to eat with a knife and fork—conspiracy, red herrings, evasive action—X gene and X gene humanity's salvation—biologically, morally, artistically.*

Magpies and pigeons enter through the broken window and kill the mice in the cages. Once again the laboratory director is airbrushed out of the family photograph on his desk. When the night watchman arrives on Sunday evening, Cosmo is lying sprawled on the workbench. All the mice have been given potassium chloride. Cosmo has given herself potassium chloride. No hearts beat in the laboratory now. Notes and dead mice are scattered everywhere and the walls are filled with lipstick slogans, lipstick kisses, and lipstick dreams. About the superiority of mouse girls, the latent violence in mouse boys, the possibility of producing only mouse girls, the future, a women's movement, and a world with only whores and mouse girls. About Elizabeth. About Valerie. About love.

I don't want to talk to any more doctors, I only want to talk to Dr. Ruth Cooper...

I don't want to talk to Dr. Fuck any longer...

I want to have my own clothes back...

SISTER WHITE: You're my prettiest patient.

VALERIE: Drs. Such-and-such and So-and-so. Dr. Shitbag. Dr. Lie. Dr. Hate. Dr. Hate-all-women-in-the-universe. Dr. Nothing. Dr. Pain. Dr. Fuck. Dr. Blame-everything-on-your-mama.

SISTER WHITE: The park is full of happy patients. Everything's going to be fine. You'll see, it'll pass. You must stop telephoning Andy Warhol. There are better things to do. You must focus on getting well and start talking about your mother.

VALERIE: Elizabeth Duncan is murdered in San Quentin. Four months later Cosmogirl dies. There is no childhood. There are no children. The state of California takes Cosmogirl's life, definitely not her mother. America has assailed all my rights, it was definitely not my mother's doing. I'm thinking of covering every public wall in New York with medical records. I don't want to talk to Dr. Fuck and Dr. Blame-everything-on-your-mama.

SISTER WHITE: No one is so great that it wouldn't be shameful, even for her, to be subject to the laws that determine normal as well as pathological processes with equal rigor.

VALERIE: I'm going to take over all radio and television stations. It's not possible to buy the universe. It is possible to customize park benches so no one can sit on them. I'm a ghost from the sixties. There's no public culture. There's pop art, fake artists, high and low and upside down. Fine art. Foul art. Nothing art. Man's art. Degenerate art. Degenerate structures. Art politicized. My hands smell of war. There was nothing I could do. There was only me. Or rather, I mean—there wasn't even me. There's no organization called SCUM. There was nothing. Maybe that's enough.

SISTER WHITE: The trial is getting closer. You mustn't be afraid, my dear. Andy Warhol has decided not to appear in court.

VALERIE: I blame myself entirely. I regard this institution as a pathological condition. I submit to an illness. The hospital illness. We can call it hospital-acquired infection, if that's easier.

SISTER WHITE: There are so many ways out of here.

VALERIE: I have nothing to get out of. This is my life. I don't want to escape my life. I am Valerie Solanas.

SISTER WHITE: Only those who can accept all their sides can be happy. Evil exists everywhere and in us all. It's about the ability or inability, as the case may be, to accommodate pain. A thin line separates us, just like thin skin between people. There is no point in denying one's dark sides.

VALERIE: My darkest sides are my most beautiful.

SISTER WHITE: I wish I could help you.

VALERIE: I'll make an artwork out of blood and sperm. They'll love it. The flimflam artists. The plagiarists. The happy, happy whore.

SISTER WHITE: The clinic can help you leave all that behind. Drugs. Delusions. Prostitution. Destructiveness.

VALERIE: Sex is a very solitary experience, not at all creative. The historical absence of men in prostitution. *Pacta sunt servanda*. La dolce vita. This is how it is. Do what you will with my mangy goddamn cunt.

SISTER WHITE: The park is full of happy patients. It may not help you at all to wear your civilian clothes. Patient clothes create a sense of community, a collective feeling, of being in a group.

VALERIE: Collective guilt. Group guilt. Buyers and sellers. Woman's body and soul. In the so-called contract there are no equal parties. They differ on all points. Her social position: none. Age: often young. Housing: none. Education: usually none. Background: none. Social network: none. Drug addiction: always.

SISTER WHITE: Of not being alone in the desert.

VALERIE: I take the entire blame. One single telephone call. One single kiss I forgot to send from New York.

SISTER WHITE: When you were given the chance to go home, you demanded that all the other mental patients should be allowed to go too. When you didn't get what you wanted, you chose to stay here with them, but you demanded your own clothes. You arranged an orchestra in the park, danced with the girls one at a time all night, finagled permission for all the patients to have cotton candy and beer.

VALERIE: Twenty dollars. The whole repertoire. The price list. No censorship for tiny God-fearing marzipan ears. Ten for a fuck. Five for a blow job. Two for a hand job. I don't sell my soul. My pussy isn't my soul. Pussy soul. Cock soul. I'm an adult, I know what I'm doing. Thirty-two years in exile. All illness can be treated. It's possible to live forever. If someone is missing, someone else is taken out in her place. There's no point in trying to escape your destiny.

THE FACTORY, LATER IN MARCH 1968

You sit on that wooden chair again, straightening your clothes and working on your makeup. The spotlight is directed at your face, so you cannot see, but Andy's assistants move around in the light. Andy is late and no one answers when you shout. A makeup girl arrives and powders your face, someone else passes with a glass of wine; their TV powder always makes you sneeze. When the girl has finished her work, you pick up a handkerchief and wipe off her makeup. The makeup girl starts again.

VALERIE: Andy fucking loser. Am I here to get made up or to make this film?
(*Silence.*)
VALERIE: Hello.
(*Silence.*)
(*Morrissey emerges from the light.*)
MORRISSEY: Sorry, Valerie. We're shooting over here. Would you like to hear some music while you're waiting?
VALERIE: Sure. Whatever. Please. Go for it. Don't feel awkward.

MORRISSEY (*puts on a cassette player*): It's the Velvet Underground.

VALERIE: Aha.

MORRISSEY: Do you know them?

VALERIE: No.

MORRISSEY: They're the sixties' greatest—

VALERIE: —Thanks for the information. It all sounds incredibly interesting, but I'm a bit busy over here with my makeup. What's Andy doing? Has he got his hand stuck in his pants?

MORRISSEY: Andy's preparing to film.

VALERIE: I can imagine.

MORRISSEY: I don't know why you think Andy's interested in you. You're not the first freak to gain admittance here.

VALERIE: No, I can see that.

MORRISSEY: Here's a tip—show a little respect. For Andy. For his art. For the Factory. For all of us, for example. Great art is being produced here.

VALERIE: Yes, so you say. Great art, I'll remember that. I only have to bow and scrape and tip my cap. It's fantastic . . . (*bows and scrapes into the spotlight*) . . . for "Great Art." Wherever it chooses to be today . . . (*looks around*) . . . Yeah. No matter where it is, I'll bow and scrape. Do you have a sandwich and something to drink?

MORRISSEY: I don't want to be hard on you, but you won't last long in the Factory.

VALERIE: We'll see. Maybe Andy's tired of brainless cocksuckers and illiterates.

MORRISSEY: You're no woman, Valerie. You're a disease.

(*Andy appears out of the light.*)

MORRISSEY: I was just saying Valerie looks fantastic today.

VALERIE: Like a disease. That's the nicest thing I've heard in a long time.

ANDY: Thanks, Morrissey. We don't need you any longer.

VALERIE: Thanks, Morrissey. We'll be delighted to be spared the sight of you.

MORRISSEY: Let me know if you need me, Andy.

Andy sets up his camera. Morrissey makes vomiting actions in your direction. You give him your prettiest smile and wave to him while Andy starts his whirring little film camera again.

VALERIE: He's really nice. That Morrissey. Your associate.

ANDY: He's okay. I want you to carry on talking about yourself, Valerie. Or, I reckon we'll start with the manifesto. Would you like to read some of the text?

VALERIE: I've thought of something, Andy.

(*Silence.*)

VALERIE: Andy?

ANDY: Carry on talking, Valerie. I'm listening.

VALERIE: I need a leader for SCUM's Men's Auxiliary. You'd be perfect, Andy. Your contacts with newspapers and television. You could be the cover boy on *Vogue* and talk about your work in the auxiliary. You love attention, you love being on television painting your nails.

ANDY (*laughs*): I'm not that political.

VALERIE: You *are* political, you just don't know it. Besides, the auxiliary—and this applies to the auxiliary's leader as well— has a full and clear agenda to follow. An agenda that's exhaustive and explicit and can be implemented with no further interpretation. We're talking about putting it into effect, Andy. The job requires neither talent nor political conviction. It requires energy and the ability to obey orders, not brains.

ANDY: I'm flattered, Valerie.

VALERIE: And what do you say? I haven't decided yet. There are other candidates, but your chances look good, Andy.

ANDY: Tell me about the auxiliary, Valerie. Is it open to all men?

VALERIE: No, definitely not. A select few.

ANDY: Look into the camera when you speak.

VALERIE: Here are a few examples of the men in SCUM's Men's Auxiliary. Men who kill men. Biological scientists who are working on constructive programs, as opposed to biological warfare. Journalists, writers, editors, publishers, and producers who disseminate and promote ideas that will lead to the achievement of SCUM's goals. Faggots—this is where you come in, dear Andy—who, by their glittering, glowing example, encourage other men to de-man themselves and thereby make themselves relatively inoffensive. Men who consistently give things away—money, things, services. Men who tell it like it is. So far no one ever has.

ANDY (*laughs*): It sounds fantastic.

VALERIE: It *is* fantastic. Nice, clean-living women will be invited to the sessions to help clarify any doubts and misunderstandings they may have about the male sex. Some other examples of the men in SCUM's Men's Auxiliary are makers and promoters of sex books and movies, et cetera, who are hastening the day when all that will be shown on the screen will be Suck and Fuck. Males, like the rats following the Pied Piper, will be lured by Pussy to their doom. They will be overcome and submerged and will eventually drown in the passive flesh that they are . . . And that's also where you come in, Andy, with your voyeuristic sex films—

ANDY: —Wait, Valerie, I just need to change the film . . . (*shouts into the light*) . . . Morrissey! We need more film. Valerie's talking about the auxiliary.

VALERIE: Being in the Men's Auxiliary is an essential condition for getting onto SCUM's exemption list, but isn't sufficient. It's not enough to do good; in order to save their worthless asses men must also avoid evil—

ANDY: —Stop, Valerie. We need more film.

(*Viva Ronaldo and Morrissey appear.*)

VALERIE: Do you have anything to drink, Morris? And maybe a sandwich. Just a small chicken sandwich and something to drink, anything at all.

ANDY: Viva. We need sandwiches and drinks.

VALERIE: Right, Viva. Sandwiches and drinks. Quickly.

(*Viva Ronaldo hurries away. Morrissey fumbles with the film.*)

MORRISSEY: It'll just take a second.

VALERIE: Do you need help, Morris?

MORRISSEY: It'll work now.

ANDY: Thanks . . . (*to you*) . . . We were on something to do with the auxiliary. Just carry on talking and a drink and sandwich will arrive.

VALERIE: You're fortunate to get a place in the auxiliary. Possibly as leader, if you're lucky. We'll have to see how it turns out, your chances look good . . . Some examples of the most obnoxious or harmful male types are: rapists, politicians, and all who are in their service. Campaigners and members of political parties. Lousy singers and musicians. Chairmen of boards. Breadwinners. Landlords. Owners of greasy spoons and restaurants that play Muzak. "Great Artists." Cheap pikers and welshers. Cops. Tycoons. Scientists working on death and destruction programs or for private industry. Practically all scientists. Liars and phonies. Disc jockeys. Men who intrude in the slightest way on any female they don't know. Real-estate men. Stockbrokers. Men who speak when they have nothing to say. Men who stand around idly on the street and mar the landscape with their presence. Double-dealers. Flimflam artists. Litterbugs. Plagiarizers. Men who harm any female in the least bit. All men in the advertising industry. Psychiatrists and clinical psychologists. Dishonest writers. Journalists. Editors. Publishers. Censors in both public and private spheres. All members of the armed forces, including the brains behind them.

ANDY: And women?

VALERIE: All women have a lousy streak in them, to a greater or lesser degree, but it stems from a lifetime of living among men. Eliminate men and women will shape up. Women are improvable; men are not, although their behavior is. When SCUM comes after their asses, they'll shape up fast.

ANDY: And rape?

VALERIE: I think we should take a break now. I'm hungry and your assistants don't seem to be very good at making sandwiches.

ANDY: Just say something about rape.

VALERIE: I hate rape. Rape is a totally male quality.

ANDY: And the imperative to kill, should we interpret that as serious or ironic?

VALERIE: Gorily serious. A woman knows instinctively that the only wrong is to hurt others and that the meaning of life is love . . . A hundred thousand murdered women and utopias float ashore. Now we'll take a break and have some chicken sandwiches and booze. We have a lot to celebrate. Your potential appointment, for example, and future position as leader of the auxiliary, maybe. Think about that while you go and fetch the champagne.

ANDY: Just one more question—

VALERIE: —A woman knows instinctively the only wrong is to hurt others and that the meaning of life is love.

MOVIE STAR 1968

And then you are the film star Valerie Solanas in *I, a Man*, in which you have made up all your own lines. Andy is very pleased with the result, you are exceptionally pleased with the result, and Maurice Girodias comes to the Factory to watch the film. You sit in the cool, dark room with the fans and the striking black-and-white sequences, the soporific sound from the film projector, Maurice's discreet cigarette glow, and it is very easy to learn to love the smell of new filmstrips.

Andy never sits still during the screenings; the wig moves round the room and his associates shift respectfully like a nervous cloud around him. But you are the star now. Andy is impressed by your improvised lines, how easily you improvised in front of the camera. *Andy, do you want to hear the line again? Gladly, Valerie. My instincts tell me to dig chicks—why should my standards be lower than yours? You're a genius, Valerie. I know, Wiggy. Have you read my play yet? Not yet, Valerie. Soon, Valerie.*

When you leave the room in search of champagne and sand-wiches, they talk about you, and you stand behind a skin-colored curtain and eavesdrop. Everything is going your way now. New York, the Factory, and Maurice Girodias are the an-swer to all your problems. The weather is fine, prospects are good, and soon you will have time to write that novel Olympia Press has given you money for. And *Tropic of Cancer* and *Lolita* and all the other shit books they publish will disappear from history without a trace.

ANDY: How's it going with Olympia?

MAURICE: Olympia's very successful at the moment. We're ex-panding. We're about to publish Henry Miller. Where did Valerie get to?

ANDY: She's out there somewhere.

MAURICE: Shall we wait for her?

ANDY: She's looking for something to eat. She's always hungry. Are you switching it on now, Viva?

MAURICE: Have you read her play?

ANDY: Not yet.

MAURICE: Her use of words is fabulous.

ANDY: Who knows, we might decide to produce it.

THE PARASITES

A. Black sun, black snow, black despair. Literary parasites, post-modern parasites. Take everything from me. Do it. That is what I want.

B. A handbag full of dollar bills. A woman in a leopard-skin dress, dark men in dark plastic suits, dark snowscapes. They really want to have you. Talk dirty, talk sweet. Money is all worth the same and has no value.

C. The sky was made of nothing that night. The stars were made of greaseproof paper. The porch seat creaked and squeaked. It was a straight story, a straight world. It was a heterosexual neurosis, there is no other way to describe it. You have to learn when you ought to leave. You have to learn to say no.

D. There were only authentic American boys. Toy presidents. Roosevelt. Truman. Eisenhower. John F., Lyndon B., Nixon. Ford. Carter. Everything is made up. Miss World. Miss Universe.

E. The American whore and the American women's movement. Reagan's spokeswoman, Faith Whittlesey, confused different types of material in her accounts of various contemporary phenomena. She described the twentieth century as one collective longing for hand-knitted underwear. There was Black Monday. The causes were sought in Wall Street and an old Hollywood film from 1947. Ronald Reagan drifted slowly into a garden of oblivion.

F. A white fake fur, white tights, always a dress slightly too short. She had her dead flowers and the sunny veranda. She had her constant hopes and defeats. All married women are prostitutes. Hey, wait, mister!

G. Because the child wished for a film projector, the mother was convinced she had produced a little artist. She knocked on doors in the neighborhood with assorted flower arrangements in jam jars wrapped in pretty paper, she read comic books to him in her incomprehensible English, and every time he finished a page of his coloring book she rewarded him with a sweet. This created a lifelong passion for painting and chocolate and for himself. He regarded his surroundings as giant coloring books and all other people as clones of his mother.

H. The whole sky was purple that night. Violet. There was a taste of plastic. I held my hands in front of my face. I am the only one here without a soul. It was a high-class concentration camp. God was not there. No one was there.

I. Metaphor. The rhetoric of sexual politics. Serious error. NOW had its roots in the American middle class and in the dreadfully boring decade that is referred to as the fifties.

J. An unfortunate metaphor. How would you like to describe that bird?

K. Metaphysical cannibalism. Predator of nature. Black birds hurtling down. A temporary deformation of the body for the sake of art. The parasitic fetus. Pathological condition. Mass neurosis. Happy housewife. Happy whore. A beautiful child.

L. August 26, 1970. Thousands of women march along Fifth Avenue. They are burning their underwear, kissing one another, and holding hands. What is on the agenda? Is there actually anything on the agenda?

M. Lunch meeting in the White House. Carter. Reagan. Friedan. The nation's military and economic plunder. Rape. Vampires. Dracula. Andy Warhol sucking blood out of people. The personal is very individual. Makeup. Beauty salon. A revolutionary in every bedroom. An Andy Warhol in every thought.

N. Mass prostitution. Mass murder. To meet is murder. Hey. Wait. Mister.

O. They take what they want. They never want it again. Hey, wait, mister.

P. Patriarchal projections. The world's oldest and finest profession. I am the only one here without a soul.

Q. Screen prints, projection screens, torture. An out-and-out man hater. An endangered species. I could have told you from the start how it would end.

R. I do not want to submit to your laws. I do not want to carry all these paper bags around. I always walk too quickly between the counters in department stores. I always steal. My mother tries to maintain normal behavior and blend in with the surroundings. Hey, wait, mister!

S. Experiences were not documented, they were eliminated, eradicated. Her signature was removed, her ideas devoured by an art factory. Loss of name. Of memory. Loss of everything. Andy's collected works: Pain. Albino. Dracula. Prosthetics. Human experiments. Machinations. Massacre.

T. What does it matter? I have doll eyes, doll mouth, doll legs, doll heart. They really want me.

U. All civilization is based on sublimation. All civilization is based on money. All civilization is based on heterosexual neuroses. c/o The Factory, New York, 1968.

V. Pornography. Prostitution. Presidents.

W. All civilization is based on repetition. All civilization is based on money, masculinity, weapons. All civilization is based on previous civilizations' mistakes. Make no mistake, make women. Make no mistake, make lesbians. Military intervention. Vietnam. Distraction.

X. Money, shopping, surface. He worshipped America and its presidents. He celebrated his birthday on Hiroshima day. Be a SOMEBODY with a BODY. Hiroshima. My love.

Y. You wanted to merge with the skyscrapers. Reach for the sky. Spread out. Not lose yourself in the night. You longed for your high-heeled sisters.

Z. Explosivity and fear are the same thing. A morbid fear of running out of ideas or a morbid fear of strange people's strange thoughts. He could not abide his earlier work. He was convinced he could outsmart death by wearing a silver-gray wig prematurely. He continued to be dependent on fictitious prosthetics. The accessories gave him a strange appearance.

LOVE VALERIE

You loved Central Park. In those days, you cycled between the trees beyond the pédestrian paths. Cosmo and you rode your bicycles into the lake and left them there. All that was long ago; now there is only the monotone melancholy of the crows' cries as they swoop down at your head while you try to walk slowly along with your shopping cart. You run across the park so fast your bottles nearly break. Thousands of cawing crows raid your possessions and your cap. When you emerge onto the street they sit in a row on the telephone lines and laugh at you. Even the crows laugh at you.

Caw-Haw-Caw-Haw

Caw-Haw-Caw-Haw

Caw-Haw-Caw-Haw

At the police station outside Central Park, there are cops everywhere and a penetrating high-voltage light. Interrogation methods, hidden microphones, false smiles and knowing looks under the table. Gripping the hem of your jacket tightly, you drum the manifesto on the interview desk.

Everything is going to shit. You cannot write with Cosmo calling all the time from the underworld, nagging you whenever you lose concentration. Andy is always busy and Maurice refers in an increasingly unlovely way to your so-called contract. You have the chance to appear on the Johnny Carson television show, but even that is a fiasco, it is obvious you have been invited so they can ridicule you. All you wanted was to send some pretty pictures home to Dorothy's television set.

And Andy never has time to read your play, even though you stand outside the Factory waiting every day, and the promise of taking part in more films imperceptibly fizzles out.

VALERIE: I want to report a crime.
THE STATE: What crime?
VALERIE: There are crows in the park. I was hunted down. Almost killed.
THE STATE: What do you want to report, miss?
VALERIE: There were no people there. A crow. It sat in the middle of the footpath and stared. Black. It refused to move when I tried to get past. Then the whole flock came. They dive-bombed my face. They were laughing at me.
THE STATE: That's no crime. We can't prosecute birds. What's your name?
VALERIE: Valerie Solanas. I flew straight into the light. I'm here to report a crime.

THE STATE: Are you on drugs?

VALERIE: You bet I am. Without amphetamines, it's like a mini–world war in here.

THE STATE: Where do you live?

VALERIE: In the docks for the time being. On roofs during summer.

(*Silence.*)

(*The State makes notes.*)

VALERIE: What are you writing in that notebook?

THE STATE: I'm recording that you were here. You're not suspected of any crime.

VALERIE: And what are you writing? A little novel about Dostoevsky?

THE STATE: I'm reporting.

VALERIE: Write that I'm an author. You can write that. Author. A-U-T-H-O-R. I'm writing a novel for Olympia Press. You can record that.

THE STATE: I'm recording that you were here, that you're on drugs, and that you have nowhere to live.

VALERIE: Write that I was here and reported my ass.

THE STATE: Hustling isn't allowed here.

VALERIE: I'm not hustling. I'm selling the manifesto. Do you want to buy one, mister? A dollar.

THE STATE: You're known to us. You've tried your shenanigans in here before.

VALERIE: For half a dollar I'll tell you something really disgusting.

THE STATE: Clear out before we arrest you.

VALERIE: Okay . . . Men . . . You owe me half a dollar, just so you know. You can buy two hundred copies of the manifesto. But no credit, no discount. Minimum order of two hundred copies. I don't like arithmetic.

THE STATE: It is you posting flyers everywhere? There are penalties for that.

VALERIE: In Washington I put up scientific texts and lab reports. Then I patrolled round to make sure no one took them down. It's been a long time since I stuck up any notes or reports.

THE STATE: That's good, madam.

VALERIE: That's good, mister. I'll come and collect my dimes tomorrow. By the way, I'm not a bag lady. I just find it unworthy to save my own ass when my people are being destroyed. When pussy souls are being sent to the slaughter. Otherwise another pussy soul will have to do the work. I might as well do it.

CHELSEA HOTEL, MAY 1968

You are in overdrive again, the colors in the lobby are unusually bright, and it seems as though everything is grotesquely large and coming at you very fast. The check-in desk is a pounding, florid heart advancing dangerously close to you, and the Little Desk Clerk is no longer there. You move along, hugging the walls, when suddenly something in your chest shatters, a crystal of silver and frost, making it easier to think, and quicker. Maurice is nowhere to be found; the office in Gramercy Park has been closed for several days.

HOTEL PORTER: Are you okay, miss?
VALERIE: I'm very much okay. Thanks for asking, but where the hell is Maurice Girodias? Has he checked out of New York?
HOTEL PORTER: Mr. Girodias is working in his room.
VALERIE: Which room?
HOTEL PORTER: We can't say.
VALERIE: Has he changed rooms?
HOTEL PORTER: Yes, miss. He thought it was too dark in the last one.

VALERIE: Why hasn't he said something?

HOTEL PORTER: I don't know, miss.

VALERIE: I don't know here and I don't know there. Miss hither and thither. My name is Valerie Solanas. Would you be so kind as to tell me what you do know, instead of overloading me with everything you don't.

HOTEL PORTER: You can't run up and down the stairs anymore.

VALERIE: I have to speak to Mr. Girodias.

HOTEL PORTER: You have to go home and sleep. You're confused, miss.

VALERIE: I have no home. I've never been clearer.

Cosmogirl would never have frequented a women's café by choice, but Cosmo is no longer here, so new rules apply. The dogs in Dolores Park play under the trees and on the hill down to the Women's Building you change your mind. The sun is blinding, but Daddy's Favorite Girl, Gloria, has already seen you and there is no way you can turn back. And in your silver coat you are too early, only a few girls on their own have arrived, the coffee makers and one or two others. The boss (*we have no hierarchies here, no leaders*) gives out jobs and makes you draw the female symbol on some moronic leaflets.

The girls touch each other's hair the whole time, braiding and stroking. But the silver coat does not fit in here, nor the dress, nor the boots that gape and smell of sweaty feet. You do not fit in at all.

The plan is that you will sit in a circle and hold hands, but your hand is perspiring and cold and you have to let go all the time to light more cigarettes. The female symbol made of plush indicates who can speak, but you have no idea what to say when it is your turn, you have absolutely nothing to say next to these four-eyed goody two-shoes. *How nice of you to come, Valerie, we would be so pleased if you came back, would love to know what your opinion is, what you think, please tell us about your manifesto.*

VALERIE: I want to emphasize that I'm speaking about all men. They'll screw any snaggletoothed hag as soon as they get the chance and, furthermore, pay for it. They're obsessed with screwing, they'll swim through a river of snot and wade nostril-deep through a mile of vomit if they think there'll be a friendly pussy waiting for them.

DADDY'S FAVORITE GIRL GLORIA: A person's biology is not her destiny. There are men who are better feminists than women are. And it frightens me, all this business with girdles, corsets, and heels that are way too high to run in. I think you should consider that, Valerie. We're not judging you. I just think you should consider it.

VALERIE: Cosmo and I are America's first intellectual whores. And if I don't do it, someone else will.

DADDY'S FAVORITE GIRL GLORIA: If you had a little boy then, Valerie, would you hate him?

VALERIE: I'd never have a little boy.

DADDY'S FAVORITE GIRL GLORIA: But if you did.

VALERIE: It would never happen.

DADDY'S FAVORITE GIRL GLORIA: Use your imagination.

VALERIE: I would love him like a daughter. I would raise him as a woman, dress him in frocks and in the evenings dance with him in the kitchen. Let him have lipstick outside his lips if he wanted. If not. No lipstick. I would love him.

DADDY'S FAVORITE GIRL GLORIA: His biology is therefore not his destiny.

VALERIE: Man is a machine. A walking dildo. An emotional parasite. A biological accident. Maleness is a deficiency disease. Man's biology is his destiny. I love black dresses. I regard it as a political act to wear lipstick outside my lips.

DADDY'S FAVORITE GIRL GLORIA: That's ridiculous, Valerie. It'll lead nowhere. Without men, we'll have no women's movement. And to dress in the way you do leads nowhere at all. It can give men the impression that you're—

VALERIE (*stands hastily*): Okay. Thanks very much for nothing. All that about the women's movement et cetera et cetera should be great. Good luck with your project for the future. It'll certainly be very nice on your mixed demonstrations. I don't have time to discuss men and male children and clothing styles. Lace or plush. One or the other. I have better things to do.

DADDY'S FAVORITE GIRL GLORIA: Can't you read a little bit from your text?

VALERIE: Definitely not. But for six hundred dollars, I'll gladly get to work in your panties.

You have a lot of shopping to do. If Andy is investigating the boundaries between art and shopping, you intend to investigate the boundaries between the abyss and shopping. Department stores are beautiful, shining palaces in the darkness. What you need now is a ship to embark. You have to buy lipstick and books for Cosmogirl; her lipstick was called Cherry Bomb and it was sticky and tasted of sugar.

The shop assistants help you test lipstick and perfume on your wrists. They are blond and inspire confidence. But you walk too quickly from one to another and the security guards want to escort you to the exit. And it is so difficult to understand why everything that was dazzling with possibilities has been turned into nothing. Andy Warhol is obviously an ignorant illiterate, because he will not read *Up Your Ass*, but just keeps looking at pictures in his imbecile fashion magazines. And all you want is to send one damn book to the desert sometime so that Dorothy can finally have something good to read.

SECURITY GUARDS: You have to leave. We'll accompany you to the door.

VALERIE: Why?

SECURITY GUARDS: You have to leave the department store immediately.

VALERIE: I'm shopping.

SECURITY GUARDS: We'll accompany you to the door.

VALERIE: Why do I have to leave?

SECURITY GUARDS: You're in too much of a hurry in here. You're dashing from one counter to the next. It makes the other customers uneasy when you race around like that.

VALERIE: I'm shopping for lipstick and books for Cosmogirl. And a powder compact for Silk Boy. A little fuck-wig for Dorothy.

SECURITY GUARDS: It doesn't matter what you're shopping for. You still have to leave.

VALERIE: You can buy the manifesto for half a dollar.

SECURITY GUARDS: Come with us, now.

VALERIE: I'm a writer.

SECURITY GUARDS: You're switching between the sales staff too much. It makes people nervous. It's time for this shopping trip to end, miss.

VALERIE: Valerie Jean Solanas. I studied for a doctorate for several years at the University of Maryland. Almost a Ph.D. in psychology. Almost a professor in the art of ruling the universe without letting on.

SECURITY GUARDS: This way, Miss Solanas. The main entrance, Miss Solanas.

VALERIE: I'm an author.

SECURITY GUARDS: It's time for this shopping trip to end now.

VALERIE: I've traveled here and there. I've done this and that. For a while I lived at the Chelsea Hotel. I mix with artists, writers, publishers, big game, hotshots, high-class prostitutes, and wealthy people with hot parties.

SECURITY GUARDS: We'll go with you to the door, miss.

VALERIE: I'm writing a novel for Olympia Press based on the manifesto.

SECURITY GUARDS: You're welcome back another day, miss.

VALERIE: I got an advance of six hundred dollars.

SECURITY GUARDS: Sure. That's great. As long as you leave the store.

VALERIE: Hey-ho. Lipstick and literature.

SECURITY GUARDS (*push you through the revolving door at the entrance*): Thanks, that's enough from you.

VALERIE: Cosmogirl calls all the time from the underworld. It's torture, I can't sleep anymore. She rings and whispers that being unloved is an act of terror and giant tears roll out of the receiver and I've moved from the Chelsea to Hotel Early and it's absolutely all right, but it's absolutely wrong. I loved the Chelsea, but I'm sure it wasn't mutual. They don't like me there. As soon as I settle down in the lobby, there they are, asking me to leave. They're planning a summer party. I think it'll be fantastic. They won't invite me, but you'd definitely be invited.

SECURITY GUARDS: Sure, sure. Thanks for coming, miss.

VALERIE: Cosmogirl says she needs more lipstick. She has my Pink Panther and she's very particular. She wants me to hang myself in Central Park or drown myself in the docks. Negotiations are currently ongoing with the underworld to find an alternative course of action that would mean I might possibly survive.

CHELSEA HOTEL, STILL MAY 1968

By the time Maurice finally arrives, with a haughty "It's okay" to the porter and no time to talk, you have waited outside in the street for half a day and the son-of-a-bitch doorman has called in reinforcements. And nobody harbors the idea anymore that you were the most wonderful guest the hotel ever had and no one remembers your favorite doorman, the polite one, but never mind. But Maurice has to stop to discuss the novel and the future with you, it is the very least a female mammal who knows she is on the way down can expect. Anything else would be indecent, unnatural.

VALERIE: I've been writing all night. I need more money.
MAURICE: Hello, Valerie.
VALERIE: I need more money for the novel.
MAURICE: Nice to see you, Valerie.
VALERIE: I can suck your dirty cock, if you like.
MAURICE: Thanks, but no, Valerie.
VALERIE: Have you spoken to Andy?
MAURICE: No, I have no contact with Andy Warhol, as you know.

VALERIE: I know you've discussed *Up Your Ass*. I know you've discussed my work. I know you laugh at me behind my back.

MAURICE: I don't know Andy Warhol. I know nothing about his play.

VALERIE: It's my play.

MAURICE: Sorry, Valerie. You don't need to worry about your play. There's hardly anyone interested.

VALERIE: I need a bigger advance. I need to discuss my work. Can I sleep in your hotel room?

MAURICE: Definitely not.

VALERIE: I can suck your ugly cock again.

MAURICE: Move. I'm on my way to the airport.

VALERIE: Maybe we could put on a show, it might earn us some cash.

MAURICE: You're disgusting.

VALERIE: You said I had talent. You said we should work together.

MAURICE: And now I regret it.

VALERIE: We have a contract.

MAURICE: That doesn't matter. You need to get ahold of yourself. Stop the amphetamines, for example. Then we can talk about it. It's impossible to talk to you when you're like this.

VALERIE: All you're bothered about are your horrible Lolita books and sex books.

MAURICE: You're not well, Valerie. Those pills you're taking make you look like an idiot, standing there licking your lips like a cow. Stop taking them, and then we'll see.

VALERIE: I've never felt better. The sun's shining. I'm writing. The natural order of things. The annihilation of men.

MAURICE: Goodbye, Valerie. I'm going to work now, Valerie. Good luck with the novel. I'm looking forward to reading it.

NARRATOR: And the question of identity?

VALERIE: Suspended identity. What's the use in being a little boy, if you're going to grow up and become a man? Giving up isn't the answer, fucking up is.

NARRATOR: I only wish I knew how to fuck all this up.

VALERIE: Artificial historiography. The story of the whore and mental illness. Of the American underwater population.

NARRATOR: And the question of identity?

VALERIE: Non-identity is the answer. Non-female females. Non-lesbian lesbians. A nonlower-class lower class. Peonies smell like magnolias. Dogs smell like dogs. And gardens smell different at different times of the year. There are no given identities, there are no women, there are no men, no boys, no girls. There's only a little puppet show. An endless shitty play with a shitty script.

NARRATOR: So it mustn't end like this?

VALERIE: You'll have to write something new, baby-writer, you'll have to find new endings. There'll be new rose gardens. Dorothy burns down a rose garden and the flowers that grow again are entirely different. A garden full of pussies, roses, fragments of text and oblivion. Now we'll close the literary factory for the time being.

(*Silence.*)

NARRATOR: Valerie.

VALERIE: Yes?

NARRATOR: I can't stop thinking about you.

VALERIE: It'll pass, you'll see. Go home and finish this novel now.

NARRATOR: The novel's just shit.

VALERIE: That's fine. Go now, baby-writer. It's going to be a nice day out there.

MAX'S KANSAS CITY, NEW YORK, MAY 1968

Summer arrives in New York in earnest. You and the wind chase along the avenues, amphetamine pumps in your blood and through the half light. Your heart keeps up its beating like a Manhattan church bell. You pass out on a rooftop after a night with sharks, and when you wake up again, the wind has taken all your papers and one shark has stolen your turquoise Swintec. Andy does not answer your calls anymore. Maurice never calls back. At the Chelsea you are stopped before you come in from the street and Cosmo makes her fevered calls from the underworld no matter where you are, no matter whether a phone booth is nearby.

You no longer sleep, because she prefers to pay you a visit when your guard is down and you cannot defend yourself. At the end of every night she is waiting for you with her pearl necklace and her pale eyes and all she wants (all she has ever wanted) is for you to drop by in the underworld. And if you have really forgiven her, why have you not been to see her?

You spend entire days at Max's Kansas City, waiting for Andy to appear and drink a toast to the production of *Up Your Ass*. Meanwhile a thin, cigar-smoking professor and a projectionist jerk off on your face in the toilet. When Andy finally arrives with a new wig, he is nervous and forgets to say hello. And he has that way of sliding through the walls and being swallowed up by the shadowy presence of his companions.

Hey you, hey you, hey you, Andy, what do you know about torture and histrionics?

MORRISSEY: Andy doesn't want to speak to you. He's tired of your telephone terrorism.

VALERIE: Thanks for the information. But I'd like to speak to Andy . . . (*to Andy who is hiding behind Morrissey*) . . . Andy Stupid Warhol?

MORRISSEY: You're vile, Valerie. Everybody hates you. No one gives a fuck what you say. We're laughing at you in the Factory. Andy's laughing. Everyone's laughing at you.

VALERIE: Read my manifesto. That'll tell you who I am. I was in *I, a Man*. Played myself. Had a role in *I, a Man*. Didn't I, Andy? You said you liked it. Didn't you, Andy? I made up my lines myself.

MORRISSEY: There isn't anyone in this city who's not laughing at you.

VALERIE: My instincts tell me to dig chicks. Why should my standards be lower than theirs? Well, not yours. Your standards are abysmal. Man lover. Faggot standards.

(*Silence.*)

VALERIE: I just want to know whether you've read my play. I want to know if you intend to produce it.

(*Silence.*)

VALERIE: Hello? Andy? If that bad Muzak you listen to has given you hearing problems, we can use sign language. The sign for lesbian is very easy. A quick stroke of the lips . . . (*signs in the air*) . . . Do you understand me now, Andy?

(*Silence.*)

VALERIE: Do you have a dollar, Andy? I need money for a hamburger.

MORRISSEY: It doesn't matter how much you talk, you'll still be filthy and vile.

VALERIE: That Johnny Carson show you lured me onto, Andy, the one where you sat painting your nails and calling yourself Miss Warhola, it was a disaster for me. I went on there to talk about the manifesto. There were bright spotlights pointing at me and spiteful laughter from the audience. That Carson guy was a killing machine under the TV powder, and all the workers in the studio were snickering. Then they cut me out. The show was never broadcast. I'm glad I refused to wear their disgusting powder. That whole program is just a means for male fake artists and male plagiarists to lie about their work.

MORRISSEY: And what does that have to do with us?

VALERIE: I don't know, but being unloved is an act of terror.

Morrissey tries to move you and there is nothing you hate more than someone trying to move you. The only thing you hate more is someone imitating your voice.

MORRISSEY (*imitates your voice*): It was really nothing special. Louis used to screw me in the porch seat after Dorothy had gone into town. The fabric on the seat cover was covered with roses and I counted the roses and the stars while I rented out my little pussy for no money. And I don't know why, but some chewing gum got stuck in my hair every time. It must have fallen out of my mouth. We used to cut out the stickiest snarls afterward and he would chain-smoke. The strange thing is I sometimes miss the electricity and that tingling sensation in my legs and arms.

Sounds of crowd laughter and individual sniggers. Andy laughs like a desert animal and tries to disguise it behind a copy of *Vogue*. The ceiling tilts toward you at alarming speed and in a flash you duck.

VALERIE: They're my words.
VIVA: You were even disgusting when you were a child, Valerie. Men wanted to screw you, because you were disgusting by the time you were seven. No wonder you're a lesbian.

Andy gets up and walks away. He never needs to say anything; like fleeting shadows they move behind him, picking up his *Vogue* magazine and his cigarettes. And he does not answer when you shout after him.

VALERIE: I want my play back.
VIVA: Valerie, that play was too dirty even for us.
VALERIE: It's not nice to steal other people's plays.
VIVA: The amusing thing about your paranoia is that you have nothing any sensible person would be interested in stealing.
MORRISSEY: Goodbye, Valerie. I hope we don't see you again. There's no point in hanging around outside the Factory. Andy still won't want to speak to you.
VALERIE: Remember . . . Remember . . . Remember I'm the only sane woman here.

THE PRESIDENTS

A. Political machines. Political paradoxes. I had my fluffy silver fox fur. High white boots. I missed all the protests and demonstrations.

B. Amendment to the Constitution. The Treaty Factory. The White House. The white president. Some things do not change. Some things never change. You have to stand still when I speak to you. You have to close your eyes and open that sexy little mouth of yours. That sexy little hole in your face and between your legs. Sexual politics. The whole world would have loved me by now.

C. They were only false promises. There never was an amendment to the Constitution. They walked along the streets of Chicago in their white skirts. They shed tears on the tarmac. A hundred thousand handbags washed up on the beaches.

D. August 26, 1980. Sarah Weddington. Eleanor Smeal. Florence Howe. Bella Abzug. Someone chains herself to the railings outside the Republican Party's headquarters in Washington. The Second Stage. Betty Friedan sucks cock in the White House. The white architecture. The white witch. Sex is, itself, a sublimation.

E. I walk across New York in my bra and girdle. Welcome to happiness. Who is president of America? I actually have no idea. The Lavender Menace. They toss their bras and girdles into the Freedom Trash Can.

F. Remember that I am sick and longing to die. Remember that I am the only sane woman here. The feminine mystique. Self-proclaimed revolutionaries. Disorders in every thought. Patriarchal hegemony.

G. Paranoid associations. They dreamed of publishing the manifesto. They dreamed of a feminist sanctuary. Time passed, publishing houses kept their bordello wallpaper, their overgrown vocabulary. In Washington, women's rights became a bad joke, embarrassing. The first wave came and went. The second wave rinsed every thought away.

H. The Equal Rights Amendment turned into a social club, where ex-suffragettes came out with their confessions. Emma Goldman was deported, cases of insanity increased, tuberculosis, diabetes, various nasty cancerous tumors on society and the social mother. Obviously, I knew they were lying to me. Obviously, I knew nothing was for real. That novel. That play. The manifesto, the satire. When I left, they laughed at me like a pack of desert animals.

I. There were only superwomen. It was the second wave. They were all courageous, they all loved sucking cock. Passion. Obviously, I knew they were laughing at me.

J. Suffragettes. One by one they joined the underworld. Lung cancer, heart attacks, shark attacks. The inquests never ended. Formalities were set aside. It was overrun with weeds around the house. There were no people left in the old house in Washington. Former HQ. Women's Party. The suffrage movement.

K. It was no game. These were not fun-size demonstrations. Miss Pankhurst chained herself to a lamppost. Rioters set fire to themselves in the street, went on hunger strikes, were imprisoned. The future. Future generations. They are dead now. Miss Pankhurst. Clark Gable. The moon.

L. The performative dynamic in those girls. Their pseudo-radicalness. The biological relationship between men and women. They always returned to that. Sexual love between men and women without martyrdom. Welcome to happiness.

M. We chained ourselves to the lampposts. We went on hunger strikes. Women died in the demonstrations. Strangers sent turds and semen through the post. They locked us up, we got out again, they locked us up, we were back on the streets. *Fuck you, Miss Pankhurst*. The white blouse. That was 1913. I had seen her on Fifth Avenue. The next summer she died from her injuries at the racecourse.

N. Atlantic City emptied of tourists and casinos and demonstrators. The Freedom Trash Can abandoned on the boardwalk.

Underclothes destroyed by rain. Of course, I knew they were all laughing at me.

O. There was not a problem I could put my finger on. Yet still I was in despair. I walked around my backyard all day long. With nothing to do.

P. It was after the revelation of the feminine mystique, after Watergate, after Agent Orange. They did their gardening on Long Island. They no longer attended demonstrations. Sexual politics. You dreamed of a revolutionary in every bedroom. You dreamed of occupying and eradicating every bedroom. In retrospect, they said: It was not political at all, it was simply personal. In retrospect, they said: It was not the enemy who frightened us; it was our violent sisters.

Q. I was dressed in a flowing white fur. High white boots. I did not fit in anywhere. I had my pockets full of filthy knives. There was Muzak playing in my ears. Flimflam artists and other sharks shouting (or wanking or pissing or crying) in my face. I wanted to go home. I cried out for someone like you.

R. The meetings were lonely white fields. The laboratory mice would have wept if they had seen you there. Samantha would have wept. Women's movement. There were no Amazons. It was a mixed gathering. An experiment. It is never too late to change.

S. The suffragettes rejected all forms of male company. I am the only sane woman here. The little songbird flew out of the doll's house. The future gave her the right. The white blouse. She threw herself in front of the king's horse. The white blouse was stained with blood then. Skirts torn to shreds. After the funeral they decided to join forces with the men, they decided to employ peaceful methods. Mixed demonstrations. You can't fight communism with perfume.

T. I had to stand absolutely still, or I would have fallen apart.

U. There were no stars. There were only crystal nights, crystal-clear thoughts, a concentration of human fluids. Take it all from me, do it, that's what I want. I should have learned to say no. Take it all from me, do it, that's what I want you to do. If he had been drinking, it was of no consequence. Another act of brutality. Brutality of the kind I do not want to remember, cannot remember. The sky was wild that night. An emptiness I could relate to. Trapped in a fool's reality, and enjoying it.

V. Sexual politics. Intimate structures. Organization of love. Organization of rape. Red-light districts. Specific areas of the city sprang up. Take it all from me. Do it. It's what I want.

W. National Organization for Women. We decided right at the start that we wanted to join forces with men. Without men, no women's movement.

X. Blue smoke between the trunks. Frost in all the trees. Burning white witches. Millett. Atkinson. Brownmiller. Firestone. Solanas. Davis. Morgan. Steinem. Flowerpots dead in all the windows.

Y. NOW's founders. Kay Clarenbach looked after her three children in a corrugated shack in the desert while her husband studied at Columbia. Muriel Fox had a husband who was a brain surgeon. (God, how unhealthy, no surprise she was an airhead.) While the first meeting took place, he waited in a hotel room nearby with the children. When she returned, the television screen was flickering.

Z. Politics. Sexual politics. Why should we care about politics? Why should we care about what happens when we're dead?

33 UNION SQUARE, MORNING OF JUNE 3, 1968, LIKE BEING IN A DREAM

It is a dream with black claws again, perhaps the last. You are back in Union Square. A smell of smoke lingers around you and you remember you have set fire to all the waste bins in the park. You and Andy are at the doors to the elevator in the entrance to the Factory. Andy has just returned from Coney Island and you have lipstick around the edges of your lips (remember it is a political act) and the gun aimed at his heart (a .32 caliber). In the dream you have been waiting there all evening and into the night and replica Andy never comes, and now it is morning and the blinding sun comes streaming in. There is a strange calm in the Factory, no complicated fancy art lamps yet, no furniture, no assistants, no tortuous psychedelic music, just bare light bulbs crackling, just you and the monster art parasite Andy Warhol, and Andy Warhol already has the marks of three gunshots on his upper body. *It seemed unreal, like watching a movie. Only the pain seemed real.* The film stars on the walls are your character witnesses, staring at you, bewitched, out of their frames: Shirley Temple, Mae West, Joan Bennett, Lana Turner, Louise Brooks, Marlene Dietrich, Kay Francis.

The desert birds screech in the desert and Andy takes off his wig and covers his chest and heart with it and cries like a forlorn child and for one burning second you wish you could save him, but the gunshot wounds are already showing on his body. There is only one manuscript, and all you need now is concentration and tunnel vision. And at that very moment in the dream (and it is always the same dream) your hearing goes and black pools of blood spread over your coat and a gigantic silver screen with all of Andy's lines drops down from the ceiling. A crystal clarity unfolds in the room. Andy holds the silver wig to his heart.

Valerie, no, no . . . Don't do it . . .

Andy holds the silver wig like a shield in front of his chest. Seconds of pain like snow on fire in your heart and the room a sea of voices around you. There is Dorothy, Cosmogirl, Silk Boy, and Sister White. The hem of your dress in your mouth, the taste of blood, a heart of stone, you concentrate on clearing the voices from your head. The reason for the amphetamine, cocaine, heroin, benzodiazepine, and the LSD has only ever been the voices that never stop booming in your head. *I do not want to die. I do not want to live. I do not want to have a story. I do not want to know how it ends.*

Valerie, no, no . . . Don't do it . . .

God damn it, Valerie. Leave. It's a stupid plan, anyone can see that. Remember New York State has the death penalty for homicide. Remember New York State hates women. Remember governors and presidents get a hard-on when they see women die in the electric chair. Drop the gun and leave.

My little horse. What are you doing here? What were you thinking just now? You have got it all completely wrong, even I can see that. I have always done everything wrong, back to front, upside down, but this, my darling, even I can see this is not a brilliant idea. You should

*be a professor, writer, president of America, not standing here, point-
ing a nasty gun at some faggoty little faggot. Or artist. Or whatever
he calls himself. I have never liked artists, actually.*

*Just run fast and don't look round, my sweetheart. To the right is the
elevator, immediately behind you, take it down to the street and go
out as quickly as possible. Go home to your hotel room, call somebody,
anybody, get yourself to a hospital. There is help, there are white nurses.*

*Come on, Valerie . . . if you drop the gun, I promise I will learn the
alphabet . . . I will read to you . . . Mr. Biondi has moved now . . .
drop it now . . . here . . . take my hand . . . silly . . .*

*Little horse . . . Little president . . . My dearest little horse . . . My
little sugar cube . . . My little Valerie . . . My little baby pussy . . . My
feral creature . . . My treasure trove . . . My little brainbox . . .*

*You hold your life in your hand. You are a girl, not an animal. A girl
mammal, a little she-child standing on the borderline between human
being and chaos. Let's face it, you have really strayed off course this
time. Do you remember, Valerie? Do you remember what we wrote
in the manifesto? A woman knows instinctively that the only wrong
is to hurt others. The only wrong is to hurt others . . . Do you remember, Valerie? And that the meaning of life is love . . .*

I will tell you how it ends, my friend . . .

*I forbid you to, Valerie. Consider that I am your mother. I never
wanted to be anyone's mother, but I wanted to be your mother.
Everything I have touched has broken, you know that. Everything
except you. You are the only thing in my life that was beautiful. I*

wish I could be a velvety embrace for you now, that we could be loop-
ing together in perpetual dreamless sleep. Oblivion. Clouds of pink.

It is like an eclipse of the sun. This is the beginning of the end, Valerie.
The moment you shoot Andy Warhol, you throw away all possibility
of being someone other people listen to, the only thing you dream about,
the writer, artist, revolutionary, psychoanalyst, rebel. There are so
many options, there is a world that can be yours out there, if only you
drop the weapon and leave. Remember, Valerie, this is New York, it
is 1968 and you have your university degree, your wild heart, your
rich talent of raw poetry and a fantastic sense of humor. You can do
whatever you want. In a few years' time the women's movement
will move into the universities and everywhere women's cafés will
appear, reading circles, feminist groups, and in San Francisco half a
million women will demonstrate, dressed in white, in protest against
sexual politics based on fear and systematic rape. A radical women's
movement will emerge and with it a radical sexual politics. There
will be a place for you there, Valerie. The new age will be your age.

FILM SEQUENCE, THE LAST ONE FROM THE FACTORY

When the voices around you clear, there is only Andy and you and the whirring, flickering fluorescent light. There are no happy endings.

Andy goes down on his knees and prays to God.

You hold the gun to his heart. Then you pull the trigger and blow a hole in his chest and a hole in all prospects for the future. You blow a hole in everything you should have been. You blow a hole in your only, tiny, silver-colored hope and your clothes are seared forever onto your skin. A sea of blood spreads out beneath your feet. *It seemed unreal. Like watching a movie. Only the pain seemed real.*

Andy is engulfed by white backdrops and disappears. You close your eyes and drop the gun into your raincoat pocket. You leave the Factory, take the elevator down. The trees outside look as though they are decked in silver tape.

You run across Manhattan, hand in hand with Cosmogirl. Her hair like dirty honey in the sunlight, her eyes ready to drown in her face. You run out of the story.

ANDY AND DEATH

During the eighties Andy was obsessed with painting revolvers. Apart from that, he made no public comment on the murder attempt. In an interview he says he has forgiven you, that is all he ever says about you. On one occasion, much later, when asked if he is afraid of death, he replies: *I am already dead. I've been dead a long time.*

At Columbus–Mother Cabrini Hospital he finally regains consciousness. Your .32-caliber bullets have damaged his chest and his stomach (liver, spleen, esophagus, and lungs). He never completely recovers physically, and afterward he suffers from severe, lasting paranoia. The Factory is a closed book. The spirits no longer go in and out of the building at will, the freaks are no longer welcome and only a few carefully chosen people are admitted to 33 Union Square.

On arrival at the hospital on the afternoon of June 3, Andy is at first pronounced dead, but when the doctors realize (with Viva Ronaldo's help) that the victim is Andy Warhol, they manage to keep him alive in an unconscious state. Five doctors then work for five hours to bring him back from the dead. It is his name that saves him, and when he dies twenty years later during a routine operation (residual complications following the shooting), he dies because he does not have a name. He is admitted to the hospital as the anonymous character Bob Roberts, and Bob Roberts dies because he is not monitored in the immediate postoperative recovery period.

People say Andy Warhol never really comes back from the dead, they say that throughout his life he remains unconscious, or one of the living dead.

You do not return from the underworld, either, after June 3, 1968.

In June 1969 you are sentenced to two years in prison for the attempted murder of Andy Warhol and his associates. What is regarded as an extremely lenient penalty is probably due to Andy Warhol's refusal to appear in court, the demonstrations outside the courthouse every day in support of your release from the hospital, and not least Florynce Kennedy's blazing defense.

In September 1971 you get out of prison and in November the same year you are rearrested for making telephone threats to a number of men, both famous and not famous, among them Andy Warhol. In 1973 you spend the entire year in and out of various mental hospitals.

In the winter of 1974–75 you return to the sun and surf of the Alligator Reef beaches. But after only a few weeks in Florida you are committed to South Florida State Hospital in Fort Lauderdale, where you spend the rest of the year strapped to beds with restraints and diagnoses.

ARITHMETIC AND SURFING II

In February 1977 you are back in New York and issue a mimeo-graphed version of the manifesto with your own introduction.

"Olympia Press has gone bankrupt and the publishing rights to *SCUM Manifesto* have reverted to me, VALERIE SOLANAS, and now I am issuing the CORRECT edition, MY edition of *SCUM Manifesto* . . . I will let anyone who wants to hawk it do so, women, men, Hare Krishna. Maurice Girodias, you're always in financial straits. Here's your big chance—hawk *SCUM Manifesto*. You can peddle it around the massage parlor district. Anita Bryant, you can finance your anti-fag campaign selling the only book worth selling—*SCUM Manifesto*. Andy Warhol—you can peddle it at all those hot-shit parties you go to . . . Minimum order for peddlers is 200. No credit, no discount. I don't like arithmetic. And don't have gang wars over territories. It's not nice."

In an interview with Howard Smith in *The Village Voice* the same year, you say the manifesto was just a literary device and there never was an organization called SCUM.

In the summer of 1977 you travel to Atlantic City in Virginia to surf. Miss America contests are taking place in the city at that time. You do not do much surfing. Instead, on the lookout for Miss America contestants, you go back and forth along the boardwalk, selling sex and losing your money in the casinos.

ARITHMETIC AND SURFING III

At the end of the seventies you are sometimes seen at Tompkins Square Park and St. Mark's Place in Manhattan. You are always hungry, dirty, and alone. You are always selling sex and always trying to sell the manifesto.

At the beginning of the eighties you hitch to San Francisco to surf in the Pacific Ocean. You never reach the sea. You end up instead in the Tenderloin red-light district.

You never return to Ventor and Georgia after 1951. Dorothy and you never see each other again.

NEW YORK STATE PRISON FOR WOMEN
IN BEDFORD HILLS, 1969–1971

I'm scared of the other inmates, Sister White . . .

Are you still there, Sister White . . . ?

SISTER WHITE: I'm always here.

VALERIE: When I was a teenage whore. I hoped I would die.
I've seen your hate. Leave my house. I don't want those underpants. I don't want those dresses.

SISTER WHITE: Valerie . . . it's not me you're talking to.

VALERIE: You suck everything out of me. You take my energy.
You're so much bigger than me. You're so much bigger than
me. Watch me disappear. Darling. I'm destroying you. I'm destroying you. Darling. I can't save you. Darling. I want you to
be on fire. I want to burn every bridge. I've burned them all.
I regret burning all the bridges. Look at me now. You're not
going to miss me when I'm gone. No one is going to miss me
when I disappear from the story.

SISTER WHITE: There is help, Valerie. There are white pills and white-clad nurses. I'm here. And nurses all smoke, more than most. There's a perception that we don't, that on the inside we're clean and white. I've always smoked. I want to get out of here.

VALERIE: Where the hell were you when I needed you? You didn't want to look at me. Let me out. What could I do in you, apart from fall? I never wanted to have you. I didn't know where to go in you.

SISTER WHITE: I dream about living somewhere quite different. In a different state, perhaps. By the ocean, maybe.

VALERIE: You suicidal goddamn bitch. You suicidal goddamn bitch. Leave her in peace. Let her go. And you did let her go. Her heels clipped the moonbeam. She laughed and smiled. And you let her go. All this has been wasted. Where were you when I needed you? Don't ask me again. Don't ever speak to me again.

SISTER WHITE: You're strong, Valerie. You're strong and bright. A ray of light. There are dead people lying in the desert, you said. You laughed and flew straight into the light.

VALERIE: I'm a killing machine. Yeah. Yeah. Yeah. I kill. Open him up, look inside. I'll bury you, darling. I'll bury you deep within me.

SISTER WHITE: You had your bag of notes. We weren't allowed to touch it. We didn't touch it. Your eyes flicked all over the walls. We kept asking you: Should we call someone? There was no one we could call.

VALERIE: Hey you, hey you, hey you, my beloved in the desert. Don't let anyone look into your eyes. You only have to die and smile at me. You know I want you. Here's what you get when you fall. Why don't you just wave goodbye? Heroin. Amphetamine. Cocaine. Who's the daughter of suicide? I'm in your eyes. I'm on fire. Now I'm on fire. Don't shut your eyes. Don't shut your eyes. Your pulse. You're sucking my scars and wounds. It's best if you open your eyes. When I come, it's best if you open your eyes. I'm coming now. I'm just getting older, just charged up. Charged up now. I'm a killing machine.

SISTER WHITE: You were incoherent. Your voice was high-pitched, cracking. Someone had left you. You said it had been a holiday, a defeat, a thunderstorm.

VALERIE: Is she beautiful on the inside? Is she beautiful from the back? Is she ugly on the inside? Is she ugly from the back? Promise her everything, even if she's ugly on the inside. That grotesque girl rabbit. So smooth and beautiful on the inside.

SISTER WHITE: There's no more mist in the park now. We can go out. We can walk between the trees. The other patients aren't there any longer. I can hold your hand if you like.

VALERIE: The blond rabbit girl has a dead rabbit in her rabbit handbag. The blond girl dissects the lab director's little family dog. Family values. Wonderlands. Wonder girls. She carries on ringing and terrorizing from the underworld. Being un-loved is an act of terror. When they've taken what they want, they never want it again.

SISTER WHITE: You laughed and flew straight into the light.

VALERIE: I laughed and flew straight into the light. I'm a sui-cidal goddamn whore. Will the story soon be over? Is Dr. Ruth Cooper coming back soon? Cosmogirl? Dorothy? Andy Warhol, is he playing dead or alive?

BRISTOL HOTEL, APRIL 25, 1988, THE LAST DAY

VALERIE: I think it's raining again.

NARRATOR: It is April.

VALERIE: What day is it?

NARRATOR: The twenty-fifth of April 1988.

VALERIE: Whereabouts are we?

NARRATOR: Bristol Hotel, the Tenderloin.

VALERIE: Where are we going?

NARRATOR: Nowhere.

VALERIE: Who's president of America?

NARRATOR: Still Ronald Reagan.

VALERIE: Oh.

NARRATOR: I wish the story had a different ending. I wish there were happy endings.

VALERIE (*smiles and coughs up blood onto the sheet*): Do you know, the little governor, George Bush junior, once asked Ronald Reagan if he'd thought about becoming president. President where? he asked. In America, George Bush said. Reagan answered: I didn't realize you thought I was such a bad actor . . . (*laughs*) . . . Then he did become president. Joke presidents. Pretend presidents. Next time they'll doubtless ask Donald Duck or Red Moran.

NARRATOR: You should have been president of America.

VALERIE: Absolutely.

(*Silence.*)

VALERIE: Nancy Reagan apparently plans her husband's duties with the help of astrology. Now that's what I call realpolitik.

(*More silence.*)

VALERIE: April is the cruelest month. It drives sirens out of the dead ground, memories and desires, stiffened roots, spring rain. You should stop crying now. You're quite silly and sentimental, toady, a namby-pamby. I want you to hold my hand when I go. I don't want you to weep. No sadness. No weakness.

NARRATOR: You mean syringa, Valerie. It's syringa, lilac, in the dead ground, not sirens.

VALERIE: I mean syringa, I mean sirens, I mean whatever. It doesn't matter anymore.

NARRATOR: I'll never stop searching for you. You're my faculty of dreams.

VALERIE: That's good, little Daddy's Girl. I'm going to sleep now. I'm going to sleep and dream that there isn't a question about death in every sentence; I'll dream about a film being made in the desert with wild horses chased by helicopters.

NARRATOR: You know, Valerie, mouse girls did finally have babies with each other. Little Japanese Kaguya. And human girls learned how to make babies with each other. The women's movement is a glowing mass moving slowly through the cities and all they wish for is wild horses and peace.

VALERIE: The lines were always covered by something plastic. The sun burned through the parasols, American dreams and nightmares, the American film, the American story, the

camera's lies, world literature's. America with its desert landscape and wild mustangs was a huge adventure. I never
understood what was in the script.

NARRATOR: How's it all going to turn out?

VALERIE: I'm going to go to sleep now.

NARRATOR: And me?

VALERIE: You just have to be patient.

NARRATOR: One last question.

VALERIE: Go for it.

NARRATOR: Why did you shoot Andy Warhol?

VALERIE: I don't know, actually. I just did. You'll have to be
satisfied with that.

(*Silence.*)

NARRATOR: Just one more thing, Valerie.

VALERIE: Yes?

NARRATOR: How will I find my way back in the dark?

VALERIE: I have no idea. But it will be better for you when I'm
gone. And there's really nothing to be sad about. I could have
told you from the start how it would end.

AMERICA, LIFE IS A COURT CASE

THE STATE: Name of the accused?

VALERIE: Valerie . . . Solanas . . . Jean . . . Solanas . . .

THE STATE: Accused's current employment?

VALERIE: Whore.

THE STATE: Previous employment?

VALERIE: Whore.

THE STATE: Education?

VALERIE: None.

THE STATE: Age?

VALERIE: Unclear. An unknown number of years in exile.

THE STATE: Address?

VALERIE: None.

THE STATE: Where does she come from?

VALERIE: America.

THE STATE: Of what is she accused?

VALERIE: Of being born. Her existence in the world. Of not being dead. Of stinking.

(*Silence.*)

THE STATE: Thank you. When did it all happen?

VALERIE: She hates herself, she doesn't want to die, and it's a supremely permanent condition.

THE STATE: And the criminal act for which she stands before the court?

VALERIE: June 3, 1968.

THE STATE: Where?

VALERIE: In America.

FLORYNCE KENNEDY (*stands*): The Factory . . . 33 Union Square . . . Manhattan . . . New York . . .

THE STATE: Thank you. Was she alone?

VALERIE: Yes. She was alone.

THE STATE: No one else present?

VALERIE: She was alone the whole time.

THE STATE: And the motive?

VALERIE: She doesn't remember.

THE STATE: And what defense does she intend to offer?

VALERIE: None at all.

(*Silence.*)

FLORYNCE KENNEDY: On June 10, 1968, I was appointed public defense counsel in the case *New York State vs. Valerie Solanas*. I described Valerie as one of the most important campaigners for the modern women's movement. Dr. Ruth Cooper at Elmhurst Psychiatric Hospital in New York described Valerie as brilliantly intelligent and . . . and Andy Warhol didn't actually die, he was only injured, he survived and he kept on being wealthy and making bad art, even though he didn't make a full recovery . . . There was her unhappy childhood . . . raped by her daddy when she was seven . . . raped six times before she turned eighteen, her mother abused and raped by an undisclosed number of men in the desert, homeless at the age of fifteen, working as a prostitute, drug addiction, mental disorders, repeated rapes in connection with prostitution—

VALERIE: —Excuse me . . .

THE STATE: What is she trying to say?

VALERIE: She only wants to say that she's reeling a bit at the prospect of all this eternity. But she wants to emphasize that she takes full responsibility for her actions. She is an adult and she distances herself from explanatory models of psychiatric illness based on the importance of the past. She prefers to project herself toward the future, rather than her dirty, piss-soaked past. Her feeling on the matter is this: There's no one to blame. There is no God, there are no happy endings, every chapter is a sad chapter. This is not a world she wants to live in, but she prefers to take the whole blame for all her actions and she would like that to be recorded.

(*Silence.*)

FLORYNCE KENNEDY: Excuse me, Your Honor . . . I should like to add one thing . . . Andy Warhol stole Valerie Solanas's play. He was a kleptomaniac, he lived as a parasite on other people's . . . wreckage and madcap ideas . . . a parasite on their bloodstained memories and experiences. She asked for her play back on numerous occasions. It was art theft, equivalent to attempted murder.

THE STATE: Does she have anything to add?

(*Silence.*)

THE STATE: Do you have anything to add?

VALERIE: Forget it.

THE STATE: Pardon?

VALERIE: Forget the play. It's plain Andy wasn't interested in it. It was a shit play, a shit script, that was obvious the whole time.

THE STATE: And what does she have to say in her defense?

VALERIE: That she longs to be able to sleep.

THE STATE: And the future?

VALERIE: She is most definitely a girl without a future.

(*Silence.*)

THE STATE: Thank you very much. The court is adjourned. The American government currently has no charges or indictments against Valerie Solanas.

VALERIE: And what about me?

THE STATE: The defendant can leave the courtroom.

ON THE OTHER SIDE OF THE ALPHABET

A. A person approaching death is often unconscious for the last few hours.

B. This does not mean, however, that your presence is not important. It does not mean she cannot hear you speak or move across the room. The last senses to go are hearing and touch.

C. A near relative or friend should be present in the last hours. If that is not possible, a nurse should care for the dying person. She should not be left alone.

D. Feel free to hold the dying person's hand, talk to her, touch her. She will soon be gone.

E. Moisten her lips with a wet towel. The ability to swallow is lost early on, but the sucking reflex remains to the end.

F. Moisten her forehead too, touch her and stroke her skin. Massaging her arms and chest will assuage the fear of death.

G. Patches of red and bluish color will appear on the chest of the dying person. This is completely normal, as the blood flows more slowly through the body, the circulation is poorer and the pulse weaker. It makes the legs and feet cold, so massage them gently. Talk to her. She can hear everything you say.

H. If there are no analgesics—they are almost always available in modern society—the dying person will often experience severe pain and cramps.

I. Let her know you are in the room, talk to her, take her hand; it will help the pain as well.

J. Right at the end, as the body temperature rises, the dying person will have a fever. Softly dab her forehead and wrists.

K. The heartbeat is now irregular, the pulse in the wrist weak. This is completely normal. Just hold her hand, talk to her; it will calm the fear and soothe the pain.

L. By now the intervals between breaths are commonly so long, it seems unlikely the dying person will take another breath. Do not be alarmed if she coughs and struggles to breathe as she fights for air, it is quite usual. The definitive cause of death is almost always suffocation. Do not be alarmed if she has urinary incontinence.

M. The dying person is often agitated at the very end. She claws at her chest, shouts, cries, tries to get air, her hands fumble with the sheets. At this stage you can take comfort in the fact that sensations and consciousness are severely dimmed. There are only faint slivers and shards of light.

N. Slivers and shards of light.

O. She can still hear your voice, still feel your hands. She is like a babe in arms now; she knows you are there, even though she does not understand. Remember, your presence allays the fear.

P. She might wake for a second immediately before death. Her gaze can be utterly clear and conscious. Perhaps she will say something, perhaps squeeze your hand.

Q. It is vital she is not alone at this moment. Now she is a tiny child, waking at night and calling for her mother. It is important someone heeds her cry.

R. Hold her hands, talk to her, talk to the one you love, soon she will be gone.

S. Touch the dying person, talk to her, soon she will be gone.

T. The last thing to happen is that her heart will stop beating and her breathing will cease.

U. Her last breaths will come after a very long pause. Without analgesics these breaths can also be very distressing.

V. Afterward (after death), the pupils are dilated and fixed.

W. The eyes remain half-closed, living, she has not gone yet. There is still time to talk to her, caress her skin. Remember, the dying person knows you are there, even though she cannot show it. The final senses to go are her hearing and touch.

X. Sometimes she will wake for a moment immediately before death. Perhaps she will say something. Perhaps she will look at you, her eyes often quite clear. Perhaps she will squeeze your hand.

Y. Feel free to take something with you to pass the time.

Z. A book, or some sewing.

The blood moves so slowly through your body and blood roses appear in pink patterns on your chest and hands, and yet it sounds like a factory site in there; the bellowing and wailing of heartbeats, thoughts, breaths, and brain. The blood roses are a bad sign, the heartbeats are the pulse in a garden of fear, a desert without desert flowers; and, just a few breaths from now, everything will come to an end. Dorothy used to steal roses from other people's gardens, roses which she later sold in the bars. Dorothy burned down a rose garden when she was mad at Moran. Dorothy was a wonderful pink panther in a nuclear dress who ruled a desert and a junk garden with only sweet wine, watering cans, and dying plants.

You dream that she is blowing you kisses across the desert and across the decades, you dream that she is standing outside her corrugated house, wearing a dress she has made from the American flag and a lunatic hat in a wasp design, waving at you. *Welcome to my garden of horror and love.*

Dorothy?

Dorothy?

DOROTHY: Valerie?

VALERIE: They've haven't combed my hair right.

DOROTHY: It doesn't matter now.

VALERIE: They've given me a side part. I don't want it like that, but I can't lift my hands up.

DOROTHY (*brushes the hair away from your face with her gentle, aging hands*): I liked hearing my child laugh in the backyard. I often dream you're young again. You have a high temperature and your eyes are glazed. You reach out for me, for the garden. My hands are caught in coat pockets. In their hair and between their legs. I loved that hardness. I missed all the appointments, I let you disappear into the desert.

VALERIE: My hands are so heavy . . . I wish I could still ride a bicycle . . . I cycled in Central Park, I wrote postcards to you from the café in Central Park, I telephoned you from Elmhurst, telephoned from everywhere, but I didn't know what to say . . .

DOROTHY: I'm an idiot. I missed all your calls.

VALERIE (*holds Dorothy's hand, it smells of soap and smoke*): Your hands have grown old, Dorothy.

DOROTHY: Never mind. I wish I'd not been so afraid of getting old and disappearing. All that longing for eternity. Moran got sick from all those gasoline fumes.

VALERIE: You left me to drown.

DOROTHY: Mr. Emin died in the swimming pool the other day. He wasn't even particularly old, or particularly overweight.

His heart just stopped mid-stroke. Do you remember Mr. Emin? You used to play by the river and he was always following you like your little tail.

VALERIE: I don't give a fuck about Mr. Emin. I don't give a fuck about Moran. I don't give a fuck about you being scared of getting old. I want to know why you left me to drown.

DOROTHY (*her face is just a glimmer, but her hands are warm and real*): I don't know anything, Valerie. I remember your hair being quite fair, I remember you catching sunbeams and tiny animals in your dress . . . You're wearing that dress again, the little white one, it's tight. I'm standing on the steps after a night in the bar. You're sitting at the back, crying. Don't leave me, you say. Don't leave me with him, you say. I always left you. And I don't know why. The sun glinting on the porch, the smell of sand and the netherworld on you when I return, and when I have to go again you try to hold me back. I leave you. And I don't know why.

VALERIE: I don't want to die with a side part, I don't want to die in ugly clothes. I want you to help me put my silver coat on.

DOROTHY: I was so happy when you came along and I remember thinking I should travel that road with Louis once a year with new babies under my dress. At the hospital I swayed my butt to ward off the pain. And then, afterward, when you were lying in my arms, the sky was all flamingo-pink. I have a memory of flamingos hurtling past in the sky outside the hospital window. Hundreds, thousands. All those skies that never come back. I'll help you on with your beautiful silver coat.

VALERIE: Will you hold my hand when I die?

DOROTHY: I'll hold your hand. I'll stay with you until you fall asleep. We'll say it's nighttime now, and nighttime is dark like a mother's embrace or an eclipse of the sun.

The highway   the lost highway   headlights shining on the tarmac

fleeting white flashes   the rain hitting the car windows   dead

animals asleep in the grass

motel signs beside the motorways   neon   rain   darkness   girls

with their handbags under streetlamps

trucks   lipstick   gasoline   desert   oblivion   America

ten thousand fathoms of ocean water

ten thousand different stories about water

lips   hands   milk teeth

drowning dresses and memories   gaggles of girls

pussy souls   pussy material   death material   lipstick

literature

prostitution   stories   horses   hegemony   dream landscape world literature   presidents   utopias   a girl can do anything

she wants

fifties   sixties   seventies   eighties   Carter   Reagan

Warhol

you know I love you   you know I love you

I'll sit here until you fall asleep

there are no happy endings

you're going to go to sleep now

you're going to sleep and dream you're flying over snow and over people

applauding

that death is like a dark embrace

        or an eclipse of the sun

when you shall pass through waters I will be with you

        the rivers shall not cover you

and when you walk in the fire

        the flames shall not burn you

ONE LAST ROOM LIT UP, ONE EXPLODING
LILY IN THE DARKNESS

Cosmo stands in the corridor with a bunch of enormous flowers in her hands. She smells of trees and water and she still remembers that you used to love lilies. Around her is a pall of smoke, or maybe frost, and little white clouds escape from her mouth when she breathes. The ceiling above you changes into sky and in the distance is the sound of the night watchmen disappearing in their clogs with their bunches of keys. She stands in the doorway to the laboratory in her newly washed white coat, and she and her towering boots take a few rapid strides toward you. And she kisses your mouth and your neck and her hands are all over your face. The color of the lining in her coat is gentle and comforting.

VALERIE: Who are the flowers for?
COSMO: We got the money.
VALERIE: What money?
COSMO: The research money. All the money we applied for. We got it in the end.
VALERIE: I don't believe it.

COSMO: It's true. We can do everything we want now. No restrictions, no limitations. We can make just mouse girls.

VALERIE: Just mouse girls?

COSMO: Just mouse girls.

VALERIE: No Y genes?

COSMO: No Y genes.

VALERIE: No walking abortions?

COSMO: No abortions.

VALERIE: You remembered the lilies this time.

COSMO: I bought lilies, I bought champagne. I forgot to buy cigars.

VALERIE: How much did we get?

COSMO: As much as we wanted. And more if we need it.

She takes your cool hand and pulls you up onto the workbench and she lies behind your back and holds you. Outside the window, hundreds of white albino rabbits are playing between the trees.

VALERIE: What are the rabbits doing?

COSMO: I let them out into the park.

VALERIE: Shall we go out with them?

COSMO: We'll sleep for a bit first.

VALERIE: You're not leaving now?

COSMO: I'm going nowhere.

VALERIE: You bought night flowers filled with sunshine. Do you remember when the night watchman chased us across the park? Your hair always smelled of rain and grass. Your hair still smells of rain . . . I remember you held my hands above my head, you kissed me so hard I thought I would break.

COSMO: Sleep now, Ruler of the Universe.

VALERIE: Where's the money?

COSMO: Shh . . . We're going to go to sleep now and dream that there isn't a question about death in any sentence. Death didn't happen and we weren't there. We're going to dream that we're not in a San Francisco welfare hotel for dying drug addicts and whores. We're going to dream that I've been here all the time. Death isn't in the same place as us.

VALERIE: Read me something while I fall asleep.

COSMO: Do you promise to sleep then?

VALERIE (*faint smile*): I swear on my breasts.

COSMO (*opens the manifesto*): You've never had any breasts to speak of.

VALERIE: Read it now.

COSMO: Life in this society being, at best, an utter bore and no aspect of society being at all relevant to women, there remains to civic-minded, responsible, thrill-seeking females only to overthrow the government, eliminate the money system, institute complete automation and destroy the male sex. It is now technically feasible to reproduce without the aid of males and to produce only females. We must begin immediately to do so.

VALERIE (*begins to fall asleep*): Keep going. I want to know how it ends.

COSMO: The female function is to explore and discover the world, solve problems, invent, crack jokes, make music; it is to create a magic world. Every woman knows instinctively that the only wrong is to hurt others and the meaning of life is love . . . Valerie?

VALERIE: —

Cosmogirl holds you in her arms and her embrace is a black expanse of velvet in which to plunge and be enfolded. Desert animals screech in the darkness, waves pound against the shores, nurses turn on the lights in the dormitories at Elmhurst Psychiatric Hospital, Dorothy sleeps her wine-induced slumber surrounded by rose wallpaper in Georgia. When Cosmogirl sees you are no longer awake, she stops reading, takes off her white coat, and drapes it over your shoulders. Then she carefully closes the book.

AFTERWORD

After the novel is finished, I visit the Tenderloin in San Francisco, that small area of affliction in the middle of the city beside the Pacific Ocean. The Bristol Hotel is still a welfare hotel under the auspices of the city and the Tenderloin is still a form of hell. The hotel is said to have improved greatly since the eighties, when Valerie lived there.

I have never been in a place that puts me so much in mind of death. The smells and the dirt, the vomit marks on the carpets and the wizened figures moving hurriedly up and down the corridors. The mangy cats and dogs, the scraps of food, the wheelchairs. Lost women, lost men.

They are all near death, they are all sorrowful, all smiling, many with the characteristic red patches on their faces; it is an incurable disease they share. Out on the street are men whispering,

"Kill me, just kill me," and women go in and out in their blood-stained furs.

The view from most of the rooms is dominated by a gigantic billboard covering the wall of the building opposite. In the entrance there is a soft drink machine and a pay phone. I visit the hotel only a few times, fearful of being contaminated by their ruin. The smells scare me and all the time I long to be sitting in a bar in another part of town, long to be by the ocean. And I never understand what that billboard is trying to sell, but the text is a simple appeal in orange capitals: S T A Y.

This novel is dedicated to the residents of the Bristol Hotel.

Sara Stridsberg

A NOTE ABOUT THE AUTHOR

Sara Stridsberg is an internationally acclaimed writer and
playwright. She has published seven books of both fiction
and nonfiction, and her work has been translated into
more than twenty languages. A former member of the
Swedish Academy, she is a leading feminist and artist in
her native Sweden and around the world. *Valerie* is her
North American debut.

A NOTE ABOUT THE TRANSLATOR

Deborah Bragan-Turner has a degree in Scandinavian
languages from University College London. She trans-
lates Swedish literature, particularly literary fiction and
biographies.